Where Hope Begins

The Cafe on Hope and Main ~ Book One

Candee Fick

Contents

"We have this hope as an anchor for the soul, firm and secure." ~ Hebrews 6:19a

"For I know the plans I have for you," declares the Lord, "plans to prosper you and not to harm you, plans to give you hope and a future." ~ Jeremiah 29:11

Chapter One

♥

A greeing to help his family should not be this painful.

Joel Dawson flipped a dozen slices of half-cooked bacon, then blinked several times. His eyes still watered from earlier that morning, but at least Mom had taken over the onions.

Thank God for that.

And that his college professors weren't here to see his fall from top of the class to the bottom rung.

Also known as a cramped commercial kitchen in a small-town diner at five o'clock on a Monday morning. Because that was normal for the diner's staff—including his parents—as they prepared for another day of business.

What wasn't normal was returning to Loveland after graduation to see Mom's deep wrinkles and slumped shoulders. Her decline had been almost as shocking as hearing Dad's request for financial advice. On Christmas of all days.

Obviously, they'd been keeping something from him. Making curiosity—and concern—the only reasons he'd even shown up this morning.

Mom scraped pieces of the vile vegetable into a metal container, then glanced his way. "Is the time change from California still messing with you?"

"Something is." Joel jerked back from the griddle and rubbed his forearm where a grease splatter had left its mark.

The cute waitress across the worktable from Mom giggled.

He glared.

She blushed a pretty pink. Probably because she'd been caught crossing the line from not-so-secret stares to outright participation in his mother's teasing.

Although he really shouldn't be taking his irritation out on innocent bystanders. In any other circumstance, he'd be tempted to get to know her better.

Just not here. Not today.

Not when she represented everything he'd worked so hard to escape.

Well, escape might be a bit harsh. More like avoid.

While the current batch of bacon sizzled under his nose, Joel's attention drifted to where Dad seemed to be in a speed-chopping contest with the new guy in his early twenties. Of course, Trevor gained an advantage when Dad paused to rub the center of his chest.

Nearby, Aunt Greta kneaded dough for either pie or rolls. At least he could look forward to those, especially if she still used Grandma Hope's recipes.

An ache grew in Joel's heart. He'd spent hours of his teen years sneaking tastes of his grandmother's cooking, but the diner felt empty without her.

Joel might have been away for several years, but some things didn't change.

Lots of busywork and lots of constant—mundane—chatter.

Because the topics so far had bounced from the weather forecast—cold with possible snow like every other January in Colorado—to the fact the older adults needed to follow-up with the Realtor about getting a new lease signed for the now-vacant space next door.

However, when the effervescent blonde started in on the future of his cousin Julie's culinary program in New York, Joel groaned. Enough.

He half turned. "What's a guy gotta do for a little quiet around here? Or at least a subject change?"

The waitress snapped her mouth shut mid-sentence and stared wide-eyed.

Trevor snort-laughed, jutting his chin toward where Dad exited the walk-in refrigerator with a flat of bell peppers. "What do you say, Frank? Think the Broncos will make the playoffs this year?"

An apt topic since Trevor could have been a linebacker on Joel's college team, complete with a reddish buzz cut and stocky build.

Dad slammed the door. "Not likely. As usual."

Aunt Greta's blue eyes twinkled as she smirked, but Mom gave him the side-eye.

Joel winced. How could he have forgotten their heated debate while watching yesterday's televised game?

For a minute, only the rhythm of Trevor's quick knife skills filled the awkward silence.

Joel's phone vibrated in his back pocket and he pulled it out to find a text from his very-ex-girlfriend Desiree.

Why had he never deleted her contact? He stared at her polished picture for a second, then swiped to read the full message.

Hey stranger! This early bird saw your application and I'm so excited that you might come to CVX Industries!! We should get together some time!!!

He frowned. Of the dozen companies holding his resume, she had to work at one of them? Wasn't she still in California? And what was with all the exclamation points? She hadn't been so thrilled to be seen with him when he'd been a poor college student on a football scholarship.

Someday he would love to stride into a boardroom in his tailored power suit and give *her* the brush-off for a change. Let her see what it felt like to...

Another series of tiny burns on his arm brought him back to the present.

And a row of bacon strips about to transition from crispy to burned.

He shoved his phone away and moved the bacon to the warming pan before adding fresh slices to the hot surface.

Someday would have to wait.

Behind him, someone cleared their throat. "So, Nancy, now that Joel's home, what are the odds he finds a girlfriend willing to put up with him?" Aunt Greta's question didn't sound as innocent as she may have hoped.

"He might need some help in that department." Mom's wry tone made his ears burn. "Have any suggestions?"

He glared over his shoulder and the duo burst into laughter.

As if his love life was any of their business. Especially in front of Trevor and the waitress.

What was her name again? Oh yeah, Lauren.

Joel hadn't recognized her at first without the braces or his cousin by her side. How long had it been? At least five years.

She wasn't his usual style with her tie-dyed shirt, dangling earrings, and designer jeans, but they seemed to fit her personality as well as her mop of shoulder-length curls and her laugh.

As if she actually liked working at Dawson's Diner.

Somewhere in the past hour, his cousin's best friend had made an impression.

A way-too-cheery-for-this-time-of-day impression.

Lauren had the audacity to smirk at him before glancing at the clock above the pass-through window into the dining room. "Any chance I can get some eggs to go with that bacon?"

Aunt Greta stopped talking mid-sentence. "Is it that late already?"

Mom laughed. "Time flies when you're having fun, right, Joel?"

Joel poked stubbornly at the bacon. "Who said anything about fun?"

Dad grunted. "Nancy? Did you buy more Tums? My heartburn is acting up again."

"Of course." Mom grabbed a bottle off the shelf near the sink. "Men. You'd think they were dying." She shook out a couple before pushing Dad toward the adjacent office. "Take a break, Frank. I can handle enough eggs for all of us."

Within minutes, trays of pies and cinnamon rolls had disappeared into the ovens and various containers of chopped vegetables were covered with plastic wrap and positioned over ice on the cold prep line.

After scrambling eggs in a bowl, Mom set to work beside him at the stove.

Where he still fried bacon.

By the time he moved the last batch to the warmer and scraped the remaining bacon grease toward the drip tray, the aroma of hot cinnamon and other spices filled the kitchen.

His stomach growled. "Can I eat now?"

He nodded to where Trevor and Lauren leaned against the prep counter with half-eaten plates of scrambled eggs, Lauren's doused in salsa.

Mom scooped a pile of eggs onto a clean plastic plate and handed it over. "Can't have the help go hungry, not if we want you to stick around."

He forced a smile and dug into his breakfast.

What if he didn't want to stay? Although he could never tell her that.

There had to be an easier way to help the diner back to solid footing. In fact, even if it took long days, he'd be gone by the end of the week or die trying. After all, he needed to be available if—when—one of his many applications led to a real job.

Lauren placed her empty plate in a rack for a later trip through the dishwasher. "I'm headed out front. How soon until those cinnamon rolls are ready?"

Dad rose from the office chair he'd dragged into the room. "Needs a few more minutes in the oven. Go on and work your magic."

"It's not magic." She patted his dad's arm. "It's the coffee."

Joel took another bite of his breakfast as Lauren tied her apron and pushed through the doors into the dining room.

At least one of them got to escape the kitchen.

Aunt Greta added her dish to the rack. "Once I finish the icing, I'll move out there."

Joel surveyed the kitchen where Mom ate, Dad dumped potatoes on the corner of the griddle, and Trevor seasoned a giant bowl of hamburger.

He frowned. "Dad, if Aunt Greta and Lauren are out front and Trevor and Mom are back here with you, what am I supposed to do?"

Dad jutted his chin toward the prep line. "You can help me over here until Trevor gets the meatloaf in the ovens. Then you can float between the front and back. Get a feel for how things work while keeping us stocked with clean dishes."

Joel glared at the mountain of mixing bowls beside the industrial sized sinks.

Onions, bacon grease, and now dishpan hands on his first day. And they wondered why he wanted a desk job.

Mom chuckled, then reached to adjust the heat beneath the soup pot. "Don't worry. I can run trays through the dishwasher when I'm not helping with prep. But you'll have to fetch the tubs of dirties yourself."

He groaned. "So I'm clearing tables too?"

Aunt Greta tucked a large bowl under the stand mixer. "We've been shorthanded since Julie moved to New York and Emma got married, but we've managed to make do without hiring someone else right away because we knew you'd be here for a bit."

Funny how they assumed that when he'd only agreed a few days ago.

She reached for the bricks of cream cheese on the worktable. "Seven might be normal, but if it includes you, six is the perfect number."

Perfect?

Not from where he stood. Not even close.

Lauren Graham paused near the swinging doors to the kitchen and surveyed the empty dining room.

From the black-and-white checkered tile floor beneath her feet to the painted walls covered in an eclectic variety of framed photographs and the burgundy vinyl booths to the metal-rimmed tables in between, this place felt like home.

Soon the room would hum with conversations punctuated occasionally with the ding of the kitchen's bell signaling another order was ready to deliver.

What would she learn today?

Whose day could she brighten?

And in the middle of it all, whatever she did for even the grungiest or grumpiest of their customers, she did for God.

Hope Dawson had taught her that. Had welcomed her into the Dawson's Diner family with open arms, despite her quirks.

So while Lauren's status-driven relatives had scattered across the country, she chose to remain behind. And until she figured out what her future held, she'd rather be here paying God's blessings forward to the community than anywhere else.

Just like Hope's legacy demanded.

After confirming Frank had stocked the register with cash and the coffee pots brimmed, Lauren crossed to the front door. With a flip of a switch and the twist of a knob, the red neon Open sign shone into the darkness.

Dawson's Diner was ready for business.

Halfway back across the room, the bells jangled and she grinned over her shoulder at one of their regulars. "Good morning, Kyle. The usual?"

She slipped behind the old-fashioned lunch counter and reached for a coffee pot.

The reporter with the local paper settled onto a padded stool.

At his nod, she turned over the cup on its saucer and filled it. "Anything new in Loveland?" she asked.

"Don't you ever read what I write?" Kyle tore the end off a packet of sugar.

"I'm up early enough as it is. Can't you give me the highlights?"

Lauren pulled out her order pad, scribbled the necessary kitchen shorthand for eggs over easy, bacon, and wheat toast. She ripped the top sheet free and faced the pass-through window, catching a glimpse of Joel beyond.

And tried unsuccessfully not to stare yet again at the dark-haired man who looked just like his picture on Julie's fridge, right down to the clear blue eyes.

Not much had changed since that Christmas five years ago when she made a fool of herself. Or a couple years later when she'd been a puffy-eyed mess at his grandmother's funeral.

At least *that* time he hadn't acknowledged her existence.

Maybe this time he'd stick around long enough for her to make a better impression. Then he would look for another job, move on, and leave them all behind.

Again.

She forced a smile back onto her face.

Moments after she placed the order on the spinning rack, Frank cracked the eggs onto the griddle.

The bells jangled again as a trio of construction workers entered, stomped their boots on the mat, and slid into a booth along the windows. They'd been in a few times over the past week as they fueled up for work on a project a couple blocks away.

A few minutes later, she added their order to the rack.

"What's the word on the street?" Kyle cradled his coffee cup.

She crossed her arms. "Hey. You're supposed to be giving me the news, not the other way around."

"That's what you say every day." He winked. "And every day you point me in the direction of a great human-interest story that spotlights the revival of downtown Loveland."

"Maybe." Lauren tapped her bottom lip. "Except the only thing I've heard lately is that no one stepped up to take over the barbershop down the block. Even the owner's son didn't want it. So there could be room for a new business soon... but you didn't hear that from me."

Kyle pulled a small notebook out of his shirt pocket and made a note, then pointed over her shoulder. "Isn't that the Dawsons' boy?"

Behind her, a soft *thunk* was followed by a resounding ding.

She turned to find a loaded plate on the counter under the heat lamps and Joel's hand still hovering over the domed chime. Almost as if he resented being called a boy.

"It sure is." She reached for Kyle's breakfast and the order ticket tucked beneath the edge. Then smirked at Joel's grimace before turning to deliver Kyle's food.

The reporter cut up the eggs and stirred them into the side of hash browns. "Heard he graduated early. Nice to see him back."

Nice to see Joel again? Absolutely.

Could she keep from getting her heart broken again? That remained to be seen.

Through the open window behind her, she caught Joel's frustrated voice. "Can you at least tell me about your cost management software? What system are you using?"

"Save your fancy words for somewhere else." Frank's characteristic grumble made her smile. "This is my business."

"Seriously. You asked me to help."

"You will. Now, make some toast."

"Ahem." Nancy's motherly tone interrupted them. "What your father means is that it's not as simple as you'd like to think."

Frank grunted. "What she said."

Lauren bit her lip. Too bad her best friend now lived in New York. The Dawsons could use another ally to bring Mr. Top-of-His-Class back to the real world.

Someday Lauren would have a graduation of her own. With classes starting again next week, maybe this would be the semester she finally found her place and made her dad proud.

The diner traffic picked up and soon she'd added three more orders to the rack.

Kyle raised his near-empty cup for a refill. "How's college going?"

She reached for the pot. "I switched my major to communications."

"I can see that with all the talking you do around here."

She topped off another nearby customer. "It's not as fancy as Joel's MBA."

Unless she specialized in journalism. Just at a bigger paper than Kyle's to compete with her sisters' accomplishments.

The reporter nodded. "All depends on what you want to do in life."

If she knew that, the rest would make sense. At least Dad didn't know that she'd changed majors. Again.

She sighed. "If that's all it depended on, I'd skip college, find Mr. Tall, Dark, and Handsome, and get my M-R-S degree." She wiggled her empty ring finger to punctuate the joke. "But this is the real world and people have expectations I keep failing to meet."

Behind her, the pass-through bell chimed again. Loudly.

She swiveled to find Joel watching with a raised eyebrow. As if he expected her to be working instead of oversharing her lack of prospects with the customers.

Heat rose in her face as she loaded a tray with plates for table three.

She risked another glance only to catch his smirk. Bracing the tray on her shoulder, she stuck out her tongue before scooting away.

So there, Mr. Smarty Pants.

What was it about Lauren that drew him in?

First, lighthearted chatter followed by a sobering statement about people's expectations. Then a refreshingly innocent blush ending with a childlike gesture that made him want to shake and hug her at the same time.

"See anything interesting?" Mom wrapped an arm around his waist and surveyed the dining room through the pass-through window.

A woman in medical scrubs entered, providing Joel an easy escape from his mixed-up thoughts.

"I'm surprised how many people come this time of day," he said.

"We'll see a wave of nine-to-fivers later, but lots of these folks have to head in early. And some, like Wanda over there, are just getting off work." Mom squeezed his side before stepping away.

Joel checked the next ticket on the spinning rack and started the requested toast while Dad scooped pancake batter onto the griddle. Somewhere behind them, Trevor continued working ahead on the lunch menu.

Through the window, he overheard the guy at the counter tell Lauren something about the city council debating the potential need for a parking garage off Main Street and the formation of a downtown revitalization committee.

Riveting news. Sophisticated order system.

Small-town life at its best.

Just like Dr. Hollaway's scathing words from Joel's freshman year. *You can't expect to succeed in business with such a small-town mentality.*

Something he'd spent the rest of his college years working to erase.

"Don't just stand around between orders." Dad pointed with his spatula. "You can work on those dishes while you have the chance."

Joel turned to find that a pile of sticky pans had joined the mountain of dirty mixing bowls.

Aunt Greta picked up a tray of frosted cinnamon rolls and headed for the dining room with his mom trailing behind her carrying a cherry pie.

They wanted him to see the full picture? It already included too many barked orders for menial tasks. Like filling a sink with hot soapy water.

This wouldn't last forever. Just long enough to help put the diner's financial books in order while continuing his own job search.

The sooner Joel found the perfect position, the sooner he'd be free.

Mom returned for an apple pie. "Another day in paradise."

Dad snagged her arm. "I'll show you paradise." He planted a big sloppy kiss on her lips right in the middle of the kitchen, making her giggle.

Joel shuddered. "I'm glad you're still happily married and all, but did you really have to do that here?"

"Where else?" Dad stole another kiss. "This place is practically home. Just like my parents before me. And your Grandma Hope's family before that." He reached for another order slip and added it to the row of clips on the wall.

Mom paused on her way out. "Maybe it's time for Joel to continue the tradition." She winked, then ducked out again.

Joel slid the worst of the pans under the water to soak.

He'd like a family of his own... eventually. But first he needed a real job that paid real money.

As Trevor disappeared into the walk-in refrigerator, Joel started scrubbing the first pan. "When can I see the books?"

Dad grunted. "Plenty of time for ledgers and receipts once we lock the door."

"But that's why I'm here." He focused on a particularly stubborn spot.

If Dad's business records were as outdated as his ordering system, Joel should start immediately. Not to mention, it was a better use of his skills than kitchen duties.

"You can't really help until you understand how we do things now." Dad's voice sounded strained.

And unexpectedly weak.

Joel turned in time to see his father clutch his chest. His heart leaped into his throat as Dad's spatula slipped from his hand.

Chapter Two

♥

The spatula clattered onto the tiled floor and time stopped for the space of two heartbeats.

With Dad's years of experience—and a grudging respect for health inspectors—he rarely dropped things in the kitchen.

Which made his unexpected behavior all the more ominous.

Mom's shoes squeaked as she came to a sudden stop inside the swinging door. "Frank? What's wrong?"

Joel surged forward to catch his Dad's leaning body before he joined the spatula on the floor. "Dad?"

Dad mumbled something unintelligible.

Mom rushed to support his other side. "Frank? Joel? What happened?"

Joel strained under the additional weight. "We were talking, then he dropped the spatula and you walked in." He mostly carried his father to the chair where he'd sat earlier after complaining of heartburn. "He did grab his chest..."

Once Joel lowered his dad onto the chair, Mom knelt in front of him.

"Talk to me, Frank." She held his hands while staring into his eyes.

"It hurts." Dad wheezed as if short of breath, his face dotted with sweat.

Mom blinked back tears. "Joel, call 9-1-1. We need help."

Help? They needed a miracle.

Joel released his grip on his dad and pulled his cell phone from his back pocket. In seconds he was connected to an operator. "This is Joel Dawson calling from Dawson's Diner downtown on Main."

"I know the location." The woman's brisk voice somehow conveyed a sense of calm.

"Something's wrong with my dad." He swallowed hard. Would speaking his suspicions make them true? "I think he might be having a heart attack."

"What happened?" A clicking sound like typing echoed in the background.

"He grabbed his chest and almost fell. Says it hurts. Earlier he complained of some heartburn but based on the giant bottle of Tums, that might be a regular thing." Joel took a deep breath and caught the distinct smell of burning food. His eyes darted to the griddle and the smoking potatoes.

"Stay with me, Frank." Mom's voice broke.

His father slumped to the side and Joel braced himself to keep him upright without dropping the phone.

Trevor emerged from the walk-in cooler and gasped. "What happened to Frank?"

Joel snapped his fingers and directed him toward the griddle.

The man grabbed a dangling spoon from a hook overhead and scraped blackened potatoes into the trash can.

Hopefully they were in time to avoid setting off the smoke detectors and triggering the sprinklers.

"Sir? Are you still there?" The operator's voice cut through the distractions.

"Um, yes. I think Dad is close to passing out. What did you say?"

"I asked about any family history of heart problems?"

A wave of nausea left him lightheaded and Joel leaned against the wall, bracing one hand on his father's shoulder near his neck. At least he could feel a pulse there.

"His dad died of a heart attack." He did the mental math based on the family stories. "At about this age."

And in this very building.

His stomach churned at the implications.

"Okay." The operator continued tapping away on her end of the call. "I'm sending an ambulance now. Please stay on the line until they arrive so we can keep them updated if his condition changes."

Changes? As in got worse? How much worse could it get when his dad couldn't stand up, let alone cook food for all the people expecting breakfast?

Breakfast.

They'd need to close.

He tilted the phone away from his mouth and looked down at his parents. "Help is on the way. Should I have Aunt Greta lock up and send everyone home?"

Dad grunted and grew agitated.

Mom yelped as he squeezed her hand. She gave him a watery smile. "Your dad is coherent enough to have a definite opinion about that. Call the girls in here for a chat."

Joel blinked. "A chat? Now?"

"Now." Mom's voice took on that no-nonsense tone he remembered from growing up.

He shook his head but moved toward the swinging doors. Hopefully *the girls* would back him. He stopped just inside the dining room, surprised to see half of the tables were already filled and another group entering as a buzz of conversation swirled around him.

They'd need to move fast before more customers got upset.

Catching Lauren's eye, he crooked his finger and motioned her closer.

"What's the holdup in the kitchen?" She gestured at the line of tickets waiting over the window.

"Get my aunt and meet me in the kitchen ASAP."

She raised her eyebrows at his demand but hurried off.

He turned on his heel and pushed back into the kitchen where Trevor was seasoning a new batch of potatoes and glancing repeatedly over at Joel's parents.

"Joel?" Mom's face paled to match his father's. "Tell them to have the ambulance come to the back door. It's closer and won't disrupt the dining room."

"Disrupt the *what*?" Was their business more important than Dad's health?

She held out her hand and he passed over the phone.

Chatter from the dining room filtered in the open door just moments before Aunt Greta's voice ricocheted around the kitchen. "What's the deal calling a meeting in the middle of the—"

She skidded to a stop beside Joel and then rushed forward to his mom's side. "Oh no. What happened? Don't tell me it's his heart. Not after what happened to our dad."

Lauren gasped and he looked down to see her holding a hand over her mouth as tears filled her eyes.

A gaping hole opened in Joel's chest.

He might have only been two years old when his grandfather died, but he'd heard the stories. And grew up in the aftermath.

"The ambulance is pulling in now." Mom handed Joel back his phone and squared her shoulders. "Joel, open the back door and let them in. Greta, can you and Trevor manage things back here until we know something?"

"Absolutely." Aunt Greta patted her brother's knee. "Don't worry about a thing. You focus on getting better, okay?"

Joel staggered toward the door he'd come through just two hours before.

Don't worry?

Didn't she realize how serious this could be?

He propped open the door and waved at the paramedics grabbing bags from the back of the ambulance before turning back inside to the comparative warmth.

Aunt Greta motioned him over to where she now stood with Lauren and Trevor beside the sinks. "Here's the plan. Long before the last five years working here, I grew up in this kitchen, so with all the prep work we did earlier and Trevor as backup ...?"

The wide-eyed man saluted. "Of course."

"Good." She nodded. "I can short-order us through breakfast, and then we can re-evaluate."

Joel tried to block out the increased noise a few feet away as the paramedics unzipped bags and worked on his dad.

"Lauren?" Aunt Greta kept barking orders like a true Dawson. "Ask everyone out there for a little patience since we've had a bit of an emergency and are shorthanded even with Joel here."

"Should I rope off a section?" Lauren shifted her weight as if eager to move.

"Closing down is a good idea." Joel watched his mom shrug into her coat.

The staff of six they'd started the day with had instantly dropped to four. If they closed, he could be there at the hospital. And with his lack of helpful experience, he might as well go—

"Pay attention, Joel." Aunt Greta's voice cracked and his eyes snapped back to find her struggling to contain her emotions. "We can't let all this food go to waste when we have loyal customers already waiting to be fed. Plus, some of us need the income to pay our bills. That goes for your parents too since they'll need every penny they can get their hands on for the inevitable medical bills. So we have to keep the doors open as best we can, for as long as we can. Got it?"

"Yes, ma'am." He squared his shoulders but resisted the urge to snap off a salute. "But can't I—"

"Good. You might be slow but that's better than nothing. Help Lauren wait tables through the thick of it and then catch up on the dishes." Aunt Greta turned to Lauren. "Show him what to do. He used to be a quick learner."

Joel opened his mouth to protest but was interrupted by the rattling of a stretcher rolling across the tile.

If only he could go with them. Make sure Dad lived another day.

Lauren shook her head. "God help us all."

Lauren latched on to Joel's chiseled bicep and pulled him toward the dining room. "Ever done this before?"

He rolled his eyes. "Back in high school, while you were in—what?—junior high? Or younger."

"Let's hope it's like riding a bike."

Near the doors, she paused and drew in a quick breath before blowing it out slowly. *God, Frank is in Your hands. Now help me to focus out there.*

She pushed through the doors and stopped near the end of the lunch counter.

The bells over the door clattered as more customers filtered in.

Lauren raised her voice to be heard. "Take a seat and we'll be right with you."

Her eyes scanned the dining room as she counted booths and tables and made a quick calculation—taking into account the area Greta had been serving—before handing Joel a spare pad and pen.

She nudged his arm with her elbow, then pointed. "You take over the counter and those first three booths along the outside wall for starters. Drink orders first. Food order on the clip. When you pick up, deliver the ticket at the same time and tell them I'll ring up their total at the register."

"You'll ring them up?" His tone oozed arrogant disbelief.

She gritted her teeth. "The register is a new one and I don't have time to teach you."

He grunted. Like father, like son apparently.

She eyed his T-shirt and jeans. "Also, you might want to grab an apron. Things can get messy, especially when clearing tables." She indicated the rag and bottle of spray disinfectant sitting next to an empty tub for the dishes.

"I'd hate to look ridiculous." He gestured toward her outfit.

She sucked in a breath. Had he really gone there again?

He shrugged. "You can pull off the apron look, but not me."

Between his muscular physique and the short haircut that accentuated his strong jawline, Joel could pass for the football player he'd been or even a Navy SEAL. And neither look fit with an apron.

Lauren forced a casual tone. "Suit yourself."

"I'll be fine." He shoved the order pad into his back pocket and moved toward the coffee pot.

Fine? Failure was not an option because they *all* needed the income.

Lauren winced. Why was she thinking about her paycheck with Frank's life on the line?

God help us all.

By choosing the multiple booths and tables with their more complicated group orders, she'd also placed herself farther from the drink station and kitchen. Time to put more miles on her shoes and polish her diplomacy skills on the disgruntled customers who'd been kept waiting far too long.

At least many of them were regulars who knew this wasn't the norm.

She pasted a smile on her face and dove into the deep end with a coffee pot in hand. Within a half hour, she had caught up most of the backlog in her sections, but a stint at the register followed by a shortage of coffee put her behind again.

A rattle of dishes caught her attention and she glanced over at Joel clearing a booth in time to see him scowl at a smear of something on the front of his shirt. She'd tried to warn him.

"Excuse me, miss?" A departing couple from Joel's section waited to check out.

"Sorry. I'll be right there." Lauren wiped her hands on her apron and hurried to take their ticket before punching each item into the register. "How were things?"

The man wrinkled his nose. "Well, the service was woefully slow, but the food was good when it finally arrived."

"Didn't your server tell you?" She gave him the total. "We're very shorthanded this morning after an emergency with the owners. It's also his first day."

"That explains a lot." The gentleman pulled cash out of his wallet. "I guess I'll leave a tip after all. Should I put it on the table or can you keep track of it here?"

"Whatever is easiest for you." She made change and dropped Joel's tip into Nancy's jar beneath the register. "Have a nice day."

"What's this about an emergency?" Wanda, a regular with a medical job, was next in line to pay. "Is that where Greta disappeared to?"

Lauren lowered her voice. "We think Frank had a heart attack and Nancy went with him in the ambulance. Greta took over in the kitchen."

Wanda grimaced. "His heart? Any updates on how he's doing?"

"Nothing yet." Lauren spotted Joel returning to the dining room and tying on an apron.

Seemed he could learn new things after all.

But would he tell her if word arrived from his mom?

Was it too soon to know anything even if it did feel like hours since the ambulance had left?

Another glance revealed a slump-shouldered Joel shoving his phone back into his pocket.

How long until they heard something?

Wanda held out her ticket. "Do you have any paper? I'd like to leave a note if I could. To let them know I'll be praying."

Lauren swallowed the lump in her throat. "I'm sure they would appreciate that." She reached beneath the counter for a spare order pad and passed it over before ringing up Wanda's ticket.

Wanda tore her note free and handed it to Lauren along with a twenty-dollar bill. "Add a two-dollar tip. Then keep the rest of the change for them."

"Thank you."

The Dawsons gave so much to the community. If she made a sign, would other customers also offer their support?

An hour later, a large recycled mayonnaise jar stood beside the register, over half-filled with a mixture of notes and cash.

Taking advantage of a temporary lull, Lauren checked the coffee pots, started another batch brewing, and tried to put the serving station back in order. A quick visual inventory let her know they'd need to run a tray of mugs soon as well as roll more silverware.

Joel deposited a load of dirty plates into a waiting tub on a shelf under the counter and straightened with a groan. "Riding this bike is harder than it looks."

"At least you haven't fallen off."

"Much." He stretched and rolled his shoulders. "Don't know why Mom and Dad do all this work for a bunch of lousy tippers."

"Lousy?" Other than the one complaint, no one had said anything bad.

He shoved a hand into the front pocket of his jeans and came out with a few crumbled bills. "Unless you think this is a fortune."

She bit her lip to stop her laughter. "There's a whole lot more in your jar under the register. Along with any tips included on the credit card receipts."

"Oh." He grimaced. "So, anything else I need to know before I show more ignorance?"

The bells on the door clattered and the entering customer headed for the counter.

Lauren scanned the dining room for any other immediate needs. "I was going to have you start a load of coffee cups, but I'll do it while you handle this one." She jutted her chin toward the new customer.

With Joel occupied with the latest arrival, she ducked into the kitchen where a drooping Greta poured pancake batter onto the griddle. "How are you holding up?"

Greta glanced at the clock on the wall. "I'll feel better when we know something." She twisted her torso from side to side. "Could you bring me a Diet Coke when you have a chance? I need the caffeine but no way do I want anything hot right now." She wiped her forehead with the back of her hand, then reached for a spatula.

Nearby Trevor flipped a couple eggs over easy, then pointed to a plastic cup of ice poised near the stovetop. "I could use more water if you're making a trip."

"No problem." Lauren moved to the industrial dishwasher and loaded a rack with coffee mugs from the various tubs of dirty dishes, followed by a tray of plates before shoving them into the machine.

"Sorry." Trevor glanced over his shoulder. "I should help with those."

"We're all working for two, but I'd appreciate it." She grabbed Trevor's glass, then detoured for the bottle of ibuprofen before returning to the dining room.

Maybe she could help ward off some of Joel's inevitable aches.

If only she could do something about the worry in his eyes.

Back behind the counter, she refilled Trevor's glass and poured a diet soda for Greta.

She shook out a couple pills for Joel. "You'll thank me later."

His grin faltered but he swallowed them without complaint.

The bells over the door clattered yet again, followed by a chirping from Joel's pocket.

He answered his phone and the color drained from his face. He muttered something and pushed past her toward the kitchen.

No way was she about to be left out again, even if customers were waiting.

"Be right with you." She nodded to acknowledge the familiar faces entering the diner.

Then with her hands full of drinks and her stomach dropping, she rushed after Joel.

Whether he wanted her to or not.

Chapter Three

♥

"Hold on, Mom." Joel hurried through the swinging doors while swiping a shaky finger across the screen. "I'll put you on speaker so Aunt Greta can hear."

His aunt turned from the griddle with a frown.

Joel reached her side and held the phone between them. "Go ahead. What were you saying about surgery?"

Aunt Greta gasped and leaned closer. "So it *was* his heart?"

"Definitely a heart attack." Mom's voice wavered, then steadied. "They gave him medications so he's stable for now. But they want to admit him so they can do more tests, see how bad the blockages are, and decide what kind of surgery is needed."

"What *kind* of surgery?" How many kinds were there?

Joel glanced over his shoulder to where Dad had eaten breakfast and spotted the clock on the wall.

Had it really only been a few hours since the ambulance had sped away?

Mom choked up but the words came anyway. "Depending on what they find, they could put in stents to hold his arteries open. Which would be a quicker recovery." Her voice cracked. "But the on-call cardiologist said if there isn't enough oxygen getting to his heart muscle, he might need open heart bypass surgery instead."

Open heart?

Joel blinked away a rush of dizziness. Wasn't that extreme?

A flurry of voices intruded on Mom's end of the call. "Got to go. I'll text updates as I can. It helps to know you are holding the diner together for us."

Holding it together?

He took in the disaster zone of the kitchen, Trevor's panicked eyes by the stove, and the mountain of dishes with eggs and syrup drying on them.

If only he could disappear and shut the door on this nightmare, but he was trapped here for the day.

Trapped?

Aunt Greta steadied the phone in Joel's shaking hand. "Tell Frank that we love him and that we'll be praying." She tapped the screen to end the call and pulled a tearful Lauren into her arms.

When had she arrived?

Joel needed to pull it together for the sake of the diner. He tucked the phone into his back pocket and took a deep breath.

Where should they start?

"Dear Father in Heaven." Aunt Greta snaked an arm around his waist, dragged him into their hug, and nodded at Trevor who turned to flip pancakes before they burned. "We ask right now that you keep Frank stable and give his doctors wisdom."

Prayer. What Joel should have been doing all along.

He wrapped an arm around each of the other women and held on.

Almost like the last time he'd been held in his grandmother's arms, her silvery hair tickling under his chin while her love seeped into the cracks of his lonely heart.

But a broken heart in college was nothing like the current crisis.

Aunt Greta's voice grew stronger. "Protect Frank's life and show Yourself strong on his behalf. Minimize the damage. Surround Nancy with Your peace."

He blew out the breath he'd been holding and felt a few of his worries slip away.

Grandma Hope knew what it was like to lose parents. To lose her husband to a heart attack. And still she modeled unswerving trust in God to her family.

Lauren cleared her throat. "Lord, give us strength to carry on here despite our fears. Take care of Frank. Heal him." Her voice caught and her body shuddered beside him.

"Yes, God, You are the Healer." Even as he monitored the griddle, Trevor was clearly a part of the same faith family.

Joel blinked away the threat of tears.

Please, God, answer our prayers. Save Dad's life.

He bowed his head. "Help us know how to make it through the rest of today."

A tendril of peace encircled his heart along with a flow of wisdom.

"Amen." Aunt Greta pulled away and turned toward the line of waiting tickets.

One by one, she'd—they'd—handle the customers.

Hour by hour they'd get through the day.

If only he had a moment to catch up instead of always scrambling hopelessly behind.

A memory tickled at the back of his mind.

"Will there be a lull sometime soon?" Joel surveyed the kitchen with the nearly empty prep table and mountain of dishes.

Lauren let out a burst of laughter. "Not for another hour."

"That long?"

Aunt Greta propped her hands on her hips. "Haven't you heard that breakfast is the most important meal of the day?"

He held up his hands in surrender. "Okay. So until then, what's the top priority? Dishes? Restock the line? Then what do we need to do to prepare for lunch? And what do we do after closing? How late do you stay?"

"Whoa." Lauren tugged on his arm, dragging him toward the dining room as if she was in charge. "First is to get back out front and let our guests know why we've been hiding in the kitchen and making them wait. After that, you and I can take turns slipping back here to start racks of dishes through the machine or help Trevor fetch for Greta."

"But—"

"Not now." She pushed open the door and raised her voice. "Excuse me, everybody. Sorry to disappear on you."

A room full of customers turned to face them.

He swallowed hard.

How exactly did one announce a personal family emergency to strangers?

Lauren released her hold but stayed beside him. "We just got an update on Frank. He had a heart attack earlier this morning but is now stable. However, he'll probably need some sort of surgery soon. I'm sure he and Nancy would appreciate your prayers just like we'd appreciate your patience."

Joel cringed as a chorus of murmurs filled the room.

As Lauren slipped past him toward the coffee pot, he noticed several tables bowing their heads.

Obviously not all of them were strangers to his parents.

He trailed behind and scanned his assigned section. Two parties waited to place their orders, three waited for food, and the rest were in various stages of finishing their meal and sipping coffee. With a glance to confirm there weren't any plates waiting to be delivered, he moved to greet the newcomers.

Despite the chaotic juggling of multiple customers, his brain raced faster with questions to be answered until he risked tripping over his thoughts and resorted to writing them down. During a quick trip into the kitchen with a tub of dirty dishes, he asked Greta and Trevor to start a list of their own if they had a chance.

If the lunch rush was anything like breakfast, they should have started preparing food even earlier in the day.

What did that mean for tomorrow because they'd still be shorthanded? Hopefully Aunt Greta—and even Lauren—had ideas.

Joel shoved a rack of plates into the dishwasher.

Aunt Greta turned slightly. "While you're in here, what do you think about doing tomorrow's baking this afternoon instead of in the morning?"

"Would it still be fresh enough?" He stretched his stiff shoulders.

"We often heat the rolls and pie up in the microwave out front so it shouldn't matter too much if they'd been refrigerated overnight."

Trevor placed a new flat of eggs next to Greta. "It would definitely help us tomorrow since we'd have to finish the other prep work with fewer people."

Joel slowly nodded. "Sounds smart."

She frowned. "Except that it means we have to stay even later today."

"If it must be done, we'll do it." He hoisted two trays of clean coffee cups and headed for the dining room.

Back behind the lunch counter, he stacked the trays beside the coffee machine and sidestepped Lauren reaching for a small pitcher of syrup. "Plan to stay late today. Greta wants to do the baking before we leave."

"Was that a request or an order?"

He rolled his eyes. "Pretty please with a cherry on top?"

She quirked an eyebrow. "You're in luck because classes haven't started yet. Otherwise, I skip out of here around one o'clock instead of closing up." She peered through the window into the kitchen where Greta and Trevor labored to fill the orders. "I can do whatever is needed today."

The bells clattered over the door and Joel bit his lip to stop the groan.

He'd pay good money to sit down with a large cola and a hot cinnamon roll and put his feet up for a few minutes. But it seemed the expected lull did not mean a break, especially today.

How did the diner staff keep up this pace every day?

The only lull he could see was fewer new customers entering and more trips to refill coffee cups for the clusters of old-timers who sat around dissecting the latest news and gossip.

He poured himself a soda and started sipping. It appeared his morning break would happen while on his feet.

He glanced at Lauren and the wide smile on her face as she talked with a departing couple.

As if she didn't have a care in the world.

As if she couldn't see the mountain of work waiting to be done or the room full of people.

She wiped her eyes as the balding man put something into that jar beside the register.

The register she still hadn't taught him how to operate.

He added the task to his list.

If they didn't have time soon, he'd have to figure it out later after they closed down, he totaled the day's receipts and prepared the bank deposit. Not that he knew how to do any of that either outside the basic theory.

No wonder Dad had gotten on his case about book learning versus real business.

This chaos did not remotely resemble anything he'd read about.

He checked his phone but there were no new messages.

Joel cleared dirty dishes from several tables and then returned with a rag and spray bottle to scrub the surfaces before resetting them with rolls of silverware and inverted coffee cups.

He didn't know where or how his dad kept records. Where was the safe and what was the combination? Would he have time to look through the files and get an overview?

At the rate his list was growing, would he ever be free to slip away to the hospital and check on Dad in person instead of taking Mom's word that he was stable?

He returned the cleaning supplies to their shelf below the counter in time to see Lauren hoist a tub of dishes and disappear into the kitchen.

His back muscles ached in sympathy since those tubs got really heavy.

How did she maintain her never-ending energy for a multitude of tasks?

Plus, she handled twice as many tables as he did.

And ran the register all by herself.

Joel squared his shoulders.

Time to pick up the slack and take over all of the dish duty. Which made sense because his tables were positioned closer to the kitchen, plus the extra activity would keep his mind off his ever-growing list of questions.

Lauren juggled her purse and the sack of fast food as she pushed through the door of her shared apartment. She made it as far as the couch before setting her dinner on the coffee table, shucking off her winter coat, and collapsing onto the cushions.

She kicked off her tennis shoes and propped her feet up beside her dinner.

Her stomach growled and she leaned forward to retrieve her crispy chicken sandwich.

What a day.

An unbearably long day.

The mixture of flavors satisfied her hunger and within minutes she had balled up the wrapper and moved on to nibble on the fries.

Her last break had been far too short and much too long ago.

Not that any of them had options.

Keeping the doors open without enough staff had been like that old show *Mission Impossible*. Especially on Joel's first day back in years.

And without a miracle, tomorrow would be more of the same.

She shook her head.

Time to erase the diner from her thoughts for a while.

She checked her phone and saw she'd missed multiple texts from her family thanks to an unfortunate group text.

She swiped the screen to learn that Lynn had passed her bar exam and was soon to be legal as a lawyer, pun intended. Lenae had offered her congratulations along with enough future stock tips to help Lynn on her way to millionaire status. Both Mom and Dad had also chimed in with pride in their daughter's accomplishments.

As if they were one big happy family instead of living in four different states, with Dad's new loft apartment in Denver the closest to her but still an hour away.

Lauren picked at a spot of dried ketchup on her jeans, then fumbled through a reply of her own.

Congrats, Lynn! I'm so happy to see your dream coming true.

At least her sisters were firmly on the path to success.

Her phone chimed with an incoming text. From Dad alone.

Great news about Lynn, right? Someday it will be your turn to shine, and soon because you've settled into the college groove. Speaking of which, I'll transfer the tuition money to the university this week.

Lauren groaned. Some groove.

What she wouldn't give for another change in topic. Or scenery.

A walk to the park would be nice, except that it was dark now... and she was too tired to move farther than the kitchen.

Guess she'd have to settle for a bowl of ice cream with chocolate syrup.

Lauren hoisted herself off the couch, collected her trash, and headed for the fridge where she found a note taped on the door.

A bossy reminder from her roommates that it was her week to clean the shared spaces of the apartment along with a sarcastic comment about the condition of her bedroom and a demand to leave her share of the cable bill on the table.

She wadded up the note and balanced it on top of the overflowing trash can.

Cleaning could wait until after her chocolate fix.

Back on the couch, she savored the first bite. Stretching out her legs atop the coffee table again, she eyed the television.

Why should she pay for a third of their subscription when she rarely had time to watch anything?

Sharing a room with college friends had seemed like a good idea until their schedules conflicted. She was now part of the 'early to bed early to rise' kind of crowd while they slept in, had midday classes, and worked in the evenings.

When they weren't at the movies or a party.

Their friendship from freshman year had faded to rare sightings and frequent notes.

If only Julie was around to share an apartment.

She reached for her abandoned purse.

Julie answered her call on the second ring. "Hey, chica."

"Hey, yourself." Lauren smiled.

"Heard you had quite the day."

"That's an understatement." She scooted back against the cushions and swirled the chocolate syrup into the melting pool in her bowl. "It's a waiting game now to see when Frank will have surgery and how long his recovery will be."

"I've been praying. Meanwhile, you're pulling a double load at the diner."

"Exactly."

Julie laughed. "Mom called earlier to complain about grease burns and a backache."

"Sounds like Joel."

"How is he?"

Lauren swallowed hard. How could she answer that question without bringing up the past?

"Lauren? I know you're there... and are probably trying to come up with a politically correct answer."

"Caught me." She scraped her bowl.

"So, is he still a know-it-all?

She choked on the last bite of ice cream. "He'd like to think so, but he was definitely out of his element today."

Images of the day came flashing back. Joel dodging bacon spatters with watery post-onion-chopping eyes. Complaining about tips. Easily hoisting another tub of dirty dishes.

Joining in Greta's prayer and his strong arm around her waist during their group hug.

"Still cute?"

"More than." She sighed.

"Uh-oh."

"Wait a minute." Lauren sat up. "I didn't mean it like that."

Julie snorted. "Really? This is me you're talking to and I know all about a certain crush you had in high school."

"Promise me you never said anything." She stood and began to pace the living room.

"It never came up. Besides, he was usually away at college. Your secret is safe."

"Whew." Lauren picked up her empty bowl and carried it to the kitchen.

"As long as you don't still have a crush..."

She growled a warning as she loaded it into the dishwasher. "It's a thing of the past and I'd like to keep it there."

"If you say so." Julie giggled. "Just be careful."

"Because he'll be moving on. I know."

"Well, he's always talked about working for a big company or running multiple businesses."

Lauren put her phone on speaker so she had her hands free, then wet a sponge and wiped down the counters. "That's a far cry from the diner."

"But now that Uncle Frank's in the hospital awaiting surgery, he'll have to stay for a while."

"True." Hopefully it would be a quick recovery; otherwise, who knew how long Joel would be around for her to resist.

"And that means you'll see him every day. All those bulky muscles and blue eyes."

"That's your cousin you're talking about." Lauren's face heated. Her best friend knew her too well.

"Imagine it. You could be my cousin by marriage."

"Enough." She grabbed a broom and swept the crumbs on the floor into a pile. "He'll make a good friend since you're out of state. But that's it, especially now that we'll be working together."

As long as she could guard her heart and ignore impossible dreams. Stomp out any glimpse of false hope.

Because falling back into crush-mode would only leave her crushed in the end.

"Friends?"

"Yes, friends." Time to shift the hot seat. "Have you made any new *friends* in New York?"

"I've only been here a week."

"There aren't any cute guys near the Big Apple?"

Julie's laughter echoed through the line. "A few."

"Do tell."

While Julie chattered on about getting settled at the culinary school campus and meeting some of the other students and even a junior instructor, Lauren finished cleaning the kitchen, took out the trash, and moved on to straighten up the living room before counting out change from her tips to cover her part of the bill.

Would her housemates notice that she'd met their demands?

A yawn caught her off guard and interrupted Julie's description of a corner coffee shop with a cute barista.

"Please, tell me if I'm boring you." Julie's dry humor came through loud and clear.

Lauren grinned. "I'd be the first. Guess my long day is catching up with me."

"Totally get it. Besides, you need your beauty sleep before facing my hunky cousin again."

"Are we back to that again?"

"Until you admit the truth."

"Enough. Miss you. Stay safe. Have fun. And good night." She caught Julie's laughter before disconnecting the call.

A moment later, her phone chimed with a text message.

Chicken.

She scowled at the screen. Maybe she was.

But she couldn't risk another broken heart.

Chapter Four

♥

D istracted, Joel slammed on his brakes at the red light.

If only he could sprawl out and sleep for the next ten hours.

He stretched his arms overhead, groaning at the stiff muscles in his shoulders and upper back.

But no. There was too much to do before he could consider passing out.

Thankfully he'd found the keys in the pocket of Dad's coat still hanging at the diner. Transportation—and winter wear—had been the least of their worries when his mom had climbed into the back of the ambulance with Dad and the paramedics.

His phone chimed with an incoming message.

With the light still red, he checked it only to find a third text from Desiree wanting to talk. If she could see him now, she'd run the other way.

His fingers flew across the screen. *Sorry. Not a good time.*

He tossed the phone back onto the passenger seat, where it landed beside the foam take-out container holding more leftover meatloaf than he ever wished to eat.

It seemed they often made too much of Dad's favorite menu item and—since it couldn't be served the next day—the staff was first in line to keep the extra from landing in the trash. But based on the speed with which the others had nominated him for today's honor, Joel might not be the only critic.

Or else they'd gotten tired of it over time.

Just like Desiree had once moved on from bargain-conscious Joel to a big-spending teammate.

Except now that she wanted to get together after all this time—and apparently also moved to Colorado at some point—it was his decision whether or not to take a bite. And suddenly a reunion was as unappealing as the dense congealing slab riding shotgun.

The light turned green and he made the final turn toward the hospital.

The radio switched to an upbeat song and Joel tapped out a rhythm on his leg, only to end up picking at a spot of dried something on his jeans. Yuck.

He really should have run home first to take a shower but was afraid he wouldn't make it past the couch.

The diner was a relentless taskmaster demanding an endless supply of food and clean dishes to meet the continual orders from the customers. No wonder Dad saved the bookwork for after they closed the doors, because there wasn't a moment to spare in the middle of the day.

And no wonder why he'd kept his old habits instead of updating his business methods.

Change took time and energy to implement.

Time they didn't have.

And energy he currently lacked.

Once parked in the visitor lot, Joel scooted aside the meatloaf to grab his phone, list of questions, and the bundle of notes Lauren had somehow collected despite the chaos.

His mom would appreciate reading the handwritten messages from their customers, most of whom promised to pray.

Inside the main doors, he limped on stiff legs to the directory.

The sooner he reached Dad's room, the sooner he could collapse into a chair. Had it really only been twelve hours since he'd yawned his way through the back door of the diner?

Joel blinked gritty eyes to focus on the map.

His day had started with a mountain of onions. And ended with the same as they'd prepared for another marathon tomorrow.

But it could be worse.

He could be fatherless right now.

Thank You, God, for sparing Dad's life.

Dad might have survived the morning, but would he be able to return to working at the diner? Or at a minimum offer advice from a distance?

And during his recovery, would Mom stay with him or be available to pitch in from time to time?

Having oriented himself, Joel headed toward the elevators.

Knowing her, she would never leave Dad's side.

So without his parents' help, they were stuck in survival mode. At least until he could somehow find and train others to take their places.

A shiver of doubt trailed down Joel's spine.

He might be stuck here for a long time.

Stuck?

His stomach churned as the elevator rose.

No. Helping his parents could—should—be an act of love, not obligation.

Just like they'd done when attending his athletic events through high school, then helping to pay for incidentals not covered by his scholarship.

The doors opened to a floor of patient rooms and he followed the signs. Near the nurses' station, he spotted his mom propped up against the wall outside a closed door.

If possible, she'd aged even more over the past few hours.

"Mom?" He hurried forward.

She turned toward him with a weak smile on her too pale face. "You made it."

He registered the dark circles under her eyes before he wrapped her in a hug. "Sorry I couldn't be here sooner. Wish you hadn't been here all by yourself today."

Her body shuddered in his arms and she sniffed back tears. "You're here now and that's all that matters."

"I'll do everything I can to help." And just like that, he knew it was true.

He was committed to the diner for the duration.

Peace settled around his heart.

There had never been a choice.

Mom eased back. "I never doubted you."

"So, how is Dad?" He tilted his head toward the door beside them.

"He had another event not long ago."

Joel's breath caught in his throat. "As in a second heart attack?"

She nodded. "It was scarier than this morning. But since he's on all those monitors, he had help right away and they increased his medications. They're planning to sedate him tonight so his body can rest before another round of invasive tests tomorrow."

"What triggered it?"

Mom frowned. "He'd been bugging me about the diner. Wanting to start a list of things to tell you..."

"And getting himself stressed out." Joel recalled his own list.

He'd felt the tension all day, and *his* heart was healthy. No way he could ask Dad about any of his concerns.

His mom's shoulders slumped. "The doctors were clear that the stress is killing him. Tomorrow's tests should show what's wrong so they know how best to fix it. But once we get past the inevitable surgery, he'll need to take it very slow. It could be a long road ahead."

"But at least he's alive." Joel searched for a chair or two where he could get his mom off her feet.

She sighed. "You know your father. He'll be so frustrated at not being able to do things right away."

The Dawsons were no strangers to overcoming challenges.

Which meant keeping Dad on the sidelines would be a battle in itself.

Joel wrapped an arm around her shoulders to help hold her upright. "He's a fighter. And there are a lot of people praying for you both. Lauren started a collection and the cash donations are in the diner safe for now, but here's the rest." He shifted enough to deliver Lauren's package.

His mom thumbed through the top few notes before clutching the bundle to her heart with tears in her eyes. "She's such a sweet girl."

Sweet didn't begin to describe the energetic waitress.

The door opened and a nurse joined them in the corridor. "He's asleep now, but you can go back in if you want."

Joel followed his mom through the door and stopped at the foot of the hospital bed. His normally robust father was dwarfed by a mass of tubes and beeping monitors.

Mom perched on a chair beside the bed and grasped the limp hand lying on a white blanket.

The same hand that earlier today had wielded a spatula in the kitchen like a general in charge of his troops.

He'd seen glimpses of that same leadership in Aunt Greta.

If only he saw it in himself.

No fancy college degree could match the authority that came with experience.

If only he'd listened to Dad when he had the chance.

"How am I going to do this?" Joel rubbed his forehead.

"Do what?" Mom twisted on her chair to face him.

"Run the diner without Dad. I don't know where to start."

Mom chuckled. "The diner tends to run us."

A bark of laughter escaped his lips. "I figured that out. But there's so much I don't know how to do." He pulled his list of questions from his back pocket. "Where do I start?"

She held out a hand and he moved to her side. "Greta and Frank grew up in that kitchen when your grandparents owned the business. And then she came back after Steve died. So Greta can run the kitchen with Trevor's talent and support."

He'd seen that dynamic in action mere hours ago.

Mom hitched one shoulder. "And Lauren's been with us for several years and knows everything there is to know about the dining room. You simply ask them what they need and trust them to keep things going while you get up to speed."

Would he always be following behind or was there something he could do to help?

He swallowed his insecurities. "What about the bookkeeping and deposits and such?"

She turned back toward the bed and the beeping monitors. "Your dad does…" Her voice caught. "Did all that. You're going to have to figure it out on your own based on whatever you find in the office. I'm just the vegetable chopper and ingredient fetcher when I'm not helping Greta with the baking."

"Mom, you're much more than that." He pulled a rolling stool over so he could sit beside her.

She rested her head on his shoulder with a sigh. "Don't mind me. It's just been a long day."

They sat in silence while his thoughts spun in circles.

But even swallowing humble pie to ask Aunt Greta and Lauren for help didn't guarantee success because Mom and Dad did so much.

What if they forgot something important?

He mentally sorted his list of questions down to the few that only his mother could answer. "Today was brutal. We need more bodies there."

Mom turned watery eyes toward him and blinked. Twice.

Then she nodded. "It will be awhile until your dad is through the worst of this and my place is with him. Especially to keep him calm and distracted."

They both knew that it was easier said than done.

She offered a weak smile. "While you can always call me with questions, go ahead and hire some people. One specifically for the kitchen to help Greta with the baking and at least one for the dining room to replace Greta and maybe a second to fill Julie's shoes if we can afford it." She pursed her lips as if that were truly a factor.

He'd have to figure out their budget in order to know for sure, but bringing the staff back up to six or seven again made sense. Except the mental tally of job descriptions left him without a clear role.

Joel forced a casual tone. "Making me the permanent floater?"

"And the manager who is available to pitch in where needed while still free to handle the office side of the business." She squeezed his hand.

If only he had as much confidence in himself.

"Thank you." He cupped her hand between his. "Enough about the diner. How can I help you here? Maybe I can sit with Dad so you can take a break or find something to eat?"

Would she appreciate the leftover meatloaf? Or was he stuck with it?

"The nurses brought me something earlier." She paused, then her eyes widened. "How did you get here? Your car is at our house—"

"I drove yours." Joel retrieved and held out the keys.

She shook her head. "Keep them. We'll figure out the swap later once I feel more comfortable leaving your dad alone. For now, I could use a nap."

He pocketed the keys again. "Consider it done."

"Give me a half hour, then you can head home for your own sleep. Working at the diner takes more energy than sitting in a chair praying." She stood and crossed the room to an uncomfortable-looking couch. "Wake me up if anything changes."

As quiet descended, Joel sat and watched his father breathe.

At least he was doing that on his own.

Thank You, Lord, for small miracles. For the gift of time.

Dad's left hand twitched a bit, and then his left foot before he lay still again.

Was the sedation wearing off?

How much damage had been done?

Joel glanced at the monitors.

If anything changed?

Too late for that.

His life had changed forever.

Lauren stuffed her phone into the back pocket of her jeans, picked up her discarded shoes and purse, and stumbled toward her bedroom.

Next on her agenda was a shower followed by a few pages of a romance novel before bed.

She opened the door to her room and stopped at the sight of the clutter.

Maybe her roommates had a point.

But after all the messes she'd cleaned up today, she only wanted to relax.

Yet relaxing came easier in an uncluttered space.

She huffed. Might as well get it done and do it right.

After hooking her purse over the inside doorknob, she collected her laundry as she crossed to the closet to drop her shoes and retrieve her spare sheets. She turned on the radio and sang along to her favorite songs while stripping and remaking her bed.

The cardstock, ink pads, and rubber stamps leftover from making Christmas cards found a new home in a shoebox under her bed alongside the remnants of other discarded hobbies. She swept scraps of paper into a small trash can and stacked last semester's textbooks in a pile on the corner of her desk.

Lauren collapsed onto the wooden chair and stared at the framed verse Julie had given her almost a year ago.

"For I know the plans I have for you," declares the Lord, "plans to prosper you and not to harm you, plans to give you a hope and a future."

If only God would give her a sneak peek at those plans.

Her gaze shifted back to the textbooks. A trip to the campus bookstore loomed on the horizon before the spring semester started, but when would she find the time?

Not that she wanted to spend hard-earned money on books for classes she dreaded. Only one of the bunch on her schedule sounded even remotely interesting.

She'd started with liberal arts like Mom suggested before switching to business to make Dad happy.

Except that her Introduction to Finance class made her head spin and reminded her that while her sister Lenae might understand the intricacies of the stock market, Lauren's brain wasn't wired that way. Last semester was a dip into Elementary Education but the constant whining during her observation experiences drove her crazy.

If only she could skip college completely.

But what else would she do with her life?

Enough.

As Greta often said, never make big decisions when tired.

And she definitely had moved past tired to exhausted.

Time for that shower and a good night's sleep.

But as she stretched her aching arms over her head to wash her hair, she wondered how Joel was feeling.

He wasn't as used to the physical demands of the diner. And somehow after the morning lull, he'd kept up with all of the dishes despite the frantic pace of the lunch service.

If he wasn't sore tomorrow, she might have to slap him.

She'd been tempted to do just that when he announced she'd have to stay late for the baking. While today's extra work would help with tomorrow's sanity, she couldn't commit to the extended hours once her classes started.

They would have to make do without her.

Her stomach cramped.

How could she let the Dawsons down when they needed her support? After all, they'd become her pseudo-family in the messy aftermath of her parents' divorce.

But she couldn't quit college either or else Dad would freak out.

God, what am I supposed to do?

Maybe she could cut back her schedule to only one late afternoon class. That way she'd still be enrolled but also able to help more at the diner.

But that would mess up things with Dad, especially since he was the one in charge of her college savings and expected her to take a full load.

Would he understand the emergency and her doing a good deed? What if she promised to make up classes over the summer? And told him that she was gaining practical experience in running a business?

Yeah, Dad might buy that reasoning.

Not that she planned to tell him right away. He'd figure it out eventually when he got the revised statement from the university's financial office.

She winced.

A good daughter wouldn't hide the truth.

But she couldn't be a good daughter and a good employee at the same time.

With a clean body but still-cluttered thinking, she padded back to her room and got ready for bed. As she plugged her phone into the charger, she saw she'd missed three calls from an unknown number.

No voice messages but a single text.

This is Joel. Call me.

For a moment, her heart fluttered.

The handsome man had her number and obviously wanted to talk to her.

What did he want?

It could only be diner business.

And probably more orders.

She leaned against the headboard and called him back.

He answered on the first ring. "It's about time."

"I was in the shower."

Blood rushed to her face. Just what he needed to know.

"Oh." He cleared his throat. "Well, I'm glad I caught you. I'm leaving the hospital and—"

"Called to give me an update. That's sweet." She bit her lip and refocused on the important things. "How's your dad doing?"

"He had a setback earlier but is okay now. They gave him more medicine so he'll rest tonight."

"That's good, I guess. How's your mom holding up?"

He sighed. "She took a nap while I was there and plans to stay all night."

"Thanks for letting me know." Maybe she could put together a care package to help Nancy through the hours at the hospital. "Is there anything she needs?"

"Um, I don't know. Actually, the reason I called was to see if you could be at the diner a half hour earlier tomorrow."

"Oh." So much for the friendly update call.

"Is that a problem?"

"No." She reached for her alarm clock to make the brutal adjustment. "I'll be there, ready to chop anything but onions."

He snorted out a laugh. "I'll reserve them for you tomorrow afternoon."

"*You* will?"

"Or Aunt Greta might give them to Trevor." He cleared his throat again. "Since Dad was asleep—and the doctors are worried about his stress levels in general—I talked to Mom about how to handle the diner. Before we start the usual morning prep, we need to discuss hiring a kitchen helper and another one or two for the dining room."

"And what exactly will you be doing?" Leaving?

"I'll be managing the business side of things in addition to floating to pitch in where needed."

"Making you the boss?" She clenched her fist around the phone.

"Maybe. Once I'm up to speed on the operation." He groaned. "As you pointed out, I obviously have a lot to learn. From both you and Aunt Greta."

"Lessons start in the morning?"

"And continue in the afternoon."

"Um, about that."

"You'll have to adjust your schedule to be there full time, especially since you're now in charge of the dining room."

Her protest over his demand faded at the realization she'd been promoted.

Sort of.

"Do I get a raise?"

"Only if you consider more hours a raise." His tone was all business.

"More hours at waitress pay or at minimum wage?" Two could play the business game. She'd eavesdropped on enough of Dad's calls to know.

"Um, I'll have to check the books before I can commit to anything."

"We can settle up later. After all, I'm only agreeing in order to help your parents out." She shook her head and disconnected the call.

More hours at the diner doing what she loved, not to mention added responsibilities, might smooth things over with Dad.

If only being in charge of something didn't come at the loss of Nancy and Frank.

They would be missed.

And in their place was their bossy son.

Lauren plugged in her phone, then flopped backward onto her mattress.

She sure hoped Joel didn't keep issuing orders.

Then again, evidence of an inflated ego could make it easier to maintain her distance... and protect her fragile heart.

Chapter Five

♥

L auren flung open the back door of the diner right over the top of her left tennis shoe, then wasted valuable seconds dislodging the bottom weather stripping from her shoelaces before limping into the building.

Two minutes late.

Why did rushing through things always make them worse?

She took in the empty kitchen, then spotted the lights on in the office.

Of course their new boss man would be holding his extra-early meeting there.

She stuck out her tongue and rolled her eyes.

Wait.

That was childish.

It wasn't his fault that she'd hit the snooze button twice.

Or that she regretted going to bed with wet hair and had to spend precious time with a spray bottle trying to wrestle her unruly curls back where they belonged and obeying gravity.

While hanging up her coat, she wiggled her injured toes.

They'd survive.

Time to act as if the diner's clock was fast.

She strolled into the office and spotted Joel behind the desk scribbling on a legal pad. "Good morning."

At least she wasn't the last one to arrive.

She stashed her purse in her locker and spun the dial before turning to face her frowning coworker.

"Is it technically morning before the sun comes up?" He scrubbed a hand across his eyes.

She pressed her lips together. "Okay if I start the coffee? Or should I order up a caffeine drip?"

"Not funny." He tossed his pen onto the desktop and stretched. "Coffee would be nice. Or a Coke since it's quicker."

"Be right back."

After a detour past the coffee machine, she returned with two Cokes to find Joel leaned back, studying the legal pad propped up on his jean-clad knee.

No one should look that good at four thirty in the morning.

She set his glass in a vacant spot on the desk before pulling out a chair from around the small table in the corner that served as their break room.

"Thanks." He chugged several swallows. "First thing we need to—"

"Sorry I'm late." Greta bustled into the room and shoved her things into her locker. "Had to convince the night nurses to let me see Frank. You'd think they didn't realize other people might be up this early."

"How was he?" Lauren nudged a chair out with her foot.

"Sleeping and hooked up to all sorts of machines. But Nancy told me he'd been mumbling in his sleep a few hours ago. Probably dreaming about this place."

"Can't imagine Frank ever thinking about anything else." Lauren took a long sip and willed the caffeine to seep into her veins faster.

"True." Joel shrugged. "But he's going to have to let it go for the next few weeks at least. Which means we need more help and the sooner the better."

"Amen to that." Greta collapsed onto the chair and eyed Lauren's glass. "Did you start the coffee?"

"Sure did." Lauren smiled as Greta clearly debated whether to get a cup. Or not. The diner—and the staff—ran on the dark brew. "Speaking of help, where's Trevor?"

"He should be here at the regular time." Joel cleared his throat. "But since you two have been here the longest, you'll be my management team as we—"

Greta snorted. "Never been called management before."

Lauren smirked. "Should we order business cards? Or new name tags?"

"Funny." He glared at them both. "As I was saying, if we're getting back up to the magic number of seven staff, we need to hire three people. One to assist Greta and Trevor in the kitchen and one or two more servers." Joel swiveled in his chair. "How can we do that the fastest and what do we look for?"

"First, dust off the sign sitting on that shelf over there and tape it in the window." Greta pointed at the red-rimmed cardboard sticking out from among a haphazard collection of binders.

"Trevor's relatively new himself, but I wasn't involved in that process." Lauren drummed her fingers on the tabletop. "We should probably find and print out a generic job application for people to fill out. And then post on Craigslist since that's free."

Joel scribbled notes on his pad and nodded. "If we don't get any workable leads by tomorrow afternoon, I'll look into an ad in the newspaper classifieds."

"Frank never took out an ad." Greta shook her head. "Thought it was a waste of money."

Joel scratched something off his list with a frown. "Once we generate enough interest, you can assist by screening the applicants before we schedule interviews."

Screening? And interviews?

What did he think this was? A big business in need of a head-hunter's services?

They were a simple diner in a growing community with a small-town feel an hour north of Denver.

But at least he'd asked for their advice.

Maybe there was hope after all that he wouldn't resort to being an impossible boss despite the way he'd once stomped on her fragile heart.

Joel waved a hand at the ancient computer and dusty binders. "I plan to have a better idea of what we can pay by the time we have someone to interview." He tapped his pen on the pad of notes. "But before Trevor gets here and we start on prep, here's my plan..."

Lauren swallowed a groan as the boss-man reared his handsome head again.

If she'd had more sleep, maybe she'd have more patience. More understanding. But for now, all she could do was chug her Coke and pray the caffeine hit her veins soon before she accidentally said something she'd regret.

"Aunt Greta? As the kitchen manager, let us know what you need prepared. Do we need to make any changes to the menu or push some items more than others? How are we on supplies?" He glanced at his list. "Didn't I hear something yesterday about a delivery coming that we'll have to put away?"

"Every Tuesday afternoon after we close." Greta eyed the door. "Let me grab a cup of coffee and I'll get my brain in order."

Joel waved her toward the door with a swipe of his majesty's hand. "Lauren? You're in charge of the dining room."

She finished off her drink instead of answering. He'd said the same thing on the phone last night.

"I learned a lot yesterday, so I can handle my fair share of the tables plus run the dishwasher."

She resisted the urge to roll her eyes and nodded instead. "Hopefully. But I still need to teach you how to operate the cash register."

He rummaged under a pile on the desktop. "I found the operations manual this morning so I can read up on the features."

"That's a good start." But it would still be better to show him.

"Now, like I had a list of questions for Aunt Greta, is there anything specific you need...?"

Lauren grabbed her empty glass. "What I need right now is a refill. Then I'll start helping Greta while you post the job listings and print out an application. Anything else can be talked about while we're doing the prep work."

She turned on her heel and left him behind with the dusty books.

Seven hours later, she delivered a bacon cheeseburger with fries and a French dip with fruit to a middle-aged couple. She retrieved pitchers of iced tea and water and started a round of refills for the lunch crowd.

On a normal day, she'd be leaving in an hour and driving to the college for her classes. But, she'd committed to another two hours until closing followed by a whole lot more for cleaning up, putting away the food order, and prepping for tomorrow.

At least there were three completed applications stacked beside the register.

Help couldn't come soon enough.

Although without the emotional overtones of yesterday's crisis, today had been much easier. Except for Joel's continued taking notes on his yellow notepad and frowning at her.

Was he ticked at her reaction to his orders this morning?

Didn't he realize the sacrifice she was making to stay longer?

He hadn't even asked if it was okay or tried to work around her plans. Then again, in chaos had she even told him about her class schedule?

The bells on the door clattered and jarred her musings back where they should belong.

On the customers.

"Hi, folks." She smiled at the family with three young children who had entered. "Seat yourself and I'll be right with you."

The father nodded and directed his brood toward a booth. The littlest girl would need a booster.

Lauren replaced the drink pitchers in their spots behind the lunch counter and retrieved a plastic chair for the little one, along with a detour to Hope's heirloom buffet for a cup of crayons and pages Nancy had ripped from a coloring book.

The antique piece of furniture had been relocated to the diner after Greta and Julie moved in with Hope, but now it was a handy spot for odds and ends including coloring sheets to entertain the kids.

The Dawsons liked to anticipate every possible need.

And now she'd have to remember to keep an ample supply.

She got the young family set up and took their drink orders before jotting herself a note to check the stock of condiments, napkins, and other items kept in the dining room.

Joel's note-taking habit was rubbing off.

She frowned.

As long as she didn't forget to be a team player, she'd be fine with a little more discipline.

Half an hour later, she paused for a moment to take a swig from her soda glass tucked next to the coffee machine.

"Why do you keep talking to them so much?"

"Excuse me?" She turned to find Joel hemming her in beside the counter. At least he had the good sense to lower his voice so they weren't overheard.

"The more they talk, the slower they eat, and the longer it takes before their table is available for new customers." He folded his arms over his chest.

"You have a problem with me talking to our customers?"

"Well, obviously you have to communicate enough to get their orders, but that doesn't mean you have to stand around chatting about how nice the weather is for January while I'm busting my rear keeping up with all the dishes."

If the furrow between his eyebrows grew any deeper, it would be a canyon.

Just like the chasm between their viewpoints.

"You haven't got a clue what—"

Greta's kitchen bell dinged that an order was ready.

Lauren glared at the know-it-all-who-knew-nothing. "You just got saved by the bell. For now."

He raised an eyebrow and she pushed past him.

Two could play the bossy role.

She gathered several plates of food and turned to face him, narrowing her eyes. "I'm in charge of the dining room. And you need a much-overdue lesson about good service."

Joel locked the front door after the last departing customer and headed for the cash register.

Finally.

Only half an hour after their posted closing time.

His stomach rumbled. They'd been too busy earlier for him to eat much of anything on his too-short break. And at this rate, it would be hours before he could get off his feet.

Joel pulled out the manual and started punching buttons on the touch screen to run the program totaling the day's receipts. "At least you flipped the sign over or else more slow eaters would have wandered in to occupy the space we should be cleaning up."

Lauren straightened from the table she'd been resetting and propped a hand on her hip. "Oh, get off your high horse."

"I'm not a cowboy and I certainly don't ride a horse." He frowned at the feisty blonde frowning back at him.

She added silverware bundles beside the overturned coffee cups on their saucers. "You know what I mean. You've been acting like serving is a dirty word."

"Well, it's a dirty job." He swiped at the remnants of food crusted on his shirt and jeans despite the apron while trying not to inhale the whiff of body odor his movements caused.

"You're impossible." She stalked to the closet near the bathrooms and rolled out the mop bucket.

"Who's impossible?" Aunt Greta paused at the soda machine with a glass in her hand.

"Your nephew belongs somewhere other than in the dining room." Lauren rattled the empty bucket toward the kitchen.

He rolled his eyes.

As if he didn't already know that.

Aunt Greta glared. "I know we're all exhausted and patience is worn thin, but can't we work together?" She filled her drink and took a sip.

Lauren aimed an accusing finger in his direction. "Not when Joel thinks we're only here to get 'em in, get 'em fed, get their money, and get 'em out."

He winced at the harsh summary.

"Really?" Aunt Greta turned on him.

He slowly nodded. "Not quite like that, but we can't serve new customers until the current ones leave."

She raised a graying eyebrow that matched the prematurely silver hair she'd inherited from her mother. "What exactly do we sell here?"

Joel resisted the urge to squirm. "What kind of question is that?"

"Lauren? Grab a couple drinks for you and Joel and let's have a seat."

"Yes, ma'am." Lauren gleefully abandoned the mop bucket.

He'd rather have a slice of pie than a soft drink, but Dad's favorite complaint was accurate. The regulars never left any. His afternoon sugar fix would be the liquid variety with a side of caffeine.

"Hey, Trevor?" Aunt Greta called through the pass-through window. "Keep an eye out for the laundry service swap. But you might as well take a break before we put away the rest of the order. I need to chat with my nephew for a bit and am going to get off my feet as far away from that kitchen as possible."

"No problem." The other man chuckled.

Joel gritted his teeth.

Why did he feel like a ten-year-old who'd misbehaved in church?

He started to balk, then gave in. The sooner her lecture was done, the sooner he could return to the real work. He followed Aunt Greta to a nearby booth and slid onto the cushion across from her.

Lauren arrived with two Cokes and took up position next to Aunt Greta.

Outnumbered and on the hot seat.

He reached for his drink as a distraction.

Aunt Greta folded her hands around her glass and stared him in the eye. "Serving is what we do here. It doesn't matter if the food tastes good or the books balance. If the customer isn't happy, they don't come back. And don't kid yourself, there are plenty of places in town to get something to eat."

His gaze darted from Aunt Greta's icy blue skewer right into Lauren's serious hazel green stare.

Aunt Greta narrowed her eyes. "We are a diner, not a fast-food joint. Part of our draw on the market is making customers feel at home and part of the family. *They* are the most important part of this business and Lauren has the gift."

Lauren's eyes widened in surprise and she turned toward his aunt. "What gift?"

Aunt Greta patted her hand. "You have a way of getting to know people and making them feel welcome and cared for. That's the heart of customer service."

Customer service?

Just like all his professors said at least a dozen times during every business course he'd ever taken.

The customer was always right... and quality customer service could make or break any business model.

Aunt Greta rolled her glass between her palms. "That's why Frank never made you rotate into the kitchen. Just being in the room and hearing your laughter is enough to brighten anyone's day. And that's good business."

"That's sweet." Lauren giggled.

Joel groaned. "She's not been very sweet to me."

"Maybe you don't deserve it." She stuck out her tongue at him.

He fought a smile at her playful gesture. Primarily because her complaints about his attitude had started this lecture in the first place.

"Maybe." Or maybe not. But he still needed to play nice for the sake of the diner. "Truce?" He held out a hand for her to shake.

"Truce." At her gentle touch, something shifted in his chest. Maybe he wasn't alone in the struggle to keep the diner open.

Aunt Greta laid her hand atop theirs and squeezed. "Joel, I know you're a numbers kind of guy, unlike my brother. But you'll do fine around here as long as you remember that anyone can cook and sell meals. But if you don't have love, you serve in vain. Just like Jesus said, whatever we do for the least of these, we've done for Him."

"So we serve because Jesus did?" Joel grimaced. "Pouring coffee isn't the same as washing feet."

Aunt Greta's smile turned back into a glare. "I'm glad your grandmother can't hear you now."

He flinched. The family resemblance was strong and he could feel the scolding as if his grandmother was still alive.

"Hope always said that serving is the highest calling." Lauren nodded as if she'd known the woman personally.

Then again, she'd spent a lot of time with Julie... at his grandmother's house.

"You're right." He took another drink and accepted the inevitable. "It's also good business. We're in an industry where customer service is everything."

"Exactly." Aunt Greta nodded. "So, when we look closer at the folks who might be interested in working here, we're looking for heart as well as skill. We need someone who will put this family first." She gestured around the dining room before chugging half her glass.

He pictured the hundreds of people who had eaten there today and vowed to work harder to deliver what they really paid for beyond their meals.

But speaking of paying.

"Different subject." He pointed at the cash register spitting out a long tape of calculations. "I was thinking about a way to streamline our ordering and checkout system."

He held up a hand to stop Lauren's sputtering. "*Not* to rush people out of here faster."

Well, maybe a little bit, but for other reasons too. Like knowing in black and white how much meatloaf they actually sold and if there were more popular menu items to promote that didn't waste as many ingredients.

But back to the argument he'd prepared while feeding racks of dirty dishes into the dishwasher.

"It could also make less work for us. And fewer mistakes." He took another drink.

Lauren and Aunt Greta exchanged puzzled glances.

Since he'd captured their attention, Joel leaned forward. "I've eaten at places where the server might take notes on a pad for themselves but inputs the choices onto a touch screen. I assume the same order shows up on a monitor in the kitchen... and later gets printed out by the computer with the total already calculated."

He paused to collect his thoughts as the women stared back.

"No more misunderstanding about what we... I... wrote down. No having to remember the menu prices. And customers can check their bill and calculate their tip before getting to the register." He shrugged. "Maybe we could ring them up and bring their change to the table when it's convenient for us rather than have them stand in a line that pulls us away from other tables."

Lauren tilted her head. "That has possibilities."

Aunt Greta frowned. "But how much would it cost to set up a system like that?"

He rested his elbows on the tabletop. "Not as much as you might think. I studied the manual today and we already have the software in place. All we need are a few more monitors to hook into a network."

Lauren slapped a hand onto the table. "I think we might have those. I remember a couple of boxes in the back of the storeroom. Bet Frank never found the time to set it all up and figure it out."

"That sounds like Dad." He shook his head. "Want to go take a look?"

"I still need to mop and clean the bathrooms. But I should be free about the time you're done with the daily deposit." Lauren slid out of the booth. "If we can get it running soon, then we can train the new staff right from the beginning."

Aunt Greta drained the rest of her glass. "As long as somebody helps this old lady figure out how it works."

Joel smiled. He might have started off on the hot seat, but he was back in control.

Things were looking up for a change.

Or at least he hoped so.

He'd had enough of life's unwelcome surprises lately.

Chapter Six

♥

C ould their new waitress handle the pressure of flying solo so soon on her first day?

"Is she ready?" Joel stopped near Lauren's elbow, his hands full of dirty dishes.

And his words echoing her doubts.

"Better than you were." Lauren bravely smirked, then angled a paper napkin in front of her on the lunch counter.

"Hey. It might have been years, but at least I'd done it before." He bent to place his load in the bussing tub.

Across the room, Clarissa Miller greeted a just-seated couple. Pointed to the menus in the condiment rack. Nodded at something they said.

How much training did someone need before being tossed into the deep end?

"Seriously. Was shadowing you for a few hours enough?" Joel straightened with a spray bottle of disinfectant and a rag in hand.

Lauren rolled her eyes. "Even if she can only handle a single table at a time through lunch, that's still one less for the two of us. But she's a fast learner."

"If you say so." He rounded the end of the counter to wash the table he'd just cleared, passing Clarissa on her way to the drink station.

Was that a compliment or continued doubt? Time would tell.

Lauren stacked a knife, fork, and spoon across one corner of the napkin, then rolled them into a bundle before securing it with a strip of gummed paper and adding it to the half-filled tub.

The redhead scooped ice into glasses, then placed the first under the iced tea spigot. "So far, so good."

"You're doing just fine. And we're here if you have any questions or need an assist." Lauren grabbed another napkin to start the process all over again.

Clarissa offered a small smile. "It helps that everyone I've met so far is much nicer—and infinitely more patient—than my brothers are at home."

"Let's pray they stay that way." Lauren grinned.

"Amen to that." Clarissa carefully transferred the filled glasses to a cork-lined tray, then made her way back out to the dining room.

Most of their customers were the hard-working, blue-collar sort who appreciated being waited on for a change. However, there were always those few who made it difficult to keep a smile on her face.

That said, if what she'd heard about Clarissa's home situation during their interview was true, the diner could be a haven as well as a source of income. Lauren couldn't imagine suddenly becoming a guardian to younger brothers while also dealing with their collective grief.

Being busy had to help, right?

Not to mention, the boys might enjoy time away from the substitute mother who'd called them mid-breakfast rush simply to make sure they were out of bed and on their way to the bus-stop.

Yes, a little distance might do them all good.

Two bundles of silverware later, Joel stowed the cleaning supplies, then depleted the freshly stocked tub in addition to grabbing cups and saucers to reset the table before the lunch crowd filtered in.

Her phone vibrated in her back pocket, then dinged to announce another incoming text.

She fished it out only to confirm that her dad still wanted a report about her first day of classes. As if he couldn't remember that she regularly worked in the mornings and attended college in the afternoons.

And since this was Monday—and the very first day of the new semester—it was impossible for her to have physically been to class yet.

She shoved her phone away along with her thoughts. Dad would have to wait until there was something to report.

Lauren's gaze swept the room, counting tables and keeping an eye on Clarissa as she wrote something on her order pad.

While they'd planned to hire two waitresses, Nancy had later balked at the extra expense. Which meant Joel was still floating between the dining room and dish-duty with plans to re-evaluate soon.

Maybe she could give Clarissa a couple more of the booths?

Behind Lauren, Greta's voice carried through the pass-through window as she continued to train their new kitchen helper, Debbie. However, aside from the occasional chop this or hand me that instructions, most of the women's chatter revolved around their kids.

Julie would cringe if she knew what stories her mother had been oversharing to a relative stranger. In front of Trevor, too.

Then again, Debbie had her own tales from raising her twins to their current driving age. The single mother might not have formal culinary training, but she had plenty of experience juggling multiple tasks at once.

If she knew him better, Lauren would feel sorry for Trevor being trapped in the kitchen with the two mothers.

Lauren smirked. Bet he looked forward to Joel's trips to run the dishwasher to at least see another man.

Clarissa returned and stopped at the new stand-alone monitor. After referring to her notepad, she tapped the screen to input the food order for the kitchen then tapped the green submit button.

She turned to Lauren. "Now all I have to do is wait."

The bells over the front door clattered.

Clarissa grinned. "Can I have another table?"

Lauren nodded toward a vacant window booth. "Sure. But seat them near your first table so it's easier to keep an eye on everyone."

"Will do." Clarissa hurried over to greet the newcomers with a smile.

Their new waitress seemed like a perfectly friendly fit.

"I'll admit it. You made a good choice." Joel joined her at the counter and reached for a napkin.

Lauren picked up her pace, making it an informal competition to restock the tub. "There weren't a lot of options to pick from on Saturday, but I felt really good about her."

Being able to start immediately shouldn't have been such a determining factor during the interviews, yet it appeared God had answered their cries for help.

Anyone who was willing to go to such lengths for the sake of their family deserved the opportunity.

Joel glanced over his shoulder toward the pass-through window. "Do you think Debbie's daughter will catch on as fast?"

Lauren nudged him with her elbow. "What's the problem? You worked here in high school. So did Julie and I. I think having another trained part-time waitress will come in handy."

Clarissa had requested weekends free so she could be at home with her brothers, but Debbie already volunteered her kids to pitch in occasionally when they weren't in school.

They'd meet Debbie's daughter on Saturday for her first day.

And hopefully she'd learn the routine as quickly as Clarissa had. Although the true test would come when juggling several tables at once.

Joel did that male head-bob motion toward the kitchen, punctuated with a grunt so much like his father's. "Her son will be a welcome addition for dish duty. Plus we need another man around here to even the odds since Trevor and I are so outnumbered."

So he'd been thinking along the same lines as she had.

But just for good measure—and because Julie would approve—Lauren punched his bicep.

He rubbed the spot as if she'd inflicted any real damage. "Like I said. Outnumbered."

She huffed. "I didn't hear you complain this morning when Debbie asked if Greta could add a strawberry rhubarb pie to the lineup."

He patted his flat stomach. "I never turn down dessert."

"Me neither." She sighed.

It was a good thing she spent her days on her feet logging thousands of steps or her waistline would pay the price for her sweet tooth. Then again, the most tempting variety—apple crumb—was often sold out before lunch.

"Grandma used to say there's nothing a slice of pie can't fix." Joel propped one hip against the counter, facing her. "But I've been thinking..."

"That could be dangerous." Lauren tried to suppress a smile.

Why was she in such a feisty mood today? Must be the extra help to lighten the load. Because she had no other excuse to be teasing him.

Or talking about anything other than work.

"Hilarious." Joel rolled his eyes. "What I meant is that rather than offer all the kinds, what if we had a featured pie of the day or week? Aunt

Greta could bake the usual favorites but we'd still have a little something different for the customers."

It wasn't a bad idea. But how many other varieties did they have to choose from?

Lauren pointed to Hope's buffet near the door and the small white board listing the daily special. "We could have a contest to collect seasonal suggestions and the winner gets a free slice."

He rubbed his chin as if seriously considering the possibility.

At least he didn't look at her like she was out of her mind before carting the tub of dishes back to the kitchen.

She visually checked her remaining tables and abandoned the silverware to collect payments from two parties that were nearly finished. While it had been a crazy transition getting the computer system set up including a few kinks to work out, the whole process had made things so much simpler.

Especially when there had been only four of them on the job.

The monitor beside her lit up with a red number twelve at about the same time Clarissa came back with a half-empty pitcher of iced tea. Food for her first table was ready to deliver and their new helper tapped the screen to acknowledge it.

The bells over the door clattered again and a large group of women entered. Lauren hurried forward to greet them and push several tables together.

Like she did on the second Monday of every month when the ladies society from a nearby church met to discuss their latest community project and continued the debate at the diner over an early lunch.

Joel returned in time to help rearrange the chairs and get the ladies settled.

She caught his amused glance over the white-haired head of the stocky woman in the lime green polyester pantsuit with the orange chunky necklace. His cousin Julie and she had shared many a laugh over the group's outlandishly outdated fashions.

"Can I start you ladies off with something to drink?" Lauren flipped to a new page in her notepad and noticed Joel doing the same at the other end of the long table.

The tiny woman with a hot pink blazer to her right spoke up first. "I'll have iced tea with lemon." She pointed a wrinkled finger at the woman across from her. "I still think we should ask for donations."

A fierce debate erupted around the table.

Beyond Joel, Lauren caught sight of Clarissa carrying a plate of food back toward the kitchen. A picky customer or had Clarissa typed it in wrong? Either way, since Lauren and Joel were occupied with the large group, their new waitress would have to figure it out on her own. At least for now.

Mrs. Lime Green raised her chin and her voice from Joel's end of the group. "We can't ask people for more money."

Lauren tapped the shoulder of a woman with an artificially red teased helmet of hair. "Ma'am. What can I get you to drink?"

"Just water." Mrs. Helmet Hair leaned her elbows on the table. "That's right. Pastor said we have to keep our projects self-sufficient and not be a burden on the congregation."

Mrs. Pink Jacket rested her properly folded hands on the table. "But how many blankets can we make right now? Is it worth the effort to only deliver a small stack to the shelter?"

Mrs. Lime Green snorted. "Any blankets are more than what they have now."

Lauren caught Joel's eye again.

It seemed he was having as much trouble getting their attention for drinks as she was. What he didn't know was that while they never had enough money for their assorted projects, they could be counted on for a good tip.

She shrugged and entered the debate as she always did. According to her dad, curiosity would be her downfall some day. "What are you making them out of?"

A silver-haired woman in a jacket covered with bright blue flowers patted her hand. "Yarn. We're going to crochet them."

"Oh." Lauren tapped her pen on her notepad. "I think my grandmother did that. All I really remember are the numerous balls of extra yarn she had stashed all over her house."

"Me, too." Mrs. Blue Flowers fluttered her eyelashes. "I'll have water with lemon, dear, but you just gave me a great idea."

"Really?" Lauren made a note, then paused as the conversation switched on a dime to asking for donations of unused yarn instead of money.

Three minutes later, she had collected drink orders from her half of the group and rescued a dazed Joel.

As they were about to make their temporary escape, Mrs. Lime Green spoke up. "Aren't you Frank Dawson's boy?"

Joel turned. "Yes."

"He's been on our Prayer Chain for a week now. How's he doing?"

Joel stared at the rest of the now silent group and his expression softened. "Thank you for your prayers. He finally got the insurance authorization and is scheduled for open heart bypass surgery tomorrow. He'll be in the hospital for another week and then it'll take six to twelve weeks for his breastbone to heal."

A flurry of questions erupted.

Lauren reached for his notepad and slipped away to start getting their drinks.

Seemed Joel had caught a glimpse of the big hearts beneath the polyester.

And based on the perpetually full donation jar by the register, the ladies weren't the only customers who cared. The encouraging notes brightened Nancy's day, but she had a feeling that the cash would be a bigger blessing the longer Frank was in the hospital.

Hours later, Lauren locked the door and turned to face the dining room.

Even after needing to help sort out a couple of Clarissa's first day mix-ups—and placate the irritated customers—the day had still been miles ahead of last week's stress.

Especially since Clarissa had learned from her mistakes and kept a positive attitude.

Lauren ran down her mental checklist. With Clarissa cleaning and resetting the last table, they still had to reload the coffee machines, refill the ketchup bottles, clean the bathrooms, and mop the floor.

Clarissa had to leave at a certain time to pick up her brothers from school, but with any luck, Lauren could also be out of there within the hour.

Giving her plenty of time to stop at the campus bookstore before her first and only class tonight.

She was in the middle of preparing the coffee when Joel pushed through the swinging doors from the kitchen and made his way to the cash register. He started the close out procedures.

Once the machine was printing out the report, he turned to her with a frown.

She tensed. "What's wrong?"

"In all the craziness last week, there's a not-so-little something that slipped my mind." He squeezed his forehead with one hand. "What do you know about placing orders?"

About as much as he did. Or so she'd thought.

Before she forgot what she'd been doing, Lauren tore a silvery package open and poured the grounds into the filter.

She switched her attention to the extra monitor they'd been inputting orders on all day. "I read the manual with you when we set up the system."

"Not those food orders." He crossed his arms over his broad chest and leaned back against the counter. "Greta asked if I could put extra cocoa powder on our next delivery as if I'm supposed to know how to do that."

She wadded up the empty packaging and tossed it into the nearby trash can with a sinking feeling. "Those usually come on Tuesdays."

"That's tomorrow. But when did Dad actually *place* the order? And how did he know what we needed? I didn't see a running list like Mom keeps on the fridge at home."

A list.

Her stomach churned.

"I'm so sorry." Lauren wrapped her arms around her waist and stared across the room where Clarissa ran the mop back and forth. "I should have remembered. But we were so busy..."

Once again, she'd messed up somehow.

"Remembered what?" His voice sounded like he was being choked.

Guilt settled onto her shoulders like a familiar blanket.

"I sometimes helped your mom with the inventory on Saturday afternoons since I didn't have school and could stay later. She had a clipboard full of checklists and I'd count stuff for her to record."

But instead of doing inventory on Saturday, she'd been interviewing potential candidates with Joel and Greta... then deep cleaning the diner since they'd spent so much time with kitchen prep in the afternoons instead.

He ran a hand through his hair, standing it on end. "So we look for the checklists. But then what?"

Her fingers itched to smooth his dark hair. She bit her lip. "After that you'd have to ask your mom."

Because she honestly didn't have a clue what happened after the inventory was complete. Which meant that instead of helping the Dawsons, she'd accidentally made things worse.

He stepped away with slumped shoulders, already pulling out his phone.

She should have known better.

It was only a matter of time before history caught up with her.

Scatterbrained misfits like her shouldn't be trusted with responsibility.

Chapter Seven

♥

J oel paced the dining room while waiting for his mom to pick up, avoiding the freshly mopped spots to avoid leaving footprints on the checkered tiles before they dried.

He'd been hoping Lauren had answers so he didn't have to bother his parents since they were focused on tomorrow's surgery.

His call rang yet again. And again.

Mom always had her phone on her, especially lately.

His heart caught in his throat.

Please, God. We need your help again...

Behind the counter, Lauren continued preloading the coffee machines. Based on her wrinkled forehead, she blamed herself.

Which was ridiculous because this latest hurdle was all his fault.

Mom's voice mail message kicked in, but Joel hung up and immediately redialed.

His list last week had contained this very question about how to order supplies. Except he'd gotten sidetracked keeping their heads above water in the short-staffed kitchen and going through potential employee applications.

Not to mention his general exhaustion from the extra long days followed by visits to the hospital to take Mom things she needed and serve as a distraction for his dad.

While simultaneously avoiding as much talk about the diner as possible in light of Dad's health and stress levels.

He sidestepped Clarissa and the rattling mop bucket, then ran a hand through his hair as the phone continued to ring unanswered.

How many other issues lurked from his abandoned list?

At the end of that first crazy day—just a week ago—Lauren had shown him the safe, deposit slips, and his dad's checklist for restocking the register's drawer. Anything beyond that minimum cash reserve was dropped at the bank daily.

Other than asking Mom what wage to offer the new help, he hadn't brought up the topic of finances with his parents either.

He sighed. Whatever happened to taking initiative to look into their bookkeeping? Hadn't that been Dad's request from the beginning?

Ugh. He could have looked into the financial records yesterday while the diner was closed for Sunday, but after attending church services on his own, he'd spent the day at the hospital then doing laundry.

No excuses.

The voice message echoed in his ear followed by a beep.

"Mom? Call me as soon as you can. Don't tell Dad, but we may have a problem with the food order."

After disconnecting, he stopped at the register to pick up the daily sales report and cash drawer, then stalked into the kitchen and ducked into the office.

Time to search for the mystery inventory checklists.

While he was at it, he should sort through the other files. See what clues he could find in the old invoices. In addition to a phone number, he might figure out the typical quantities and types of items Dad ordered.

He had gathered several stacks to organize further when Lauren entered carrying a Coke.

She set it down and slid it toward him. "Thought you could use an apology pick-me-up."

"I did. I mean the caffeine, not the—"

His phone rang and his mom's picture flashed on the screen. He snatched it up. "Thanks for calling me back. Did you—"

She started in on a long description of why she'd been away from her phone when he'd called.

"Mom? I need—"

She continued telling him in full detail about the pre-op instructions and meeting with a physical therapist to discuss post-surgery exercises.

He'd have to wait for her to wind down before trying to get another word in.

Across the desk, Lauren rocked back on her feet with a smirk hovering on her lips. She'd worked with his mom for a while so the chattering probably wasn't a surprise.

Clarissa entered, got her things from a locker, waved, and left.

At least *she* was the lucky recipient of today's container of leftover meatloaf. Hopefully her brothers were willing to eat it.

Ugh. Those unsold ingredients had to be cutting into the bottom line. If only he had a better idea of the diner finances and their profit margin.

Then again, the wasted meatloaf was obvious.

Was it too much to hope they might run short on ground beef and be forced into a menu change even if it was temporary?

Maybe he'd ask Aunt Greta and Trevor about creating a different make-a-batch-ahead recipe? Something like lasagna? Or a soup that could be served the next day?

And still Mom babbled on as if she hadn't had anyone to talk to all day.

But he didn't have all day.

"Mom? Could I ask—"

Lauren rolled her eyes as she rounded the end of the desk. She patted him on the shoulder as she reached past him to the bookshelf and retreated with a clipboard. She flipped through the pages before pointing at herself and out the door.

He nodded and tried interrupting again. "Mom. Stop. I have a problem."

"What? I didn't listen to the message. I saw that you called and thought you wanted an update on your dad."

"I did. Do. But right now, I need help and don't want to worry Dad."

"Just a minute." He heard a shifting in the background noise as if she'd left his father's room and stepped out into the hall.

He reached for the glass of Coke, preparing himself for bad news. "Lauren said you do inventory on Saturdays."

"I do. I have lists of absolutely everything we use—or have ever used—in the diner. They're sorted by the different areas and kept on a clipboard on the top shelf of the bookshelves behind the desk in the office."

Right where Lauren had found them. "Go on."

"Each item is labeled on the sheets with how much we typically need in a week. So, every Saturday, I go through the walk-in cooler, freezer, and storage room to fill in the box with what we have on hand."

Joel swiveled the chair. "How does that translate into the order from Foothills Food Supply." He eyed the stack of invoices on the desktop.

Mom gasped. "Uh-oh."

"How bad is it?" He held his breath.

"Do you have any idea how many eggs we can go through in a single day? And bacon? Even with a built-in cushion, if you ran out then breakfast could be a dis—"

"Mom! Stop." Joel rubbed his temples. "Lauren's doing the inventory right now. I just need to know what to do with those numbers."

She sighed. "Your dad takes the order form—there should be extras in a folder on the shelf near where I keep the inventory sheets—and subtracts what we have from what we need and adds one unit for cushion. He always faxes it before we leave on Saturday afternoon so they have it waiting in their inbox first thing Monday morning."

"So an order placed Monday morning gets delivered Tuesday afternoon." Joel did a quick calculation in his head. "If I send them an order tonight..."

Mom's sigh echoed over the line. "You'll have to ask them about that. They might be able to rush the delivery for a fee."

He groaned. It was a good thing they didn't have a third new crew member to pay right now. "Thanks. I'll give them a call about our options and see you later."

He disconnected then dialed the number on the invoice.

Within a few minutes, he received condolences from the customer service representative at the distributor but no good news. An order placed by the end of the day would be delivered Wednesday afternoon. Period.

He thanked them and hung up before dropping his head onto his hands.

With the amount of fresh produce—plus the bacon and eggs Mom had mentioned—that the diner went through in a day, they could easily run out of key ingredients before the delivery arrived.

Which meant he might have to go shopping at the local grocery store—at retail prices—to bridge the gap until the delivery arrived.

What a disaster.

God, I could use a whole lot of help about now.

When had his faith become a constant plea for help? Was this the reality of praying without ceasing?

He had no other choice but to trust God to work out the details one step at a time.

But the first detail he could take care of by himself.

He fished around in the desk drawers and found a red marker. Pushing aside the papers covering the desktop calendar, he made a note on every Saturday to avoid future problems.

Time for damage control.

He headed out into the kitchen to where his aunt, Trevor, and Debbie scoured the grill and the prep stations. "Aunt Greta?"

Her smile faded. "What's wrong?"

"Do I really look that bad?" He shook his head. "Never mind. Thanks to your earlier question about cocoa powder, I figured out that we're going to be a day late on the order."

She gasped. "The inventory! That's always been Frank's department and I've been so busy trying to keep up in here that—"

Trevor patted her shoulder. "You're not the only one who forgot." His green eyes turned toward Joel. "As the kitchen newbie, he had me help him get a head start once, but now that I'm on the line..." He shook his head.

Joel had been surprised to learn they had a highly trained chef in their midst... and were using him to chop vegetables and assemble meatloaf. Once they were past crisis mode, they'd have to brainstorm ways to use Trevor's skills better.

For now, he eyed the worried staff. "No one's to blame. It happened... and it won't happen again. And I think if we could keep this place open over the past week with just four of us, I'm sure six of us can work together to make it an extra day without a food delivery."

Thank God he wasn't facing this crisis alone.

He focused on his aunt. "Lauren started doing the inventory so I can place the order later, but what I need is for you and Trevor to make a list of the essentials you'll need between now and Wednesday afternoon. Then I'll make a special shopping trip later... and we can re-evaluate after closing tomorrow to see if we've miscalculated anything."

"Um, Greta?" Trevor shuffled his feet. "I'd really like to help today, but I have to—"

A sympathetic smile crossed his aunt's face. "Take your mom to her oncology appointment."

Right. His mother's health was the reason Trevor had passed up more prestigious posts in the Denver area and moved back home after culinary school.

And fighting for one's life—like Dad was—mattered more than how much bacon cost at the regular store.

God, heal him. Them.

"You're a good son." Aunt Greta squared her shoulders. Shoulders that knew personally what it was like to battle alongside a mother with cancer. "Don't worry about us. Show Debbie what's left for clean-up before you leave and I'll do my best with the rest."

"Thanks." Trevor nodded and got to work.

With Aunt Greta working on the emergency shopping list, Joel headed to the storeroom to help Lauren with the rest of the inventory so he could pull together the official order.

He found her perched on the top of a step ladder counting packages of napkins in a large cardboard box.

She jotted a note on the pages and looked down at him with a smile that made his heart skip a beat. "I take it your mom finally listened?"

"Finally. Wish it was good news." It took less time to fill Lauren in on the problem and plan of action than it took to inventory the items on another shelf.

She stepped down to the floor. "At least we figured it out before we ran out of something right in the middle of a rush."

"True." He moved the step ladder and climbed up to count Styrofoam to-go boxes.

"And we have time to fix it." She checked the time on her phone and then slowly slid it into her back pocket.

"It could have been worse. Three and a half boxes of the large sized."

She recorded the tally, squared her shoulders as if she'd made a decision of some kind, then nodded. "I'm free for the remainder of the evening so I'll help you finish the inventory and go shopping for Greta's list."

"You don't have to—"

"I know I don't have to." She rolled her eyes. "But two of us can do it a whole lot faster. Besides, after helping you set up the touch screen monitors, I'd like to learn more about how to do this part of the business, too."

He glanced into an opened box, then shifted it to read the labels on those behind it. "Two and a half of the small take-out boxes." He moved down the ladder and started counting giant cans of green beans. "Thanks."

Especially today.

Because the sooner they got the order faxed and shopping done, the sooner he'd be free to stop by the hospital to see his dad before tomorrow's critical surgery.

Maybe even have time to come back here and uncover whatever other secrets the office held.

They might have averted one disaster, but how much impact would regular grocery store prices have on their bottom line?

Too much, he feared.

Because he still didn't know how slim their profit margin might be.

Wednesday morning, Joel set the plate containing the last cinnamon roll on the desktop and collapsed onto the chair.

Only fifteen minutes before he had to be back in the dining room so Lauren could take her legally required break during the temporary lull.

Just fifteen minutes to search for the passwords into the payroll program and the diner's online banking account.

He glanced around the office. Yesterday he'd spent hours sorting through the binders on the bookshelf and had discovered several years' worth of bank statements, invoices, inventory sheets, and payroll reports.

While it seemed Dad had started to update his business model—albeit with an outdated desktop based on the mere size of the hulking monitor, he still printed out and saved everything on paper.

Which had turned out to be a good thing since Joel was still locked out of the computer programs.

And with Dad recovering from yesterday's successful surgery—and on heavy pain medications that made him extra drowsy—he didn't want to bother him.

Especially if the question would trigger any additional stress.

In the meantime, while there was nothing a piece of pie couldn't fix, Grandma Hope's cinnamon roll recipe was a close second.

He forked a bite of gooey buttery deliciousness into his mouth and started a deeper search of the desk.

Where would Dad have hidden the passwords?

The top drawer on the left still contained a mess of office supplies like tape, staples, and pens while the middle drawer held envelopes, extra order pads, and a rubber-banded stack of blank time cards.

But where were the filled-out ones?

If there were any to be found.

He certainly hadn't been keeping track of his hours over the past chaotic week and a half.

But, according to Mom during their whisper-filled emergency conference Monday night, payroll went out every other Friday based on the two-week period ending the Saturday before.

Which meant that after unloading their delayed food delivery this afternoon, he needed to get a jump on the payroll since it would take longer the first time he did it.

Not to mention that the government would be looking for last quarter's estimated tax payment by the fifteenth. Which fell on a holiday this year and so would have to be paid early.

Unfortunately, Mom did the filing and tidying up but said Dad did all the rest. She didn't know any passwords, only that he had written them down somewhere after complaining about getting old and forgetting things.

Although she might be able to casually ask, she'd already been taking the brunt of Dad's frustrations and now walked a different tightrope. It wouldn't be easy encouraging Dad in his long recovery while keeping him from scaring away the very people trying to help.

Especially since the doctors said to keep him calm.

No, he'd only ask if no other options remained.

Joel took another large bite of roll and pulled open the bottom left-hand drawer to find an odd assortment of pictures, dumbbells, and supplier catalogs. Moving on to the right-hand side he found a first-aid kit, collection of vendor business cards, and finally a batch of files in a dilapidated hanging rack.

After a glance at the time on his phone, he fingered through the manila folders labeled with his mother's handwriting. Insurance policies. OSHA regulation bulletins. Health department inspection reports. Blank I-9 and payroll deduction forms and a file for each employee with completed forms and contact information.

Including updated files that Lauren must have made for their new employees.

All important to have but not what he needed today.

If he could get into the computer programs, he'd feel better.

After all, he was the one with the master's degree in Business Administration. Yet he couldn't even do the basics like keep the inventory stocked or pay the employees.

Then again, most business administrators delegated tasks to competent people instead of running everything by themselves.

Some day he hoped to run his own company but that was years into the future after he'd gotten real experience with a big company and saved enough to invest in his dream.

But for today, experience of a different kind contributed to a killer headache.

He checked under the keyboard and mouse pad on the center pull-out tray.

Nothing.

This was getting old.

He finished off his sugary treat and prayed for wisdom.

Where else would things like passwords and time cards be?

If only he could ask Dad.

But that was impossible because any hint of trouble at the diner would only raise his blood pressure.

Joel sucked in a deep breath and blew it out.

This was supposed to be his break, not a time to spike his own stress level.

Where hadn't he searched?

He studied the room at the small row of employee lockers and table with chairs. The walls held a few posters and more shelves holding dusty document boxes labeled with years gone by.

That left the desk with the huge computer monitor, large calendar, phone, stapler, notepad, cup of pens, and the remnants of his snack. He lifted the calendar to make sure nothing was underneath.

No papers, sticky notes, or missing time cards.

Just a single phrase written on the back in his dad's handwriting.

LvIndians_16

Joel grinned. His old high school, mascot, and football number.

Hopefully, this likely password was the one he'd been searching for. And with any luck, his father had used it with multiple programs.

Before he had a chance to find out, his cell phone rang and he answered the call.

"This is Devon Grant with CVX Industries. Denver branch."

Joel sat up straight. They were calling now?

His mind spiraled in wild circles.

Of all the lousy timing to hear from his dream job.

Chapter Eight

♥

J oel's pulse raced at the mention of one of the corporations holding his resume.

He coughed. "Hello, sir. What can I do for you?"

CVX Industries had been at the top of his list. At least until he'd learned Desiree worked there.

He winced at the memory of the many missed calls and texts he'd meant to answer when he had time. And instinctually braced for the inevitable backlash when—if—he responded.

Could he risk working for the same company? Willingly board the emotional rollercoaster again?

Even a path of friendship would be littered with potential potholes.

A rustling of papers came through the line before the man—Mr. Grant—spoke again. "We have an entry-level opening in our administration department and our human resources officer forwarded your resume to my office. We're scheduling interviews for early next week and would like to offer you an appointment if you're interested."

Interested? Absolutely.

And with a full staff at the diner again, they could probably cover a short absence in order for him to interview.

But he couldn't take a permanent job, especially right now.

His imaginary strutting brush-off toward his ex-girlfriend was just a daydream since he was needed here.

Joel sank back. "Sir, I appreciate the invitation but unfortunately I am no longer available for a full-time position at the moment." He weighed his words. "My father had open heart surgery yesterday and I'm elbow-deep trying to keep his business running."

"Really?" Mr. Grant sounded skeptical.

Joel swiveled in the office chair. "Inventory. Payroll. The quarterly estimated tax payment. Hiring more staff and updating the computer system."

He eyed the outdated equipment nearby. At least a few of those were under control now.

Or would be, once he had the chance to test the just-discovered password.

"Sounds like quality on-the-job experience." The man chuckled.

Joel relaxed. "Frankly, it's proving to be quite a challenge. While I regret missing this current opportunity to gain more experience and contribute to your company, maybe I could still be considered for a future opening. After my father is past this crisis."

Did that sound professional enough? He'd hate to burn unnecessary bridges.

"I appreciate your honesty." A tapping noise carried over the line. "Tell you what. I'm making a note to place your resume on hold so it doesn't get misplaced in our system. I anticipate multiple openings this year. So when you're available, just let human resources know and I'll fast-track you into an interview."

"Thank you for the open door. I hope to talk again soon." Joel disconnected, then took the last bite of his cinnamon roll in celebration.

Now back to what he'd been doing before the phone call.

He jiggled the mouse to wake up the computer screen.

Outside the office door, he heard Lauren's laughter followed by Aunt Greta's.

If Lauren was in the kitchen, his fifteen minutes had expired.

And once her break was over, he'd be back washing dishes instead of conquering the payroll and tax payment. So, while the accounting would have to wait until later, at least *dishes* were something he could handle alone.

·❤·❤·❤·❤·❤·

The delayed order had arrived not a moment too soon.

Lauren stacked two bags of coffee pouches on the almost-bare shelf under the lunch counter, then reached into the box for more.

Clarissa had taken over the mopping, so hopefully there wouldn't be too much of an additional delay this afternoon before Lauren could clock out.

"Can I ask a favor?" Joel's shoes squeaked as he came to a stop nearby.

"Depends. What do you need?" She glanced up.

"Help." He swiped a hand through his hair, standing it on end.

Too bad he looked so cute when he was frazzled. Especially when it confirmed she wasn't the only misfit.

Then his words sunk in. Because Mr. Big Shot needed her. Again? Mark this date on the calendar and circle it in red.

"Pretty, please?" He folded his hands under his chin as if begging.

Her internal resolve melted and she bit her lip to stop a grin. "With what?"

"Figuring out the payroll."

"The p-p-p-ayroll?" She rose to her feet. "I don't know anything about your dad's accounting system. And if you can't do it, what makes you think—"

"Calm down." He grasped her shoulders and squeezed. "You might not know how to run the program but you've gotten paid for years and can help me unravel what the numbers mean."

"Maybe." She stared into his blue eyes and took a deep breath. "Okay. I'll try after we put this order away."

"Thank you." He released her arms, but the warmth remained.

"Don't thank me yet." She knelt beside the box of coffee she'd been unloading. "I might not be any help at all."

"If you're not, then we're in big—" His cell phone rang and he fished it out of his back pocket. He answered it with a smile. "Hi, Mom."

She rolled her eyes and shooed him back toward the kitchen.

Joel was a good son and had been going above and beyond to be there for his family. As tired as she'd been over the past week, all *his* free time was spent at the hospital.

Too bad the gorgeous package also contained a generous heart.

It made him harder to resist.

Even more so when he treated her as if she actually knew something about how to run the diner.

Except, whenever he asked for help, it meant tougher choices for her.

She sighed. Monday night's inventory and emergency grocery trip had caused her to miss her first class.

Now, while the delayed order had arrived in time to avoid another crisis, she'd hoped it wouldn't interfere with today's seminar. But Joel's payroll question was sure to take up additional time she couldn't spare.

As Frank always said, things were never boring at the diner.

With Clarissa's assistance, she finished putting the dining room in order, then flattened the boxes before carrying them through the kitchen and out back to stack beside the dumpster.

After saying goodbye to the few departing employees, she returned inside to find Joel emerging from the storage room and only a small stack left outside the open cooler door.

"Aunt Greta said she'll finish up in there since this is a good time to do some rearranging."

"Didn't like how Frank did it?" Lauren grinned.

Greta exited the cooler and crossed her gloved hands over her coat-clad arms. "I heard that. And as a matter of fact, yes. Trevor and I have been talking about it all week. Just don't tell Frank." She glared at Joel.

"Wouldn't dream of it." He laughed as his aunt disappeared back inside with a flat of tomatoes. "Shall we?" He gestured toward the office.

"Why didn't you ask Greta to help you with this?"

"Seriously?" Joel bypassed her and dropped onto the rolling chair behind the desk. "Don't you remember how hard it was for her to learn the new computer system?"

"True." Lauren grabbed a chair from the break table and squeezed into the small space with him so she could also see the monitor.

Was it the proximity of bumping elbows or the looming challenge of the payroll program that had her stomach fluttering?

Seemingly oblivious to her dilemma, Joel pointed to an icon on the screen, double-clicked to open it, and then typed in the password.

"Took me forever this morning to find it." He flipped over the calendar and showed her where Frank had written it down.

Her pulse raced. He trusted her with the password?

Only family should have access.

Then again, she knew the combination to the safe hidden in the floor drain where they kept the extra cash.

As they waited for the program to finish loading, he swiveled in his chair and bumped his knee into her thigh.

What was her problem?

They'd been as close as this many times while working.

Why did her palms start sweating now?

Don't make me fall for you, Joel!

He clicked a few things on the screen. "Here's as far as I got this afternoon before I realized I needed help. This is the report for the last payroll. Mom and Dad make a salary as the owners but the rest doesn't make sense." He pointed at the monitor.

If she leaned closer, she could make out the numbers.

"For example, this is what you made, but it's broken out into different codes." He turned toward her. "What do they mean?"

Her shoulders relaxed. "That's an easy one. I'm on two different pay scales. One for time working in the kitchen area with a full hourly wage and a separate rate for time serving in the dining room because out there I also earn tips."

"Okay..." The furrow carved into Joel's forehead betrayed his confusion.

She leaned across his arm to point at another place on the screen. "Most of my hours are serving or tip-earning while Trevor's are all full rate in the kitchen. But, because the others sometimes rotated as needed with the staff changes, they could have days with no serving and some days with more."

He nodded. "What is this other lump sum payment on your paycheck? Is that the total from the clipboard next to the tip jars under the register?"

"Not quite. You're right that those are reported on the honor system, but..." She tapped a spot on the screen. "Cash from the jar goes in this box here so it gets tallied for my tax form, but isn't included in my pay."

"So this lump sum is—"

"The tips collected from credit card receipts that are being passed on to the individual server."

Joel swallowed hard and reached for the register tape on the desktop and scanned down the length. "So this number at the bottom here isn't the gross receipts?"

"No." She shook her head back and forth slowly.

Did that mean he'd been estimating the diner's income off inflated numbers?

She wiggled her fingers in the direction of the printout. "Let me see."

Since she'd been the one to input both Clarissa and Joel into the system as servers, it was easy to recognize the cluster of initials.

And soon Joel had a page of notes—along with a lot of mumbling about staying late to update the paper ledger correctly.

"That answers my questions about wage types and tips, but..." He sighed. "Another dumb question. How do I know how many hours everyone has worked? I hate to mention it after a week and a half, but I don't have a time card." He pointed to the bottom drawer. "Or any tax forms filled out."

"What?" She blinked. How could that have happened?

Joel nudged her knee aside and pulled out several papers from the drawer. "At least I figured out where they are."

The same place where she'd gotten the financial paperwork for the new employees as part of their training.

"Sorry about that. I assumed your parents had..." She winced. "Except your first day fell apart early on."

He ran a hand through his hair. "And it's been falling apart ever since."

She laid a hand on his forearm, her fingers tingling at the close contact. So much for a comforting gesture.

"Give yourself more credit than that." She stood and moved to the pocket taped on the end of the lockers—out of sight from the door and desk—and returned with three narrow time cards.

His eyebrows rose. "I never would have looked there."

"Now that you mention it, it does seem like an odd place to keep them." She shrugged and then pushed her completed card in front of him. "Like the others, I keep mine in my locker and update it daily. At the close of two weeks, when it gets full, I total up the two types of hours, put it in the pocket, and get a new blank one."

He tapped a drawer to his left. "Did find those."

"Hand me one and we'll retroactively fill it out for you based on my hours. Except it would only be for one week in the pay period."

He handed one over and she started transferring the numbers.

She gasped at another thought. "Your parents take a salary instead of hourly wages, but what are they going to do for income if they aren't working? They still have bills to pay, especially now."

He rubbed a hand over his face. "As absentee owners, they should receive a share of the profits. But since I just got into the programs today, I haven't had time to calculate how much profit there actually is."

"You'll have it figured out in no time." She offered a weak smile.

"Thanks." He squeezed her hand and tingles ran up her arm again. "It's good to have another brain to bounce ideas around with." He released her hand and reached for the mouse. "Now, to finish the payroll."

She added his improvised time card to the small stack. "How can I help now?"

He clicked back to the report he'd shown her and soon the printer whirred to life. "See if you can use this to figure out a rough calculation of what the payroll will total this time. Since I just located the password this morning, I still need to log into our online banking and compare our current balance with the ledger program."

Using the previous report as an example, she found it relatively simple to write the current numbers beside each line, adding a row for Joel's estimated hours, then starting to add them up with the calculator app on her phone. "At least we don't have to pay the new girls this period."

"True." He groaned.

"What?"

"I found an automatic payment that isn't recorded in the ledger because I didn't know about it."

"But now you do." She patted his shoulder. "You can do this."

"Eventually." He mumbled something and jotted a note on both the desk calendar and a scrap piece of paper before clicking over to a new program.

She watched the screen and found the process eerily similar to checking her own banking balance and balancing her checkbook.

Just on a larger scale. With much more at stake.

A business could not afford to bounce a check.

"Good." He nodded and wrote something else down on the calendar. "This is starting to make sense since we have several deposits from the credit card companies that I hadn't recorded. I definitely need to do this every day to avoid unpleasant surprises."

"Once you catch up, it won't take very long, right?" She skimmed the bank account balance. "Looks like there's plenty there to cover the payroll and then some."

"Except that we have to also make an estimated tax payment based on last quarter..." His voice trailed off as he clicked around in the ledger program and made more notes. She slid her page of numbers closer and he added them to his own scribbled list before pulling a calculator out of the top drawer.

She sat back and waited for him to finish mumbling. "What's the verdict?"

He dropped his face into his hands. "We're too close for comfort."

"So, how do we fix it?"

While it wasn't really her problem, she'd do anything to help Joel carry the burden. For the sake of his parents, of course. Not because of the stress carving lines in his forehead or the fact he'd asked.

"I just won't pay myself this time. After all, I never got my tax paper-work filled out and I don't need money for room and board since I'm staying at my parents' house."

"That's one way to make sure they get their full salary amount, but don't you have any bills of your own like car insurance or a phone bill or college loans?"

He groaned.

She slapped his arm. "I really wish you'd stop doing that whenever I say anything."

"It's not you. I'm the idiot." He rubbed his hands over his face. "I don't have any loan payments but I do need some sort of income for the stuff you mentioned. I'd rather not dip into my savings."

"What about your tips? Is that enough?"

"Only one way to find out." He reached for the calculator again.

As Joel punched buttons and scribbled numbers, her eyes fell on the payroll printout and the calculations for her upcoming paycheck. A total significantly more than her usual because of all the overtime hours she'd worked.

But now, seeing the diner's bank balance and a rough expense sheet? If he could sacrifice, so could she.

She nudged him with her elbow. "Since it would help, subtract the extra above my normal for this pay period."

"You don't have to do that."

"I know. Consider it a gift to your parents."

He dropped his pencil and reached for her hand. "It would make a big difference. But just this once, until I'm sure we won't bounce any checks."

"As long as you promise to pay yourself next time." She laid her free hand on top of their joined hands. "You deserve to be paid what you're worth."

"And so do you."

A spark passed between them and her heart skipped a beat.

The slamming of the cooler door out in the kitchen area interrupted the moment and Lauren glanced at the clock on the wall.

Dread pooled in her stomach.

She was about to miss her second class this week.

And she could already hear the disappointment in her father's voice if he ever found out she'd chosen the diner over college.

Again.

Chapter Nine

♥

O f all the exhausting, never-ending weeks.

Hopefully, it wouldn't be much longer before Lauren could put it behind her and get away from the diner for a while.

She ran her fingers across the packages of napkins. "Seven here." She closed the cardboard flaps and shifted on the metal ladder to see behind the current box. "Plus another case."

"Got it." Joel's voice came from near her hip. "This is going a lot faster than last week."

"Especially since you divided up the sheets by area and we only have the store room left." She peeked inside another box at the stacks of take-out boxes.

It made sense for the kitchen crew to inventory the cooler with their normal closing routines. Meanwhile, she'd gotten a jumpstart on the dining room tallies before Joel had even locked the front door.

Lauren held onto the edge of the metal shelf and leaned to her right to see more boxes. "Because the quicker the inventory's done..."

"The quicker we can—"

"Get out of here." As much as she loved her work at the diner, she desperately needed a change of scenery.

"Two and a half of large boxes and only half a case left of the small ones." With the top shelf counted, Lauren started down the ladder.

"Hmm." Joel made the note. "Might need to adjust our order if we're running out this soon."

"It's the pie." She paused her descent and faced him. "With our new 'pie of the day' program, I've noticed more customers saving room for dessert by taking part of their meal home."

He tapped his pen against his chin. "I've been doing the calculations, and the profit on pie is worth the extra boxes."

"Hopefully Greta can keep up with the demand." Her phone rang and she pulled it out. Her heart sank. "It's my dad."

And she could guess why he was calling.

"Go ahead. I can finish this." Joel gripped her elbow to help her down the ladder.

Tingles spread up her arm even as dread pooled in her stomach.

Before she lost her courage, she swiped the screen to answer the call while Joel set his clipboard on a shelf and moved the ladder further down the aisle.

Dad's voice thundered in her ear. "The university sent a strange bill. What's this about dropping out?"

Her gaze wandered over Joel's muscular arms and the pull of his T-shirt across his shoulders as he climbed up and shoved large cans of vegetables around.

Perhaps the view would make the hard conversation a little easier?

Even though Dad couldn't see her, she raised her chin. "I didn't drop out. There was an emergency at the diner."

Joel peered over his shoulder with questions in his eyes.

She ignored the rising heat in her face and turned away in order to concentrate on the call. "They needed my help here in the afternoons. So, since there's no way I can leave early like I used to, I had to cut back on school."

Leaving the store room behind, she paced the kitchen floor.

"Cut back? That sounds like quitting to me. Did your mother have anything to do with this?"

As if.

Other than occasional quick comments in the group text, Lauren hadn't talked to her mother in months.

She blew out a long breath. "No. It was my decision."

Dad huffed in her ear. "Well, you're being ridiculous."

She flinched. "It's only for a semester and it's not every class."

Except she already missed the only remaining course on her schedule twice. And yesterday's lecture on organizational rhetoric had been so boring, she was tempted to drop that course too.

If only Dad understood her heart. But since he had his own demands, she braced herself for the coming judgment.

He snorted. "You're throwing away your future on a dead-end job that pays nothing."

Tears burned in her eyes. "I'm needed here and I'm learning more than I ever imagined. Besides, the Dawsons are like family to me."

"Their opinion matters more than mine?"

"That's not fair." She swallowed the lump in her throat.

"Call me when you come to your senses."

She leaned against the wall beside the coat hooks and took a deep breath, blinking back fresh tears at the way he'd hung up on her. She should be used to it by now. After all, she didn't fit the mold of a driven lawyer or stock broker like her sisters.

Creativity like her mother's always seemed to be a strike against her.

Once again, she'd been rejected for being herself and doing what she thought was right.

Greta's laughter trickled out of the cooler and the sound of a ladder scraping across the floor caught her attention. She shoved the phone back into her pocket.

She had a job to do in a place where she was needed.

In a place where she made a difference.

Lauren rounded the corner into the storage room and spotted Joel by the last shelf. Nearing the ladder, she reached up to take the clipboard.

She tugged, but when he didn't release it, she peeked at his face.

"Everything okay?" Joel stared.

"Fine."

"Are you sure?" He tilted his head and waited.

As if he cared.

But there was no escaping her reality.

She widened her eyes to keep another round of tears at bay. "You heard the part about how I had to cut back on my class schedule. Dad doesn't understand why being here is so important right now."

"Well, I certainly do." He released the clipboard. "Can you imagine this place without your help over the past two weeks?"

A warmth spread around her heart. Amazing what a little acceptance and appreciation could do.

Joel held up one finger at a time. "No coffee? No one to operate the register or train a new waitress? No lettuce?"

She found a smile. They had survived a lot of problems together. "No paycheck?"

"No tips?" He waggled his eyebrows. "No impossibly handsome boss."

"No impossibly bossy boss." She shook the ladder a bit even as her face heated once again. "Point made. Now, are you about done?"

"Almost."

They finished the last counts, then he stowed the ladder away while she wandered out into the kitchen to find Debbie and Monica getting their coats.

Lauren approached the teenager who had shadowed her all morning. "So, do you feel comfortable taking a shift on your own next Saturday?"

The girl glanced at her mom. "I think so. It's harder than I thought but interesting too."

"That it is." Joel joined them with a chuckle. "I remember my aching back like it was only last week."

Lauren elbowed him in the ribs. "It *was* last week."

"Time flies when you're having fun." He smiled down at her while the others laughed and she fought to calm the butterflies in her stomach.

"Did someone say fun?" Greta handed Joel her inventory sheets as Trevor closed the cooler door.

"Yeah." Joel winked at his aunt. "We all think it would be fun to take tomorrow off and not come back here until Monday."

"I can live with that." Greta turned toward the others. "Come on, everyone. Let's get out of here before Mr. Bossy Britches changes his mind."

Lauren giggled at Joel's stunned expression. Only Greta—as family—could get away with calling him that to his face.

"Not so fast." Joel stopped Lauren's retreat with a warm hand on her shoulder. "I think you should stick around to compile the order while I prepare the bank deposit."

Her eyebrows rose. "You do?"

"Whatever happened to wanting to learn more about how things worked? Besides, the quicker we're done, the quicker we can—"

"Get out of here." Not that she had anywhere special to go. "Okay."

"Good." He handed her Greta's sheets before leading the way to the office.

Once inside, she collected the inventory tallies and a blank order form, then set up to work at the small table.

But the numbers jumbled before her eyes as her attention drifted across the room to where Joel counted the money from the cash drawer and entered stuff into the computer.

The computer where just a few days ago they had worked side by side.

Get a grip. He might be cute and a simple hand on her shoulder or a wink might send her heart dancing, but they were just friends.

Friends.

She focused on the task at hand and soon laid the completed order form on the desk.

He skimmed the page, then swiveled to the fax machine in the corner.

"Don't you want to check my numbers first?"

"You know as much about this as I do. Plus I trust you." He fed the pages into the tray and the machine whirred to life.

Lauren ignored the warmth spreading around her heart as she stored the inventory sheets away for the next week.

"I feel like celebrating."

"Because you sent a fax?"

"Because I survived the week." He tapped consecutive fingers as he made his points once again. "Payroll. Tax payment. Inventory. Order." He grinned. "And nothing diner-related to do until Monday morning."

"True. Just church tomorrow. But plenty of time for catching up on laundry. Cleaning my apartment." She crossed to her locker and twisted the knob.

"Don't remind me." He groaned. "Shall we procrastinate?"

"What?"

"Mom said Dad's extra tired today and while he's resting, I need a change of scenery. You don't have any plans do you?"

"Ugh. Thanks for reminding me that I have no social life." She made a note on her time card before fishing her keys out of her purse.

"Most of my high school friends have moved away or we've lost contact." He logged off the computer, set the bank deposit bag on the corner of the desktop, and straightened the remaining items.

Aside from her roommates who had their own plans, her only friend was Julie... in New York. Then again, Joel was turning out to be a decent replacement, especially since they spent so much time together.

As long as she remembered that no matter how attractive he might be, Joel would only ever be a friend.

"What are you thinking?" She shut the door on her locker and spun the knob.

"Drop off the bank deposit first then..."

"What about something outside?"

"In this weather?" He stopped at the edge of the desk.

"You've got a coat, right? Or have you gotten—"

He held up a hand. "Please don't call me soft."

Her eyes drifted across his chest. Nothing soft about those muscles. "Just for a bit. Maybe a walk around Lake Loveland or the sculpture park. I need to be somewhere without walls or tables or food."

"Hey. We might want something to eat later."

"As long as someone else is cooking and serving it."

"Deal." He gestured for her to lead the way out while he turned off the lights. "I noticed you don't live too far from the bank."

"You noticed?" She paused by the back door and glanced back to where he shrugged into his own coat.

"I may have seen the address listed in your file." He picked a loose thread off the sleeve and avoided eye contact. "What if I pick you up after I stop by the bank?"

"Sure." She fought her growing smile before slipping out into the chilly afternoon air.

Calm down. So he had looked up where she lived and wanted to spend time with her, but it could only be as friends. Because all of his had moved away.

Just like he would be moving on once Frank was back.

Still, as she slid behind the wheel of her car, she couldn't help but laugh.

What would Julie have to say about this development?

Joel inhaled the crisp air and felt peace settle around him, a peace as deeply rooted as the towering trees beside the water at North Lake Park. "This was a great idea."

"Thanks." Lauren laughed. "I've been known to have them from time to time."

He glanced across the top of his older-model-but-completely-paid-for car at her teasing smile. A smile that still tempted him to discover more about what made her so unique.

She zipped her coat up under her chin and tilted her head to the north. "What about looping around the sculpture park?"

"Lead on." He tucked hands in his pockets along with his keys and crossed the parking lot toward the paved path.

A glance at the Rocky Mountain panorama stopped his progress. "I've missed this view. With all the hours at the diner or at the hospital, I haven't actually faced west during the day in too long."

Hadn't hiked his favorite trails in years longer than that either.

"Speaking of the hospital, other than needing more rest, how's your dad doing?" Lauren nudged his side and they started walking again.

"His pain appears to be mostly under control and yesterday he had his first visit from the physical therapist." He snorted. "Or the 'inflictor of torture' as he called him."

"That sounds like Frank."

"Some things never change." He kicked a rock off the sidewalk. "But as Mom says, a lot will *need* to change. With his diet, exercise, and stress levels. It's why she made me promise to do something fun today and not head to the hospital room to sit with them."

"So, this is forced relaxation?" Her voice sounded strained.

"Well, it's no fun by yourself." He nudged her shoulder.

Her smile slowly returned. "Glad to be of help."

With a glance in both directions, they jogged across the street to where the path continued around a pond full of dormant cattails.

Joel pushed his hands deeper into his pockets. "But I get her point. Other than Sundays when the diner is closed, I don't think they've taken a day off in years."

"True. Your mom has the gift of hospitality, just like your grandma did." Lauren tilted her head back to face the sky and took a deep breath. "I can't count how many times she invited me over for Sunday lunch along with Greta and Julie. There was always somebody from church there too. And that was her only time away from the diner."

"She's always taking care of other people." He smiled at the memories of folded laundry on his bed and a cookie jar full of his favorites while growing up.

Things that had been missing lately.

Lauren frowned. "But if she's always so busy serving others—like at the diner and now at the hospital with your dad—does she ever make time to pamper herself? I mean, if you don't take care of yourself, at some point you have nothing left to give."

"Hmm. And then your health collapses, like Dad's did." He clenched his jaw. "And for what? A diner that can barely turn a profit? That's not what I'd call a successful business."

In preparing the quarterly tax payment, he'd seen the truth in black and white. And it was too close to red when he factored in his parents' salaries.

No wonder Dad had been willing to ask for a second pair of eyes and advice.

Lauren slowed her steps, seemingly lost in thought and completely ignoring the assorted bronze sculptures that lined the path. "It all depends on what you consider success. My dad says it's a financial number. But your grandma—and even Greta—say it's doing what God uniquely created you to do and helping others in the process. That's when you deserve the 'well done, good and faithful servant' reward in heaven."

His professors' lectures had centered on profit margins and to be honest, he still wanted a real job so he could afford a better car without the burden of payments. But his grandmother had been wise, especially when it came to their faith.

It had been too long since he'd considered God's plans for his life.

He gazed at the woman beside him. "How do you know what God created you to do?"

Lauren pursed her normally smiling lips. "I'm still trying to figure that out, but you? You're good at the numbers side of business. Use that to help people."

"Like making sure they get a paycheck?" His attempt to lighten the conversation felt flat.

She nudged him with her elbow. "That certainly helps me. But paying the diner's bills makes sure the lights are on, the heater works, and that there's food to serve a hungry customer who in turn finds a small oasis in the middle of their own stressful day. It's why we have so many regular customers."

"That's *food* for thought."

"Very funny." She rolled her eyes.

But that didn't change the fact it was still true.

He'd spent hours over the past week juggling reports at his dad's desk while tackling a parade of problems.

But unlike the sterile paperwork he might see at a corporate office, he knew what the numbers represented. Payroll had a face and the delivery invoice guaranteed more hours of chopping and baking ahead.

If he ever ended up with a true office job, the whole hands-on diner experience would make him a better leader.

After walking in silence for a few minutes, Lauren sighed. "I guess it's all about balancing the be's and do's."

"The what?" He almost stopped at the sudden turn in conversation.

Then again that seemed to be how Lauren's mind worked.

Her voice grew wistful. "On one hand, God says, 'Be still, and know that I am God' while on the other hand, we tend to stay busy doing all the things on our to-do list and trying to get ahead. But if true success is living out the way God created us, it makes sense to keep connected to the real boss so we know what He wants us to do."

"So it's a good thing we're taking time to just walk and *be* in the moment."

"Exactly." She breathed deep and exhaled slowly. "I feel better already."

Not so surprisingly, so did he.

Then again, they might feel better now, but Monday morning would bring another marathon of relentless work. It was easier with the extra help they'd hired and the business routines caught up and in place... but the diner income still had to support non-working people like his parents.

It was tempting to keep collecting only his tips, but he'd promised Lauren he'd pay himself.

How could they trim a few expenses and build their bottom line? Or how could they increase revenue short of raising the prices and driving away customers?

His stomach tightened. They needed to do both.

Which meant he really should pull Trevor aside soon and pick his brain about lowering food costs and waste since ingredients were their biggest expense. Surely the man's culinary training had covered how to run a successful restaurant.

Lauren giggled and crossed the grass toward a sculpture of children playing in a circle. An open spot begged them to join in the game.

Right. They were here to relax and not think about the diner.

"I wonder how hard it would be to make something like this?" Lauren ran a hand over the rippled metal of a little boy's hair.

"Probably way harder than you think."

"Spoil sport." She stuck out her tongue at him.

If only he could capture a fraction of her joy. "How do you stay so happy?"

"Prayer." She frowned. "I know that I can't do much of anything very well—"

"Nonsense."

"Not according to my dad or my roommates." She shrugged and rejoined him on the sidewalk. "I do the best I can and leave a lot in God's hands for Him to handle."

Her words spun around in his brain for a minute or two. "I've never prayed so often as I have in the past few weeks."

"I once heard someone say that prayer is like breathing. Exhale the troubles and inhale His power."

"I guess I always had my list of things to pray for."

"You and your lists." She smacked his arm with a smile.

"Hey. I keep a list so I don't forget."

"Bet you follow a strict Bible reading plan too."

"Guilty. After I read a chapter or two, I pray—"

"Then brush your teeth, comb your hair, and head out the door?"

He frowned. "When you put it like that, it doesn't sound very good."

"I'm more of a free spirit." She twirled around with another laugh. "More like I've accepted the gift of grace in a relationship instead of a bunch of rules. Like a song I heard said, more like falling in love than something to believe in."

"You and your romantic dreams." His recall of her earlier M-R-S degree antics definitely colored her current words.

Someday there would be a lucky guy in her future.

"Don't knock my dream. Your grandma introduced to me my Prince Charming." She pointed to the sky. "He thinks I'm to die for."

He groaned at her pun even as he envied her faith. "You make it sound so easy."

Her smile faded. "If only my dad was as easy to please as God."

The memory of her teary eyes after her dad's phone call made him wish he could wrap an arm around her. He shoved his hands deeper into his pockets instead as they continued to walk the loop in silence.

As they neared his car, Lauren rubbed her nose. "Thanks for indulging my whim for something outside, but I'm ready to head somewhere warm."

"What? Are you—"

"Don't call me soft." She imitated his earlier words complete with a frown that dissolved into a wide grin.

He smiled back.

Mostly because she lightened his spirits. Challenged his beliefs.

And somehow over the last few days had become a friend.

While she was nothing like the women he'd dated in the past—and he still didn't plan to stay small town forever and would only end up hurting her when he left—that didn't change the fact he didn't want to say goodbye quite yet.

Which was his only excuse for the next words out of his mouth.

"What about an early movie and giant bucket of popcorn?" Joel swallowed a groan.

Based on the surprised—but hopeful—look on her face, he'd just implied more than he'd intended with the invitation.

Had he just accidentally screwed up their working relationship?

Was it too late to take it back?

Chapter Ten

♥

Almost three weeks after their walk in the park and spontaneous movie, Lauren was still firmly in the friend zone with Joel.

Which made the pink and red decorations in the windows—and those along the street outside—all the more ironic.

Had she gone overboard this year?

Probably. But she didn't care.

Lauren scraped remnants of hash browns onto one plate and stacked the rest of the plates underneath it before sliding the used forks into an empty water glass.

Joel approached carrying a plastic tub. "All these hearts are already getting on my nerves."

"They'll only be up for a few weeks, but you gotta love Loveland as we head into February." Lauren eyed the handmade paper hearts she had taped above the booths while Clarissa took a turn rolling more silverware.

With Lauren's birthday a couple days before Valentines Day, she liked to imagine everyone decorated just for her.

It beat the unfortunate reality that any gifts she might receive from her family would reflect the holiday-heavy selection at stores. Assuming they even remembered.

Joel added the dirty plates and glasses to the tub. "Giant red hearts on the light poles and the newspaper full of stories about re-mailing valentines with a special postmark. We've got two weeks to go and already I can't go to the grocery store without tripping over the flower and card displays."

"What? You're not a romantic?" She squirted disinfecting solution from the bottle dangling from her back pocket and wiped the surface clean with her rag.

"It's enough to make a bachelor skip town." He rested the tub on the corner of the just-cleaned table.

"Or make a single lady eat chocolate ice cream straight from the container."

Lauren longed to be part of a special relationship but thanks to her extra hours, she had no time to date or even get to know someone as more than friends. Most of the men at the diner were taken or old-timers like the mid-morning batch that had just left.

Meeting men her own age was one perk about the college scene. Not that there had been any good prospects there either.

Even before she finally acknowledged the inevitable and dropped her last class before the deadline.

Lauren repositioned the dollar store vase of fresh pink carnations next to the condiment collection. The blooms had come from sweet Ethel's shop across the street. Too bad she was failing fast...

"Hmm. Is that an admission of guilt?"

"Can I plead the fifth?" She nudged Joel aside and headed back to the lunch counter.

Joel laughed as he trailed behind. "Only if you'll help put away the delivery after closing."

"I would have anyway and you know it." Just like the past few weeks, the newest staff members ducked out on time and the core crew went off the clock to empty the boxes.

"I know." He continued on to the kitchen with the dirty dishes.

After stowing the cleaning supplies, she scanned the nearly empty room. Clarissa was on her break. And all the vacant tables were clean and ready for when the lunch crowd started trickling in.

Which reminded Lauren that she needed to move the salad dressings from the main cooler to the refrigerated case behind the counter.

The door opened and one of their lunch regulars—an appliance repairman if she remembered correctly—made his way to his usual spot two stools down from her.

He glanced around the room for a few moments before leaning to peek through the pass-through window to the kitchen. His shoulders drooped as he reached for a menu. Like he didn't always order the daily special with a slice of pie.

He cleared his throat. "How is Frank doing?"

Lauren poured him a cup of coffee. "It'll be awhile yet. After that infection set back his recovery, they decided to move him to a rehab facility for a couple weeks so he'd have help as he regains his strength. But he should be able to go home soon."

She couldn't imagine the bill for those extra days, but they couldn't put a price on his life.

"Good to hear." The man nudged his glasses further up on his nose.

She took pity on him and lowered her voice. "Did you *really* want to know about Frank?"

"Just wondering when he'll be back here..."

"And when Greta will be back out front to serve your pie?" She pressed her lips together to stifle her grin as his ears reddened.

Her romantic prospects might be non-existent, but why should that keep her from playing Cupid when she had the chance?

Making a quick decision, she turned to the window. "Hey Greta? If you've got a minute, there's someone here to see you."

The older woman swiped the back of her hand over her forehead, then glanced at her watch. "I could use a break." She handed her spatula to Trevor and disappeared from sight.

Lauren pivoted in time to see Greta come through the swinging doors, stop in her tracks—was that a blush?—and bustle forward to fill a glass from the soda machine.

"It's been awhile since I asked." The man's voice cracked, then regained strength. "Greta? Will you marry me?"

"Not today, Clay." Greta chuckled, but moved to join him at the counter. "Other than a slice of my pie, what brings you around so early?"

"Oh. You noticed?"

Lauren ducked into the kitchen for the salad dressing cups.

When she returned, Clay was showing Greta a few photos on his phone. Apparently he was taking his niece and nephew to the movies later while his sister went somewhere.

Hopefully she didn't end up in the same situation as the fun aunt. Even with their high-powered careers, her sisters were still more likely to get married and start families before her.

Ugh. Birthday connection aside, Valentines season was often a depressing reminder that she couldn't find anyone to put up with her personality quirks for long.

The bells on the front door clattered and she welcomed the distraction.

At least until she spotted the statuesque brunette in a short-skirted business suit.

The woman quickly scanned the diner, then strode purposefully toward Lauren, her black heels clicking on the checkered floor. Her sleek hairstyle and flawless makeup triggered a spurt of jealousy that caught Lauren by surprise.

If Lauren didn't work in a diner, she might be able to maintain her own appearance and attract a guy's attention. Then again, who was she kidding? Her flyaway curls had a mind of their own on a good day.

Lauren lifted her chin as the new customer approached and smiled. "Welcome to Dawson's Diner. Can I interest you in some coffee or—"

"Desiree?" Joel had returned from the kitchen with an empty tub, bypassing a retreating Greta. "What a surprise. I never thought I'd see you here."

Lauren pried the forgotten tub from his grip and slid it onto the designated shelf.

Of course the hometown hunk would know all the gorgeous girls. And despite their growing friendship and Saturday outings the past three weeks, this beauty was more his style.

Especially when it came to being a potential romantic interest.

Ugh. Stupid, stupid past crushes that didn't know when to quit.

Lauren's foolish hopes deflated further as the woman—Desiree—bent a finger and summoned Joel nearer.

"Do you have a minute?" Desiree tilted her head toward the bank of windows. "We need to talk."

Joel glanced over his shoulder at Lauren. "Clarissa should be back from her break in a few minutes. Okay if I start mine now?"

"S-s-sure." Lauren's gaze bounced from Joel's pleading eyes to Desiree's raised eyebrows.

"I thought you were the boss." Tiny wrinkles furrowed the woman's forehead.

Joel pointed his glamor girl to an empty booth. "Let me grab something to eat and I'll be right there." He turned toward Lauren with a weak smile, opened his mouth as if to say something, then snapped it shut with a reddening face.

Was he embarrassed to be found working at a diner? Or because he wasn't bossy enough? He'd issued orders like the best of them the first week but had toned down over the past month.

Instead of him being the boss, they'd become almost partners.

Lauren narrowed her eyes at a new thought. What if he was embarrassed for having been friendly with her when he could have been spending time with such a beauty?

Lauren snatched the coffee pot and retreated into the dining room to check on the customers far away from where Desiree perched on the vinyl seat. By the time Lauren returned behind the counter, Joel sat with a cinnamon roll and soda across from the woman as they engaged in an animated conversation.

Had he offered her anything or was that Lauren's job?

Her heart sank. Despite her personal feelings of rejection, customer service ruled.

Lauren rounded the end of the counter and approached the booth in time for Desiree to reach forward and grasp Joel's hands.

Joel forced himself not to cringe as Desiree's nails bit into his palms.

She leaned forward. "I know I ruined things back in college, but I never forgot you. And since you were always talking about Colorado, I moved to Denver after graduation to see it for myself. And then Valentines reminded me of your cute little town traditions."

Had he really talked about home that much? Except she didn't seem that complimentary of things he was only now coming to appreciate.

He tugged one hand free and reached for his glass. "So what brings you here? Today?"

"Can't I just want to see you again?" She giggled. " But mostly I had to find out why you'd do something crazy like not interview for the perfect job. It was an amazing opportunity."

Joel leaned back. "I told your boss why. My dad had a heart attack and I'm needed here while he recovers from open heart surgery."

"At least I saw your resume is flagged for consideration for our next opening. That way we can still get our second chance." She clutched his remaining hand and batted her eyelashes.

Ah. The real reason she wanted him to take the job at CVX Industries. A month ago, he would have savored this moment but her current desperation no longer flattered him.

Beside their table, Lauren cleared her throat. "Can I get you anything to—"

"Iced tea with lemon. And is it too much to hope for a grilled salmon or tilapia fillet with wild rice?" Desiree's focus never left Joel's face.

He glanced apologetically at Lauren.

"I'm sorry, but we don't have any grilled fish options." Lauren's smile looked forced. "However, if you look in the menu found in the holder next to the window, you'll see that we offer several lighter fare items including—"

Desiree gasped. "Lighter fare? Do I look like I need—"

Joel coughed to cover his laugh and pulled his other hand free. "Why don't you take a look at the options while Lauren gets your tea?"

"Good idea." Lauren pivoted on her heel and retreated behind the counter.

Desiree tugged the laminated card from the holder and quickly dropped it onto the tabletop. She nudged it with a single fingernail, then rubbed her fingertips together as if the menu had been covered in syrup. Or worse.

"What's your problem? The menu's clean."

"Are you sure?" She raised a plucked eyebrow.

He rolled his eyes. "Yes, I'm sure. I washed it myself not a half hour ago."

"What's the point? The people willing to eat here wouldn't care anyway."

He sucked in a quick breath, ready to defend the diner, then realized the irony. Not too long ago he'd felt the same way, yet now, four weeks after being shoved into the deep end, he ran the place.

And after talking to Trevor—and starting to make a few changes—he was finally getting better at it. One might think he actually embraced the challenge, to the point the back office seemed like his instead of his dad's.

However, as he glanced around the room, this time he noticed the chipped and well-worn surfaces on the tables. And the fact the walls could use a fresh coat of paint and maybe even taking down some of the pictures displayed there. It wasn't like they had a celebrity visitor wall-of-fame to spotlight.

Joel's mind drifted back to Dr. Holloway's class freshman year.

It should have been a relatively simple project as part of his entrepreneurship final, but he'd poured his heart and soul into the plan for his father's diner, creating a roadmap to modernize and expand the business that had been in his family for generations.

Only to have his professor tear it apart in front of Joel's classmates, dismissing his ideas as naive and unrealistic.

You can't expect to succeed in business with such a small-town mentality.

As if the man knew anything about the blood, sweat, and tears that had gone into that diner over the decades.

Still went into it.

Because even small businesses deserved attention and care.

Desiree waved a manicured hand toward the vase on their table. "Even cheap flowers can't make this place any less of a dump."

Lauren picked that moment to return with a glass of tea. And based on her hesitation, likely debated whether she could get away with an accidentally on purpose spill.

Joel shook his head to stop her, then reached over to finger the soft petals. "I kinda like the hint of spring in the middle of winter." He smiled at Lauren before taking another bite of his cinnamon roll. The sooner he was done eating, the sooner he could excuse himself from this not-so-restful break.

Lauren set the glass down firmly in front of Desiree and pulled out her notepad. "Are you ready to order?"

"I'll take the turkey sandwich on rye. Just mustard, no mayo. With a side of fruit instead of fries. You can't mess that up too much." The irritating woman slid the menu back into place, then reached for a napkin to wipe her fingers.

"Very well. I'll turn this in right away." Lauren retreated.

Time to change the subject before his temper got the best of him. "So, what exactly does your job entail?"

The polished woman across from him began a vivacious monologue about her position in the human resources department. But the whole time she rambled about how she might have used her influence to route Joel's application to the appropriate person, she also proceeded to examine the silverware, wrinkling her nose in a way he'd once thought cute.

Her sophisticated clothing and impeccable makeup screamed success while her behavior radiated her opinion of his inferior choices.

He shoved another bite of roll into his mouth as he tuned out a rambling description of her new loft apartment in downtown Denver. And the rent payment she could now afford after her latest raise.

There had been a day when he would have bent over backward to impress the woman across from him. Or be thankful that she had greased the wheels to get him an interview.

Now he worked to keep the business checking account in the black firmly enough to build up an emergency reserve.

His priorities had changed and failure had taken on a whole new level of meaning, especially if the disappointed look came from his dad, aunt, or Lauren.

Did Desiree really think he was a failure for choosing to work hard to support his family? Since when was physical labor a bad thing?

And since when did financial success allow her to be rude and condescending?

What was it that Lauren had said during their walk through the sculpture park? Success was using the gifts God gave you and helping people along the way.

He'd once thought the same as Desiree and his professors.

Still remembered an argument with his dad about ridiculous roundabouts and meatloaf. Only to be interrupted by a gentle hand on his arm.

Grandma Hope's eyes glistened with unshed tears. "I suppose college life has stretched and challenged your beliefs, but I've found that life teaches the most important lessons. Always remember that our family has weathered many storms by relying on our faith. And each other."

The fight slowly left his body and he'd vowed to stop tearing down the very people who had sacrificed everything so he could succeed.

Now, as Desiree polished her fork with her napkin, he realized her opinion of him no longer mattered.

At all.

Instead, he was free to be the man God had made him to be, right here wearing comfortable clothes in a diner filled with happy customers served by friendly waitresses.

A familiar laugh echoed across the room.

His heart stirred at the sound and he glanced over to find Lauren smiling at a man in an expensive suit. The twinge of jealousy caught him by surprise.

Joel turned his attention back to the woman in front of him.

The fashionable woman talking about a trendy restaurant she wanted to visit.

The two women couldn't be more different.

And that gave him even more to think about.

Because taking another chance on love was a calculated risk.

Especially when the last rejection had left his heart broken, his ego bruised, and his confidence shaken for far too long.

Desiree hadn't been worth the pain she'd put him through.

He might be willing to try again—to take that risk—but only one particular woman came to mind.

Was she worth the potential heartache?

Chapter Eleven

♥

L auren couldn't resist another peek at Joel sitting with his fancy, sophisticated woman. The same one who'd just offered him a second chance.

Something in Lauren's chest twisted into a knot.

Jealousy? Envy?

Then again, what was keeping her from finding her own match? Could the diner atmosphere serve up someone for her to love?

Someone who could love her?

Ignoring her casual attire, Lauren approached a businessman seated in Clarissa's section.

The dark-haired man appeared to be in his late twenties or early thirties. If the assortment of numbers on the papers scattered beside his empty plate was any indication, his job had something to do with finances. And with his tailored suit, he likely had a matching resume guaranteed to impress her father.

She stopped near his elbow. "Can I get you anything else?"

"A refill..." He slid his mug closer with his left hand.

A hand with neatly trimmed nails and a noticeably bare ring finger.

"And..." He looked up with twinkling gray eyes. "The recipe for your cinnamon rolls. My grandmother's birthday is coming up and I need to stay on her good side."

She laughed. "I'm pretty sure that's as much a family secret as the one for our apple crumb pie. But I'll pass your compliments to the baker."

"It was worth a try." He offered a crooked smile before turning his attention back to his paperwork.

"I'll be back with more coffee." She couldn't stop her smile as she retreated to fetch the pot.

The man definitely qualified as a candidate for someone's tall, dark, and handsome—plus charming—valentine's wish.

What was it they said about a suit making the man?

What would Joel look like in a suit? She'd only seen him in T-shirts and jeans. Or with battered tennis shoes propped on the desk as he scribbled notes on a legal pad.

She couldn't picture Joel in a true business setting. At least not anymore.

But that didn't change the fact that a fitted jacket would likely emphasize his muscular build.

Something second-chance glamor girl was already familiar with.

Behind the lunch counter, Lauren combined the half-filled pots and started another batch brewing. While deliberately ignoring the booth where the couple sat and intentionally letting a just-returned Clarissa greet the new table of construction workers nearby.

Instead, she focused on the executive-type waiting for coffee.

As she poured, she caught a whiff of delicious cologne.

Now that was something Joel could improve upon. Bacon and onions and dish soap weren't the most romantic scents.

"Hey, watch it." The man quickly scooted back.

Lauren righted the pot before she overflowed the steaming liquid into his lap but still ended up splashing a few drops onto the man's papers. "Oops, sorry about that."

She stepped back before she could cause any more damage, then offered an extra napkin from her apron pocket. "Looks like I could use another cup myself to wake up. Or maybe the jitters show I've already had too much?"

"Could be." He accepted her offering and dabbed at the spill.

Except his frown resembled her dad's whenever he thought she was incompetent.

If she'd wanted to be memorable, she'd succeeded. Just for all the wrong reasons.

Lauren hurried back behind the counter with the pot, but not before catching a glimpse of Joel's glamor girl. And Desiree's wrinkled nose of disgust.

If that was the corporate world, give her the diner every time. At least here people didn't have to put on an act.

But acknowledging the woman's presence brought to mind both her snarky attitude and a few bits of the conversation she had overheard. Something about a future job opening. And that second chance at romance.

Jealousy churned in her stomach. If that was Joel's normal type, Lauren didn't have a hope of catching his attention.

Except, like Julie loved to remind her, she was fearfully and wonderfully made by God. And someday someone would see that.

Father, help me to remember the truth. Especially on days like this where I feel unloved. Unlovable.

By the time Desiree's food appeared in the pass-through window, Lauren was counting the moments until her own break in the back room.

In fact, she had already placed an order for a basket of chili-cheese fries. Because some days a girl needed grease, particularly if there wasn't a carton of chocolate ice cream available.

Lauren braced for another confrontation as she approached the booth.

"Even if you won't believe that I've changed... Even if you never forgive me, you still have to think of yourself and your future." Desiree's pleading tone grated on Lauren's nerves. "How much are they paying you?"

Joel rubbed his temples. "Enough. We've already been over this. You can't put a price on love or family. And as long as I'm needed, I'm staying here."

Lauren slid the loaded plate in front of the obnoxious woman and forced a smile into her voice. "Here you are. Let me know if you need anything else." She laid the ticket upside down at the edge of the table. "And I'll be your cashier whenever you're ready."

Desiree removed the decorative toothpick and lifted a triangle of toasted rye bread to study the layers of sliced turkey, cheese, lettuce, and tomato beneath. "Appears tolerable enough."

As if they didn't have a professionally trained chef in the kitchen along with years of favorable reviews?

The bells over the door clattered and with that perfect excuse to escape, Lauren took two steps backward.

Except Clarissa intercepted the newcomers first.

Joel pressed his palms against the tabletop. "As nice as it's been seeing you again, I really need to get back to work. If you'll excuse me..." He slid out of the booth and gathered his empty dishes before turning toward the kitchen.

Lauren rolled her eyes behind his back as she followed him.

Nice to see her again? Only until the woman opened her mouth and belittled everything the Dawsons held dear.

Was the man blind or simply being polite?

Joel stopped at the end of the counter. "Why don't you go ahead and start your break while it's still slow. I'll take care of her for you." He tilted his head at the woman busy picking at her sliced fruit with a fork.

Yet something in his eyes caught her attention.

Almost as if he wished things were different. That he wasn't needed at the diner after all so he could pursue that second chance.

Ugh. She needed distance.

"Deal." She re-filled her glass of soda from beside the coffee machine, pocketed a bundle of silverware, and picked up her order of comfort food.

Time to retreat to the table in the office.

And pray Desiree was gone before Lauren's break ended.

Joel signed the invoice and removed the yellow-colored customer copy before handing the clipboard back to the driver. "I hope we didn't get in your way today, Ethan."

The middle-aged man's muscles stretched his company-branded shirt as he shrugged. "Never going to turn down help unloading."

Joel had worried about the delivery status for fifteen minutes too many before calling the company only to learn there was a new driver taking over the route. But when the truck had eventually pulled in, all of the kitchen staff were on hand to check and sort the order as soon as it came off the back.

Ethan waved to the to-go container now sitting in the cab. "And if being a half hour later than your old guy results in free baked goods, I'll either stall on purpose or rearrange the schedule."

Joel smiled. "It worked out well for everyone." Because handing off other leftovers—like meatloaf—was a sure recipe for poor customer service.

"Anyway, better get moving for my next stop." Ethan tossed the clipboard onto the upholstered seat, then swung up behind the wheel.

"Any requests?" Joel caught the truck's door before it closed. "I mean, in case we were to accidentally forget to sell out of apple pie or cinnamon rolls next Tuesday?"

"Now that's what I call thinking ahead." Ethan chuckled. "I'm always up for a quality cinnamon roll."

"Noted. We'll see you next week." Joel waved goodbye and headed through the back door. He bypassed the mountain of boxes beside the store room and slipped into the office to file the invoice.

Thinking ahead.

Seemed all he did lately was hustle to stay ahead of problems at the diner.

Then Desiree waltzed in and accused him of not thinking about his future. Even more-than-hinted they could have a second chance, as if he hadn't been burned enough the first time.

As if mostly ignoring her texts for the past month hadn't sent a clear message.

Even if she'd changed since their break-up, so had he.

He slouched in the chair behind the desk and leaned his head back.

Did she really think his ultimate dream was to fill a high paying job like the one he'd been offered an interview for several weeks ago?

It would have been a good starting place to gain experience.

And income.

But only until he could leverage his savings to start building a portfolio of businesses to rival that of any accomplished entrepreneur.

Except CVX Industries had lost its appeal if Desiree was the one who had elevated his application like she implied. Couldn't he at least have earned the consideration on his own merits?

The whole encounter had left a sour taste in his mouth, and even more so after, intentional or not, she'd practically rubbed his nose in the fact he was still greasy-spoon material.

He shoved away from the desk and headed for the mountain of boxes. Better to lose himself in work than thoughts that went nowhere.

A few minutes later, Lauren stopped in the storeroom doorway. "Do you still need help?"

Joel lifted another large can of green beans and approached the ladder. "I could use a hand."

"There's still a small pile outside the cooler, but Greta should be finished soon." She ripped open the next box. "I have to ask. Who was the glamor girl earlier?"

He twisted toward Lauren to find her holding up another can. "An ex-girlfriend from college."

Her eyes widened. "She lives here?"

"No. The Denver area." He took the second can from her hands and climbed to the next-to-highest shelf.

"Oh. That's not too far." Her voice rose a bit at the end as if fishing for his opinion.

He shoved the cans into place, the metal skittering across the wire shelving. "Not far enough."

Behind him, she snorted. "My feelings exactly."

He turned. "Really?"

She wrinkled her nose and raised her voice into a falsetto. " 'Even cheap flowers can't make this place any less of a dump.' " Lauren practically growled as she reached into the open box. "Oh, you don't know how close I came to spilling her tea in her lap."

"You showed great restraint." His smile at the memory faded.

Because for a moment he'd been tempted to do the same. At least to accidentally bump the table at just the right—wrong—moment.

"So, why was she in town looking for you?"

Was that a hint of jealousy or protectiveness in her tone?

How could he explain it?

She held up another two cans. "Sometimes it helps to talk to a friend, if you want. I do some of my best thinking out loud."

He took the canned vegetables and pivoted away. "Around graduation, I submitted resumes to a handful of big companies and one of them has a branch office in Denver."

"Go on."

"Well, several weeks ago, right in the middle of our payroll confusion, I got a call to set up an interview."

She gasped. "So, you..."

"I turned it down—nicely, of course—because I'm busy here for the time being. The guy who called said my resume had been forwarded from their human resources department." He descended the ladder. "Evidently—if I can believe what she hinted at—one of his employees tampered with the applications and promoted my resume herself."

Lauren turned toward him, this time with two plastic jars of cinnamon in her hands. "Then she showed up here?"

"And was mad that I'd declined the interview." He paused on his way down. "Didn't even try to understand when I explained about Dad's heart attack and why I'm needed here."

Lauren put a hand on his arm, her comforting gesture erasing the ache left behind by Desiree's visit. "You're doing the right thing. We need you."

He blew out a frustrated breath. "After a glimpse of her manipulations, I'd much rather be stacking cans of beans and flattening cardboard boxes than running around an office trying to impress certain people so I can get ahead and make lots of money."

And watch that money disappear to pay for the trappings of an expensive wardrobe and rent in the best neighborhood.

"My dad sometimes calls it the corporate hamster wheel. Trying to get ahead but only running in circles while dodging rival backstabbers." She reached into a box for another load of baking supplies. "He thinks it's worth the effort, but to me it sounds like a lousy way to live."

"Some days it might be easier to sit at a desk inputting numbers than have your parents' livelihood resting on your shoulders."

She propped a hand on her hip. "You'd back away from the challenge?"

"No, even if the only ladders I'm climbing are made of aluminum." He slapped a palm against the metal before reaching for a carton of napkins.

Back in college, many of his friends had been obsessed with the corporate ladder at all costs. He'd been sucked in for a while, but the journey home again was opening his eyes.

Family mattered more.

And putting a smile on the face of a loyal customer brought more satisfaction than compiling a balanced earnings report.

After a minute, Lauren broke the silence. "If she's an ex-girlfriend, why'd you break up with her?"

He winced. "She dumped me."

"What? Is she blind?" Lauren's gaze swept over him and he resisted the urge to flex his muscles.

"You're good for my ego." He grinned. "Truth is, she had her eyes on someone else at the time."

Or at least on their wallet.

Lauren stood wide eyed. "Yet she came back here hoping for a second chance?"

"You heard that?" He tilted his head.

She blushed and glanced away, her tousled curls brushing against her rosy cheek.

Slivers of past rejection pierced his heart. "She was a tutor for the football team at college."

"That's convenient." She rolled her eyes.

"I thought so." He waggled his eyebrows.

She laughed.

"We started dating a few weeks into my sophomore year, but by the time I was a junior, she'd moved on to a guy who scored more touchdowns and had his name in the paper. Not to mention had a fancier car and a bigger budget for restaurants or roses."

She hummed. "Sounds shallow."

Joel knelt beside one of the last remaining boxes. "It was. Guess my hometown-style pizza dates weren't enough incentive."

"Tsk. Anyone who doesn't appreciate pizza isn't worth keeping anyway." Lauren propped her hands on her narrow waist and shook her head, setting her dangling earrings swinging.

"Come to think of it, I should have thanked her for the escape."

"But you didn't because rejection always stings." Her voice cracked with emotion.

"I didn't cry over the loss. Much. But I sure worked harder in the gym, at practice, and in the classroom." He had vowed to himself that he would someday land a high-paying job.

That instead of being the guy stuck working on Saturday while his friends went to a concert or to someone's cabin for the weekend, he could afford to go wherever he wanted.

"I was determined to be the best and failure was not an option."

"Because if you fail, someone else gets your girl... or your potential rung on the corporate ladder." She swiveled between the boxes and the shelves.

His girl.

Earlier he'd been sitting across from Desiree, a magazine-worthy, image-conscious woman offering a high-paying job while she scowled at the simple diner that had become a second home.

While being served by the friendly waitress with the big smile who cared more about her customers than the ketchup stain on her jeans.

There was only one he wanted to spend time with.

A woman of faith and hospitality just like his grandmother.

He shook his head as he flattened the last box. "I wasted years worrying about my image instead of what really matters."

"They weren't wasted. They prepared you for this moment and this place."

He straightened and studied the neatly arranged shelves with a sense of pride.

Why hadn't he seen what was here all along?

He wrapped an arm around Lauren's shoulder, peering down at her tousled curls. "Thanks for listening and understanding."

"No problem. That's what friends are for."

He pulled her into a full hug that completely soothed the rough spots in his heart. Through the doorway, he spotted the stainless-steel counters and ovens waiting for another day of service.

Lauren squeezed his waist before easing back and gazing up with shining hazel green eyes.

There was no place he'd rather be than here.

With her.

In a movement as natural and automatic as breathing, he lowered his head and covered her lips with his.

She stiffened slightly, then relaxed and leaned toward him.

His pulse raced as he tasted her lips, his fingers tangling in her soft curls.

The clanging slam of the cooler door brought a dose of reality.

He broke off their kiss and stepped back.

What was he thinking?

Kissing a coworker? While on the job?

He'd acted on instinct. Without a plan.

Something no true businessman should ever do.

He took a deep breath to slow his racing heart. "I shouldn't have done that."

The dreamy eyes that had been staring at his lips filled with pain. Lauren glanced away and mumbled something about checking on Greta before she hurried out the door.

"That wasn't what I meant." Joel's shoulders drooped.

Too late.

She was gone.

Leaving him alone to regret his words, but never their kiss.

Chapter Twelve

♥

Lauren blinked to clear her vision, her pencil tapping the empty box where the number of jars should be noted on the sheet.

Inventory shouldn't be this difficult.

All because the murmur of Joel's voice outside the storeroom door affected her concentration more than she wanted it to.

Mostly because she was mere feet from the spot where he had kissed her. Then apologized.

And since ignored her for days on end.

She huffed out a breath, rested the clipboard on the ladder's top step, and started counting the spices.

Again.

Cinnamon. One, two, three.

Nutmeg. One, two.

"That was Mom." Joel stopped at the foot of the ladder and crossed his arms, his biceps bulging. "Dad's coming home today instead of Monday."

A month after collapsing in the diner kitchen, Frank would finally sleep under his own roof again.

"That's great." She found a genuine smile at the news. "We should celebrate."

Joel nodded. "Just family though. And you, of course."

If only that didn't make her feel like an afterthought.

But she would still do the right thing for the family that practically adopted her when her own had left her in the dust.

She stepped off the ladder and away from Joel's tempting bulk and contagious smile. "Can I bring something? Do anything?"

"If you can finish the inventory and place the order, I'll get the bank deposit ready and head to the rehab center to help Mom load the walker and stuff."

"I can do that. Plus I'll lock up here when I'm done and then head to your folks' house."

Thanks to the previous weeks of experience, she could handle it alone.

Joel moved to the doorway. "Hey, Aunt Greta, come here a minute."

"Hold your horses." Greta's muffled voice grew louder. "I was just saying goodbye to the others. What's the rush?"

"Dad's coming home today and we were thinking—"

"Praise the Lord." Greta leaned against the door jamb. "We need to throw a party."

Joel's lips quirked. "Or a glorified family dinner. But what should we serve?"

As Greta rattled off an impromptu menu, Lauren repositioned the ladder and climbed it again.

Might as well do her work while they planned.

But when Greta started grilling Joel about the condition of the house, Lauren bit back a smile.

At least she wasn't the only one on the receiving end of the clean-up-your-mess lecture.

She made a note on the inventory sheets and descended again. "I could do the shopping on my way over if Greta wants to get a head start on the cleaning."

"What? Now you're ganging up on me." Joel raised his hands in protest. "Why do you assume it needs cleaning?"

Greta patted his shoulder. "I know it's not how Nancy normally keeps it. Not when she's been spending so much time with Frank."

Lauren inched closer. "Don't turn down free housecleaning."

"True." Joel wrapped an arm around each of them to create a circle like that crazy day over a month ago. "The most important thing is getting Dad home so he can continue his recovery."

"Amen to that." Greta tipped her head back and closed her eyes as if praying.

With Joel's arm around her waist, warmth spread through Lauren's body.

She glanced up and caught him staring at her.

He winked.

Heat rose in her face.

It was so hard to keep her heart from dreaming. From hoping.

All because of the kiss she couldn't forget.

Joel was right.

He shouldn't have kissed her, because it was all she could think about while continuing to spend so much time with him at the diner and trying to stay professional.

She looked away.

With Frank improving, Joel would soon be free to leave.

She had to get control over her emotions before the rest of the family picked up on them.

Lauren broke away from the huddle. "We'd better get back to work. The sooner we're done—"

"The sooner we can leave." Joel and Greta spoke in unison, then laughed.

A few minutes later, Lauren entered the office with the last of the tally sheets to find Joel shrugging into his coat. "Call me if there's anything your Mom needs me to pick up while I'm at the store."

"Will do. Thanks." He smiled and her heart jumped.

Because she was able to help those she cared about, right?

It had nothing to do with his charm, friendship, or good looks.

Or her impossible hope that he might actually be interested in someone like her.

Almost an hour later, she parked behind Greta's car on the street in front of the Dawson's home and hurried up the driveway with arms full of shopping bags. She rang the doorbell with her elbow and after a moment, jostled the bags enough to twist the door knob.

From the smell of lemon cleaner inside and sight of vacuum lines on the carpet, Greta had been hard at work.

Based on her memory of past gatherings as Julie's guest, she crossed the living room to reach the empty kitchen.

"Greta? I'm here." She raised her voice as she set the groceries on the counter.

"Hold your horses, girl." Greta rounded the corner. "I just finished the bathrooms and moved a load of laundry into the dryer."

"I think I got everything you need." Lauren placed the package of frozen meatballs next to the box of multigrain pasta and jar of sugar-free marinara sauce. Despite the cost, she'd bought all the necessary ingredients rather than wonder what Nancy had on hand.

"These never taste as good as homemade."

"There wasn't time, plus we're tired." She wrapped an arm around Greta's waist. "Besides, this celebration is more about the people than the food. Except I did try for heart-healthy options and made sure there's enough for them to have leftovers tomorrow. Didn't want Nancy to have to cook after church tomorrow if she didn't want to."

Greta hugged her back, then reached for the bagged salad. "Smart girl. What's in the other sack?"

Lauren pulled out a package of balloons. "What's a party without decorations?"

"Frank will grumble." Greta grinned.

"I know." Lauren giggled as she escaped the kitchen with her supplies. He might complain, but he liked her anyway.

She soon had a homemade welcome home banner hanging on the wall opposite the front door. With the help of a dining room chair, she added twisted red streamers radiating out from the center light fixture and a few balloons.

After snapping a picture on her phone, she sent it to Julie. ***Decorating underway. Wish you were here to celebrate.***

Was it only a few days ago that Lauren cried for an hour on the phone with her best friend trying to make sense of the kiss and apology. At least Julie promised not to say anything to her cousin.

Lauren sighed and looked around the room. She'd visited here before over the years, always with her best friend at her side.

Her gaze slid to the corner where the Dawsons' Christmas tree had stood that fateful year and she caught her breath.

No. She'd grown up and things were different now. History did *not* have to repeat itself.

No doubt she and Julie had looked silly in the bell-rimmed red-and-green hats with pointed elf ears her own mother had sent. But that was no reason for Joel to curl his lip. Or to snap at all of them.

While glaring at her.

His generic apology back then had rung false.

Which only reminded her of the current dynamic between them.

If Joel was going to apologize for kissing her, it didn't matter if he thought her party decorating tendencies were over-the-top.

Maybe a couple more balloons beside the banner?

Her phone rang and she pulled it out of her back pocket.

Joel's face filled the screen, reminding her of his wink earlier.

There might be a vague hope for a repeat kiss, but no chance of a future.

She erased his face with a swipe to answer the call.

"We're on our way. I'm following Mom right now. Is everything ready?"

"Greta's busy in the kitchen and I put up some decorations."

"Good. But we need to be careful. Dad seemed pretty worn out by the time he got to the car."

"We can help get him settled. Then all he has to do is sit and rest." She studied Frank's favorite recliner.

"Sounds good. See you soon."

Oh why did her heart have to skip a beat?

No, she was here for Frank's benefit, not her own.

After letting Greta know they were on their way, Lauren made a final sweep through the house in case anything else needed doing.

Along the way, she glanced into Joel's bedroom and shook her head. Why did his room have to be neater than hers? Then again, it didn't look like he had as much stuff.

She retreated to the front window to watch just in time to see the Dawsons' sedan slowly pull into the driveway.

Ready or not, here they came.

And her focus should be on Frank alone.

Almost home.

Joel positioned the rolling walker beside the open passenger side door. "Is this right?"

Dad rotated until his feet were on the pavement. "Closer." He reached for the handle and scooted his body forward. After a rocking motion for momentum, he was soon vertical but leaning heavily on the support.

It was hard to imagine Dad had really regained both strength and energy over the past few weeks. The post-surgery infection had taken its toll, although some of the weight loss could be attributed to the required dietary changes.

Joel gave his dad room to maneuver, shut the car door, and shadowed him toward the front door where Lauren waited.

If only her happy smile was for him and not for his mom who had reached her side. Then again, it was his own fault.

Because ever since Tuesday he'd been tongue-tied about how to make things better. How to get back to the easy friendship they'd forged.

All because of a kiss Joel couldn't forget.

And could never regret.

At the stairs, Dad teetered a bit as he transitioned his hold to the railing instead of the walker.

Joel offered a supporting arm. "Careful."

"I'm not an invalid." Dad's characteristic grumble held more bite than usual.

Joel glanced at his mom waiting for them.

She squared her shoulders. "Nobody's babying you. We just don't want to wear you out before you can enjoy what the girls have prepared."

Dad grunted and continued toward the door.

At least once he got inside, it was a ranch-style house and should be easy to navigate.

"Welcome home, Frank." Lauren offered a quick hug, then stepped back to hold the door open. "Almost there."

Joel hurried to move the walker back into position and soon Dad was officially home.

Where he promptly stopped in his tracks.

"What's all this nonsense?" Dad waved his hand at the colorful streamers and balloons.

Lauren had been busy. But the festive look couldn't quite mask the worn and tired interior. From the lumpy couch to the faded photographs on the walls, his childhood home—like the diner—seemed trapped in time.

So many reminders of difficult seasons where his wishes for things as simple as a new bicycle had gone unfulfilled as their meager profits were funneled back into Dawson's Diner.

Was it any wonder he had dreamed of more?

More than playing college football. Of getting the first degree in his family. And even beyond securing the diner's legacy.

Ever since meeting an entrepreneur during a high school career day, Joel's ultimate dream had been to build a portfolio of successful businesses. And why? So he'd always have enough money to never go without again.

Lauren's warm laughter filled the room. "It's a party and you're the guest of honor. I thought red was your favorite color."

Right. The decorations.

And welcoming Dad home.

"Used to be." Dad grunted. "Until they went overboard decorating at the hospital."

Joel snorted. "Good thing you haven't seen the diner lately."

How soon until the green of St. Patrick's Day could replace the never-ending reds and pinks splashed everywhere?

Lauren just frowned, shifting her attention to Mom. "Do you have a chair that will be easier for Frank to get out of later?"

Mom brought one with arms from the dining room and set it next to the couch. "Let's try this one for now and save the recliner for another day."

Aunt Greta appeared briefly with a hug for everyone and the promise of appetizers, then she disappeared again.

Once Dad was settled, Mom turned toward the door.

Joel nudged her to the couch instead. "Sit down and relax. I'll unload the cars."

During one of the many trips, he carried clothing bags down the hall to his parents' bedroom and heard the dryer running.

Probably Aunt Greta's doing.

As much as her pointed questions had irritated him earlier, having help with the house was nice. Especially since Mom had been—and would continue to be busy helping Dad with his exercises and monitoring his diet.

It would be good to have everyone under one roof as a family again.

Yet another reason to celebrate the small victories because there was still a long road ahead.

Joel re-entered the living room to find Lauren perched on the couch beside his mom and offering to stop by in the afternoons to give her a break or the chance to run errands.

"Thank you." Mom patted Lauren's knee. "You're such a sweet girl to think of me."

Lauren was certainly sweet.

He could still recall the taste of her lips.

If only things were different—if he weren't basically her boss—he could date her.

But was that really true? After all, his parents had made the diner kitchen their own romantic paradise.

His gaze bounced between Mom and Dad as hope rose, then sank.

He couldn't risk messing up their work dynamic now that it was finally clicking.

Joel found a seat in Dad's recliner where he could see everyone and get off his feet for a while. His stomach rumbled at the smell of garlic wafting in from the kitchen.

The kitchen where Aunt Greta still worked.

He was about to stand and help when Dad asked Lauren the question Joel dreaded most.

"How is the diner really doing? Joel won't tell me anything."

Lauren glanced at Joel, then smiled at his dad. "Joel has everything under control and we're just fine."

Good thing they'd talked about not worrying his dad.

And that she didn't know *everything*.

Lauren patted Dad's hand. "Greta's handling your spatula like a pro but Trevor is right there with her. And I've heard that Debbie, the new kitchen helper we hired, is a multi-tasking whiz keeping everyone stocked."

His dad mumbled something in reply.

Lauren just kept on smiling. "She's the one who suggested we add a pie-of-the-day in addition to the usual favorites. One of these days when you're up for an outing, you'll have to stop by and have a small slice."

Joel exchanged a glance with his mom.

Pie might not be on the approved heart diet, but the occasional incentive might make Dad more cooperative with his rehab exercises.

"What else is new at the diner?" Lauren tapped her chin with one finger and grinned. "The Great Minds Club is still trying to solve the problems of the world. In fact, just yesterday Dennis and Roy got into it over whether Loveland's Miss Valentine should visit the state capitol or not when there are more serious issues to discuss."

Joel sat back as Lauren recreated the debate complete with accents.

Somehow the exchange was funnier today than when he'd been trapped behind the counter making more coffee to fuel the heated discussion.

And based on Dad's wide smile, he was more like Grandma Hope than Joel had ever imagined.

After she'd stopped working at the diner in order to take care of Julie while Greta went back to work, Grandma had been the one craving all the gossip.

And the community news was something they served almost as much as coffee.

Lauren launched into a description of the Ladies' Group and their yarn project debate from a few weeks ago. She even described the wardrobe of each participant in hushed tones as if she were an announcer at a fashion show detailing the runway attire.

Mom and Dad were soon in tears from laughter.

All the fun and friendly side with no mention of all the hiccups in the first weeks or all the work involved before and after hours.

Or the still-too-tight bank balance he'd been keeping a close eye on.

The diner's family atmosphere was healing for Dad, even when he wasn't there.

Dad darted a glance at Mom. "I still want to see it for myself. And since I need to meet with the Realtor about Uncle Alex's side, might as well get some pie too."

"Pie?" Aunt Greta stopped in the doorway to the kitchen. "Only if you don't give Nancy unnecessary grief here at home."

Dad grumbled something about the diet police.

Aunt Greta narrowed her eyes. "Don't waste the second chance Dad never got. Your only job is to get healthy enough for a comeback."

A comeback? Joel's heart skipped a beat. He'd been counting on that eventual outcome, but now? Did he really want to move on when the time came?

Aunt Greta wagged a finger at her older brother. "And in the meantime, we're doing just fine without your meddling."

"I don't meddle. *You're* the meddler, just like Mom." Dad peeked at his wife as if recruiting an ally. "Won't be long until Nancy is begging me to get out of the house."

"You only just got here." Mom chuckled. "But about that comeback, I've enjoyed letting someone else get up way before dawn for a change. I'm in no rush even if sometimes that hot kitchen was our paradise."

The warmth in Mom's eyes triggered Dad's special smile reserved only for her.

Who knew that the blunt grump and the easygoing homemaker were such a perfect pair?

Please, God, help me find a love like theirs.

Lauren fidgeted on the couch beside them and his thoughts shifted.

Over the past month plus, his practical knowledge of business had been inspired by her vivacious creativity. As if she brought color to a black-and-white world.

And then there was that spontaneous kiss he couldn't stop thinking about.

Joel caught Lauren's gaze. Maybe his parents had the right idea.

Maybe he had something worth sticking around for.

Lauren blushed and quickly looked away. "Would it be easier to eat in here or in the kitchen?"

Mom peeked at Dad. "We have a few old television trays that should work just fine, especially so Frank doesn't have to move." She stood. "Enough relaxing for me. Greta, how can I help with the food?"

Soon they were all gathered again with plates before them, this time with him and Lauren seated side-by-side on the couch.

Joel cleared his throat and bowed his head. "Father God, thank you for the chance to celebrate Dad's recovery and his coming home. Continue to give him strength and motivation to face physical therapy in the days ahead. Thank you for Aunt Greta's cooking and this food. Amen."

And, Lord, please give Mom extra patience as she cares for Dad alone while I'm at the diner.

As they ate, the conversation drifted from his cousin Julie's latest phone call to updates about his parents' church friends. His mind tuned out the details as he simply absorbed the banter.

It reminded him of almost every other family gathering they had.

But this one had Lauren right there beside him in the middle of it all.

He glanced her way.

She not only fit him, she also fit with his family.

And she was already best friends with his cousin Julie.

In fact...

He nudged Lauren with his elbow. "Do you know what this reminds me of?"

She eyed the group now discussing breakfast ingredients. "The diner?"

"No, Christmas. Like the one where you tagged along with my giggling cousin." He jutted his chin toward the corner where their tilted tree usually stood.

She followed his gaze and the color drained from her face.

He paused to think. "What did I say?"

"That was a painful year. For a lot of reasons. So being included as a small part of your happy family was exactly what I needed." She swallowed hard. "Until..."

"Until?" He tried to remember more of the details but came up empty.

She blinked rapidly. "Until you had to go and ruin it by mocking me and my hat in front of everyone."

"I mocked your hat?"

She bit her lip and looked away. "Never mind. It's old news."

He pushed away his half-empty plate.

Whatever he'd done in the past still stood between them.

And until he figured it out—and made amends—there would never be another kiss.

Chapter Thirteen

♥

The little old pair sitting side-by-side in a booth, making heart eyes at each other was a definite example of couple goals.

Something Lauren was even further away from ever claiming for herself.

"What's your secret?" Lauren set two plates of the lasagna special in front of them.

The woman smiled adoringly at her husband. "No secret to it at all. Other than learning how to love and serve each other better."

The husband pursed his lips as if in serious thought. "Love keeps no record of wrongs, so I've been letting her always be right for the past forty years."

"Oh, hush." The wife elbowed his ribs.

He waggled his eyebrows. "A sense of humor doesn't hurt either."

They were too cute.

His wife beckoned Lauren closer and lowered her voice to a whisper. "My secret weapon is keeping breath mints under my pillow."

Lauren laughed as she placed their ticket upside down on the table. "Well, enjoy your Valentine's Day lunch. Let me know if there's anything else you need."

The man patted his wife's hand before winking at Lauren. "I've got all I need right here."

His wife blushed, then leaned in for a kiss.

Lauren made a quick escape.

Who knew diner food could be romantic? Guess it all depended on who you were with.

Then again, lasagna was a huge step up from meatloaf.

Customers loved the new addition so much she had yet to taste Trevor's dish. Mostly because there weren't any leftovers for the staff to fight over.

Which apparently was the goal based on a discussion she'd overheard between Joel and the chef. Not that terms like cost of goods sold or revenue to expense ratios made any sense.

Bottom line was that their guests left smiling and that's what counted in her mind.

The bells over the door clattered and she turned to find her roommates entering along with another girl she didn't know.

Had they ever visited her workplace before?

She hurried forward with a smile. "This is a welcome surprise. Would you like a table or a booth?"

Stacey glanced at the others. "Booth."

Lauren led the way and waited until they were seated. "Today's special is the lasagna and the soup of the day is broccoli cheddar. The rest of our options are right there." She pointed at the laminated cards in the condiment rack beside the window.

Rachel passed them around, avoiding making eye contact with Lauren.

That was strange.

Lauren held her smile and professionalism in place. "While you're deciding, what can I get you to drink?"

With three orders for iced tea, Lauren left them studying the menu and hurried back behind the counter. She was reaching for a third glass when a trill of laughter erupted from near the windows.

"Do you know them?" Joel nudged her aside to replace the coffee pot.

"My roommates and a friend of theirs."

He raised an eyebrow at a burst of profanity.

"I know. Not exactly my style but I met them in Freshman English my first semester. Julie was still living at home so she wasn't available to split rent but when my dad moved to Denver, I needed a new place to stay. They asked me to move in and the rest is history." She filled the last glass and gathered them into a triangle between her hands.

As she headed back to their table, Lauren eyed her roommates and their friend. Now that they'd shed their jackets, they were all dressed in the same style with low-cut necklines, tight-fitting shirts, and miniskirts. Heavy makeup painted their faces beneath straight hair.

Her typical jeans and T-shirt, tennis shoes, and tousled curls did not fit into their crowd.

Not that it mattered. She was rarely around them anymore.

Lauren delivered the drinks and pulled out her notepad. "Have you decided?"

Stacey took the lead, as usual, ordering a grilled chicken salad with fat-free dressing on the side.

Rachel chimed in with the same.

The newcomer stared at Lauren while adding her similar order then nudged Stacey with her elbow.

Something was definitely wrong.

Lauren frowned. "What's up?"

Stacey shrugged. "Actually, since you're not going to college..."

Lauren winced. "It's only for this semester."

Stacey waved her off. "Renee needs a place to stay in a couple of weeks."

With a glance around the table, the dots began to connect in Lauren's mind. "So, Renee is moving in."

Not that there was much room in the small apartment for another person but they could work out those details. And the rent would be cheaper split four ways.

Lauren briefly checked on her other tables. She'd be fine lingering here for a few more minutes to discuss the arrangements.

"And you're moving out." Stacey's voice sliced through her thoughts.

"I'm what?"

That's what she got for trying to multi-task instead of paying attention.

Stacey flicked an imaginary crumb from the tabletop. "Moving out. It's just not working anymore. Never really did since you had to be up so early to work here and we never hang out together. Plus you were late pitching in on the utilities. Again."

Lauren bit her tongue on her excuse. She'd been busy and didn't see the note someone had left taped to the television she rarely watched.

Rachel coughed. "And you have to be reminded to clean up. Even before that messy mud on the table."

Lauren folded her arms. "I've been doing better and the sculpture project was only one night."

After her walk in the park with Joel, she'd tried to be like her mom. But her attempt at art had collapsed.

Just like this conversation was falling apart.

Stacey shrugged. "My name is technically the only one on the lease and our agreement was majority rules. We ruled. You need to be out by the end of the month."

Dismissed.

Rejected.

Lauren stared past their smug faces to the mocking hearts taped on the window.

She'd rip them down after work.

Valentine's Day was over... along with the love of so-called friends, even if she didn't quite fit in with their crowd.

She swallowed the lump in her throat and fought for dignity. "I'll go turn in your order."

She stiffened her spine and retreated to the ordering screen to stab in their desire for diet food.

Maybe if they ate more fried foods, they'd have adequate brain cells to appreciate the finer points of social interactions.

Blindsided by her roommates while at work.

Stabbed in the back.

Broadsided by life.

"Whoa. What's with the scowl?" Joel nudged her side.

"I'm not in the mood."

"You're certainly in *a* mood."

"Very funny." She turned to face him, aiming her back at the table of giggling girls.

His smile faded. "What happened over there?"

"They're kicking me out." She sucked in a quick breath and blinked to avoid the threat of tears.

Can't show weakness.

Don't let the pain show.

"Really?" Joel's eyes widened as he stared over her shoulder at the traitors.

"Making room for the new girl by getting rid of the old."

His gaze shifted back to her. "Can they do that?"

"Legally, yes." Her shoulders slumped. "Although a little more notice would have been nice."

It was already mid-February so she had less than two weeks to find a place to live.

"At least they waited until after my birthday to deliver their lovely gift." Tears filled her eyes.

"Your birthday?" He frowned. "When was—"

"On Monday, but it's not a big deal."

"It should have been." He stared into her eyes as if it mattered.

As if *she* mattered.

She fought the wave of emotions threatening to pull her under.

The bells over the door clattered and Trevor slid a few plates into the pass-through.

Right. There was work to be done and lunches to be served.

She squared her shoulders and blinked several times. "I can do this."

"That's my girl." Joel squeezed her arm and then stepped away to deliver the latest order.

Her stomach fluttered at being called his girl.

Reality returned.

She was a failure.

Rejected once again for being herself.

A road-construction worker and his friends in matching bright-orange vests found seats around a table near the door in her assigned area.

Two businessmen exited from Clarissa's section.

If only she could walk out the door and not look back.

A fresh start somewhere was tempting, but that would upset her dad even more.

He'd already rejected her enough.

Not to mention that she wasn't a quitter and she wasn't going to turn her back on the Dawsons... or Joel.

But where on earth was she going to find a place to live in two weeks, as well as come up with a deposit and full rent payment?

Normally, she would ask Dad for a loan. But other than a text in the group chat with belated birthday wishes—something only today's date had reminded the others about—he was still not talking to her after her college dropout decision.

And the last she'd heard, Mom still lived somewhere in New Mexico learning Native American pottery techniques.

Maybe she could stay at Greta's for a few days in Julie's old room.

However, that was risky because she'd be even closer to Joel's family.

Could her heart handle getting more attached?

What if he rejected her, too?

As he ran the daily sales report, Joel kept an eye on Lauren restocking condiment trays near the front door.

Instead of her normal chatter, she had hardly said anything beyond basic interactions with customers for the past two hours.

Ever since her friends—not friends, roommates—left.

"Is she coming down with something?" Clarissa dumped used coffee grounds into the trash can.

"No. Just had a rough day."

"I heard that." Lauren growled from across the room.

"What should I do?" The waitress lowered her voice. "I just want to help."

Joel smiled at the redhead. "Finish prepping the coffee machine and you can head home."

She glanced toward the door. "Are you sure?"

"I'll take care of her." That's what friends were for.

Even if it involved a lot of tears.

He'd been around girls enough to learn they thought crying solved problems. Personally, a long run or a tough workout was the quickest way to feel better.

He watched as Lauren disappeared into the women's restroom with a bucket of cleaning supplies.

She needed a friend who hadn't just kicked her to the curb. Julie was out of state and Aunt Greta would mother her to death.

I can do this.

With the cash drawer in hand, he headed to the office to record the receipts. After locking the money in the safe, he spotted a box of tissues on the employee break table and grabbed it on his way back through the kitchen.

"What do you need those for?" Aunt Greta stopped him by the cooler door.

He tilted his head toward the dining room and the rattling noises of the mop bucket over tile that filtered through the pass-through window. "Somebody had a rough day."

Aunt Greta smirked, then patted his arm. "And you're going to fix it?"

"Or die trying." He took a deep breath and stepped forward.

Time to do his own mopping up, even if Aunt Greta got a chuckle.

He pushed through the swinging doors to the dining room and looked around. Lauren knelt on a bench seat ripping down the Valentine's Day decorations and peeling tape off the outside window.

Halfway across the room, he heard her sniff.

A few steps later, he held out the tissues. "You might need these."

She glanced over her shoulder. "Take a hike, Joel."

At least she took the box.

"A hike sounds nice, but the weather's not quite warm enough." He slid into the next booth and reached for a red construction paper decoration. "Since I'm staying inside, I'm a good listener... if you're in the mood to talk about whatever is on your mind. I think it was a wise person who once told me they do their best thinking while talking."

She crushed a heart into a ball, then relaxed her hand to let it fall to the table. "Is there something wrong with me?"

Wrong with her? Was she crazy?

He studied her from the top of her curly hair, past the earnest hazel eyes pleading for an answer, to the pink usually smiling lips that he'd tasted.

And wanted to taste again.

She started to frown.

He coughed. "Absolutely nothing is wrong with you."

Lauren was not only a hard worker, but also a woman of faith with a vibrant personality.

If only he knew how to put the sparkle back in her eyes.

"I think I'm too much like my mother."

"And that's a bad thing?"

She sighed. "What exactly do you know about my family?"

"Just that your parents split up when you were younger." He picked at a stubborn piece of tape on the glass.

"Dad was a sales manager for a big software company. Mom stayed home with the three of us girls."

"Three?" There were more like her around town?

Lauren crumpled a few paper hearts and tape into a ball in her fist. "Two older sisters. You might have gone to school with them, but one's a brand new corporate lawyer in Chicago while the other is making tons of money as a stock broker."

He blinked at the unspoken contrast to Lauren's current job as a waitress, but when he tried to picture Lauren stuck behind a desk, he failed.

"Mom is... an artistic soul who is currently somewhere in New Mexico learning about pottery." Lauren moved to the next booth in line. "Anyway, as we got older, my sisters were hyper-focused on getting into the right college and once I needed less supervision, Mom started painting and other crafts until her hobbies took up more and more of her time."

"Uh-huh." He stuffed the removed pieces of tape into the pocket of his jeans, then started work on the next heart.

"I still remember coming home from middle school one day to find Mom curled up on the couch crying because Dad had moved out."

"Just like that?" He caught her glance and winced at the raw pain in her eyes.

"I'd heard them arguing the night before. Dad had complained about all her ridiculous ideas and projects. Even asked why she couldn't get a normal job. Couldn't she see how she was messing up my life too?"

Joel frowned. "Is that what he told you to explain why he left?"

"No. He never bothered to say goodbye at all. Guess he assumed Mom would tell me, but by leaving me behind with her, it felt like he'd rejected me too. Like he thought I was hopeless and destined to be messed up just like Mom." She sniffed.

"I'm sorry." He reached toward her, but with a table and two bench seats between them, he couldn't even touch her arm.

She nodded. "He did eventually step in. But only after Mom pulled me out of school and dragged me around the country for a year. When it was obvious I wasn't actually getting an education, he petitioned the court for custody and brought me back here." She waved a hand out the window as if indicating Loveland.

How had he missed knowing that about her?

"Not that it felt like home anymore. Especially since my sisters had moved on and he was gone so much for work himself." She picked at a piece of tape. "But having to repeat a year of school was a hidden blessing because that's when I met Julie and we became best friends. She'd just lost her dad and it seemed like I didn't really have one either."

He'd been shocked to learn his uncle had died as the result of a car accident. And blindsided again when he discovered his aunt and cousin had lost their home and needed to move in with Grandma Hope.

No wonder Lauren had been glued to Julie's side that Christmas.

The Christmas he'd apparently ruined somehow...

Lauren chuckled for the first time in hours. "But meeting Julie also meant meeting Hope. And that's when I met Jesus. I can't be sad about that."

Joel gave a wistful smile at the testimony that mirrored his own.

Because anyone who'd ever met his grandmother saw her infectious faith in action and soon found themselves making a decision.

Lauren shrugged. "Anyway, I've always been more creative, like my mom, while my sisters obviously took after my dad. So, sometimes I find myself trying to be something I'm not in order to get his attention or earn a simple compliment."

"Something you're not?"

What did that mean?

"By going to college to get an acceptable degree in something he thinks will make a lot of money when I'd much rather be learning about other less-boring things. Or talking to people. I like putting my faith into action instead of serving the almighty dollar." Lauren tossed several wadded hearts onto a tabletop and moved on to the last booth.

Would she stop talking once the decorations were down?

She folded her arms and stared out the window. "I've spent years trying to fit the mold of his expectations instead of being myself."

"There's nothing wrong with being creative or enthusiastic." He finally conquered the last strip of tape and collected the shredded scraps of paper.

"Except when I feel rejected." Her voice broke.

"So when your roommates..." He passed by the booth where they had ambushed Lauren earlier.

"It feels like I'm not good enough the way I am."

Joel tossed his trash onto the closest table top and turned her toward him. With hands on her shoulders, he stared into her tear-filled eyes.

Why couldn't she see how special she was?

"You are perfect just the way you are."

Why hadn't some other guy snatched her up by now?

Why not him?

She rolled her eyes. "Be serious."

"I am." He shook her gently. "I see a talented woman who has the gift of hospitality."

"You mean the gift of gab."

"You're beautiful inside... and out."

The truth wound deeper into his heart. Despite their working together at the diner, it might be worth the risk to get to know her better.

To see if they could build something special.

Tears overflowed her eyes and the abandoned box of tissues was several tables away. "You used to think I was ridiculous too."

"What? When was that?" His brain scrambled to replay their conversations at the diner as he wiped the drops from her cheeks.

"There was this certain Christmas..." Her voice caught. "Being part of a laughing, loving family gathering was exactly what my heart needed."

He nodded. She'd mentioned it before, but maybe he'd learn the rest of the story.

Her damp cheeks lifted with a hint of a smile. "And then Julie's hunk of a cousin showed up from his first year away at college... and I developed a bit of a crush."

He recalled all the staring and fought his own smile. "A crush, huh?"

She trapped her lower lip between her teeth. "You had to have known. After all, Julie kept teasing me about it whenever you looked our way."

"All I seem to recall was a lot of giggling about something and thinking Julie needed to grow up."

The image of two teenagers whispering behind cupped hands rose to the surface of his memory along with the flash of silver from the blonde's braces every time she smiled. And every time she ducked her head, there was a jingling sound.

"I may have said something about your crazy floppy hats with the elf ears."

"Mom had sent those from somewhere. Thought they would make for a festive touch but those jingle bells were super annoying." She rolled her eyes. "But your verdict about them being ridiculous destroyed my self-confidence for years."

Surely she was joking. But ridiculous? Yeah. That sounded like something he might have said.

She pantomimed the melodramatic action of stabbing herself in the heart. "Still haven't fully recovered from the pain."

He saw through her playfulness to the truth beneath and winced. "I'm truly sorry I didn't take you more seriously. Please forgive me."

"Seriously? I was fifteen. And we *were* giggling. A lot." She pulled away from his grasp and turned toward the pink hearts in the window.

The last decorations to be removed and the end of their conversation.

The end? Not if he could help it.

Because it seemed he had developed a crush of his own somewhere along the line. And now that he realized it, Joel couldn't stop himself where she was concerned.

Joel joined her in picking at the remaining tape, recalling where their conversation had started. "Just so we're clear. There's nothing wrong with you. With others perhaps, but definitely not you."

"That's a sweet lie." She rolled her eyes.

"I'm telling the truth. And I can prove it." Inspiration struck. "Would you like to go see the Eagles play hockey on Saturday night?"

"Another one of your friendly get-out-of-the-diner outings?" Lauren stilled as if his answer truly mattered.

As if she hoped for more.

"No." His smile grew. "As a belated birthday present. But also as a 'could we be more than friends, spend time with a pretty woman,' real date."

She gasped and whirled to face him with wide eyes. "Really?"

"Yes."

"With me?"

"Absolutely." He grinned.

The tears he'd thought were gone reappeared.

"Why tears? Is there something wrong with me?" He raised an eyebrow.

"No way." She shook her head.

"No to the date?" He frowned.

If only he hadn't put her on the spot.

But, now that he knew for certain what he wanted, she wasn't going to escape easily. Somehow he would change her mind.

"There is absolutely nothing wrong with you." Her gaze trailed over his face as if looking for reassurance.

As if gauging his sincerity.

Or waiting for him to say he was only joking.

He held his breath and waited.

Would she forgive his past mistakes? Trust him now?

Finally, her smile widened further. "And there is no way I'm going to turn down your invitation."

The tension left his shoulders.

She'd agreed.

Now he just needed to deliver the perfect date.

If such a thing was possible.

He hadn't dated anyone since Desiree—hadn't wanted to—and rusty skills aside, a date with Lauren meant more than he'd ever thought possible.

Chapter Fourteen

A s perfect dates went, this was the ideal venue.

Or it should have been.

On Saturday evening, Joel gazed across the cloth-covered table to where Lauren angled her menu toward the dim light.

What had changed since he'd seen her just a few hours ago at the diner?

Their inventory and order preparation activity earlier should have been routine, except for the shy glances she'd sent his direction. The near-constant biting of her lip whenever she caught him watching her.

If they hadn't been surrounded by coworkers, he might have stolen a kiss in the storage room. Except he feared rejection if he pushed too far too soon to bridge the chasm between friends and more.

So he'd contented himself with the occasional wink that triggered a pretty pink blush across her cheeks.

Followed by a cowardly text message reminding her what time he'd pick her up for dinner.

Dinner at the kind of place Desiree had always insisted on. Then again, her expensive tastes had forced him to aim ever higher in an attempt to fit a mold he no longer found appealing.

Joel wiped sweaty palms on the legs of his khaki slacks. Paired with a blue button-down dress shirt, he knew he was overdressed for the hockey game to come, but at least he fit in here at the restaurant.

Felt more like the successful businessman he'd studied to be.

Maybe that was Lauren's problem?

Even though she'd had time to clean up after work, did she feel uncomfortable in simple jeans and that green sweater that highlighted the color of her eyes? Should he have specified what to wear?

Had he complimented her when he arrived at her apartment? Or when he'd escorted her to his car and opened her door?

Since when had his dating skills gotten so rusty?

Then again, Desiree had done the pursuing—until she hadn't—and after their breakup, he'd been too focused on school and chasing success so he'd be worthy of being somebody's boyfriend again.

And now that he was finally ready to build something real? He'd reverted to high school.

No. Time to behave like the man he'd become.

Joel shifted on the high-backed wooden chair. "In case I forgot to say it earlier, you look beautiful tonight."

Lauren lowered her menu. "Thank you. You too... I mean—"

"Have you decided?" Their waiter's gaze bounced between them.

Color flooded Lauren's face before she turned to the server. "I'm stuck between the lasagna and chicken parmesan. Which would you recommend?"

"Both are delicious, ma'am, but I'm partial to the lasagna."

"Perfect." Lauren set the menu aside with a smile. "Then I'd like that with a caesar side salad."

"Excellent. And for you?" The waiter barely spared him another glance.

Joel stared down at his neglected menu but the words jumbled on the page. "I'll have the same."

Their waiter disappeared, leaving them in yet another awkward silence.

Joel cleared his throat. "So we're having lasagna, huh?"

Lauren tucked several shiny curls behind her ear. "You could have picked something else but it did come with a recommendation. Besides, I haven't tried Trevor's version yet because we keep selling out. But just in case I ever get the chance, I'll have another chef's recipe as reference."

"True. Although I have a feeling Trevor's current diner dish is a mere shadow of what he'd like to cook. But it's also at a fraction of the cost."

"I bet it still beats the taste of meatloaf." Lauren's eyes sparkled.

"And sells more too." Joel's grin faded. "Except here I am already breaking my promise to myself that we wouldn't talk shop tonight."

Lauren took a sip of her water, her gaze roaming to the other tables around them.

His muscles tensed.

Did they have anything in common outside work and his family?

What did normal people talk about on first dates?

A random thought crossed his mind and Joel grabbed hold. "Would your ideal vacation involve the mountains or the beach?"

"Really?" Lauren smirked. "That's what we're reduced to?"

"Um." More sweat coated his palms and Joel resisted the urge to tug at his collar.

She reached across the table, fingers wiggling until he laid his clammy hand in hers. "Relax. It's just me."

Joel's throat spasmed. "I want tonight to be perfect so you'll agree to a second date. I don't want to scare you off."

"That's my line." Lauren stared at their awkwardly joined hands. "I still can't believe I'm here. With you."

Joel squeezed her fingers. "It's true. Although I think this might rank as the strangest date ever."

"I've had worse." She peered up between lowered lashes.

"Really?" He raised his eyebrows. "Now that's a story my ego would love to hear."

"Maybe later." She slipped her hand away from his and reached for her water again. "But in the meantime, I'll answer your question... as if I were you."

"Mountains or beach?" This should be interesting.

She pursed her lips as if lost in thought. "I already know you went to college in California, so that and the fact you used to date a villainous supermodel could make someone believe you'd prefer the beach."

The accurate description of Desiree begged for a reaction but he worked to keep his expression blank.

Lauren tilted her head. "But I also know that your college decision was based on football and financial aid. You're definitely an outdoors guy who runs for fun." She shuddered dramatically. "And when we were at the sculpture park, you kept staring at the mountains."

Joel rolled his lips inward. She'd been paying attention.

"Not to mention you applied for jobs in the Denver area." Her smile dimmed slightly. "So mountains it is."

"Final answer? Should I lock it in?"

Her eyes sparkled as she laughed. "What do I get if I'm right?"

"Bragging rights?" He tapped his fingertips on the tablecloth. "Or we keep swapping questions through dinner and the winner—whoever knows the other best—picks their prize at the end of the evening?"

Even if he lost this contest, seeing her enjoy the evening would be reward enough.

He could already imagine their goodnight kiss if he won.

Lauren held out a hand as if to shake on it. "As long as we can pick the questions for each other to answer."

"Hmm. That could get interesting."

And potentially embarrassing.

But he was quickly becoming addicted to this woman and it was worth the risk in order to discover more about what made her so unique.

"We have a deal." Joel shook her hand, then slowly released his grasp, letting his fingers drag from her wrist to her palm to her fingertips.

Simply because he had to test their chemistry. To see if she felt the same sparks whenever they were close.

She shivered. Then blushed.

And reached for her phone.

"I'm going to find a list of questions to stump you with."

He pulled up his notes app to keep score. "You're officially up one to nothing, so don't make it too hard."

"Yet." She wiggled her eyebrows. "I intend to claim the prize."

Joel grinned. In his opinion, this game of theirs could have no losers.

Perhaps this could be the perfect date after all.

Especially if the questions happened to get more serious, if they went beyond the superficial to touch on matters of the heart.

An hour and a half later, Lauren's nerves were still on edge as she followed Joel down the concrete steps toward the white area where the two teams warmed up.

Dinner had started awkwardly, then a lighthearted game had opened the door to a surprisingly deep conversation.

Joel had been so adorably nervous when he arrived at her apartment. Had been trying so hard at the restaurant to make her feel comfortable. Been so intentional in his pursuit of a perfect date. Of ensuring she'd agree to another.

As if that were a question.

Didn't he know how difficult it was to resist his charms? Especially when they were aimed at her. And now that she'd seen more of what lay beneath the surface, she was hooked.

He paused at the fifteenth row and checked the tickets in his hand before stepping out of the aisle. He led her past a father and son duo and beyond a couple of empty seats, then stopped.

"Made it." He started to sit, then stood again. "Did you want to take your coat off?"

Such a gentleman.

"I think I'll keep it on a bit longer. It's kind of chilly in here."

He laughed. "Must be that giant slab of ice."

"Must be." She gnawed on her lip and sat.

If she didn't get her act together soon, she'd sabotage her chances with Joel with more stupid observations and not-so-witty comments.

Was this how he'd felt earlier?

Trying to maintain a semblance of calm, Lauren looked around the arena.

They were positioned along one straight side but near where the rows began to curve behind the netted goal where the team in the mostly white uniforms aimed their shots.

The clear plastic barrier on top of the wall surrounding the ice split part of her view but at least she wasn't staring through a giant net like those with seats on the end.

"Would you like a snack? Some popcorn or nachos?" Joel rubbed the palms of his hands on the knees of his pants.

She darted a glance at the man beside her. "Maybe later. We just ate, remember?"

"Right."

The slapping crack of the sticks against the pucks echoed above the swish of skates and the murmur of the crowd continuing to filter into the arena.

The speakers overhead crackled and music started to play. It must have been a signal for something since the players left and several giant machines drove onto the ice, one carrying a load of rowdy fans.

A minute later, Joel drummed his fingertips on his leg. "Well, let me know if you're thirsty or anything."

It seemed they'd both reverted to the gangly, pimple-faced, teenaged versions of themselves. Hadn't they talked their way out of the awkwardness back at the restaurant?

"Relax, Joel." She laid a hand on his arm. "It's just me."

"Exactly." He covered her hand with his own and turned to stare into her eyes. "It's you... with me. How'd I get so lucky?"

She grinned. "I think I'm the lucky one."

The overhead lights flickered and dimmed as the announcer introduced the choir from a local high school who would sing the national anthem.

As they stood, she was aware of Joel's warmth and strength beside her.

If only this evening and feeling could last forever.

With the anthem over, the announcer began to hype up the crowd with the names of the starting line-up.

All around them, rowdy fans cheered for their favorites while a group of women in skimpy outfits danced on a piece of blue carpet near one end.

She nudged Joel's side. "Since when does hockey have cheerleaders?"

He glanced over and his eyes widened before darting away. "So, it should be an exciting game. I heard the team from Idaho is pretty good."

The players took up position on the ice, more loud music played, and the crowd went wild.

Too bad she didn't know much about hockey rules. All she knew was one team tried to shoot the puck into the other team's net while pushing, shoving, and sometimes fighting before getting sent to time out.

Joel reached for her hand.

Who cared about hockey rules anyway?

Warm tingles spread up her arm and coiled around her heart. A smile grew on her face.

Was this a fairy tale date emotional moment or was she really falling in love?

She glanced over at Joel and he smiled back.

Then winked.

Her pulse double timed and heat rushed to her face.

He squeezed her hand, then broke the moment to follow the action on the ice.

Ice.

Someone needed to cool down.

She could take off her coat, but then she'd need to let go of Joel's hand.

Maybe later.

At the end of the first period, the lights brightened.

Along with others around them, she and Joel stood to stretch.

Joel rested a hand on her back and leaned in to be heard over the music. "I was thinking about getting some popcorn and hot chocolate. What would you like?"

"That sounds great." She stepped backward to give him room to squeeze past and out their row.

Given the opportunity, she removed her coat and draped it around her shoulders before sitting back down.

As the minutes ticked by, she watched the other people in their section. A trio of teenage boys played keep-away with one of their hats while a toddler girl in an over-sized team jersey giggled as she shook a souvenir bobble-head. Several couples spent the break stealing kisses.

Since this was a real date, would Joel kiss her goodnight?

Lauren pressed her lips together in anticipation, then realized how dry they were. She fished lip balm out of her coat pocket and applied a generous layer. Just in time for Joel's return.

"The lines weren't as bad as I thought they might be." He handed her their drinks while he maneuvered back into his seat with the container of popcorn.

Once he was settled, she exchanged one cup for a handful of buttery kernels.

A young boy seated in front of them spotted their treat and tugged on his father's arm.

Lauren sipped on her hot chocolate and shared a smile with Joel over the debate brewing before them.

He scooped a large fistful from the box propped between them. "What time should I stop by tomorrow to help you move into Aunt Greta's?"

"I'm mostly packed already and planned to attend the early service, so I can be ready to start moving by ten thirty."

As thankful as she was for the excuse to spend more time with Joel outside the diner, she was equally glad for a place to stay, even if it was Julie's unoccupied room for now.

Plus moving out of the apartment a week ahead of the deadline would be a relief from the ugly tension.

Joel tossed a few kernels into his mouth. "How about I pick you up before church and we make a day of it?"

"Even better." She removed the plastic lid from her cup and swirled the melting whipped cream into the remaining chocolate before taking another sip. Tilting it further for the last swallows, she ended up with a little whipped cream on her upper lip.

She licked her lips, glancing at Joel to find him watching her closely.

The lights dimmed and the crowd cheered. The teams may have returned for the second period, but she didn't care.

She could stare at Joel all night.

He swallowed hard. "The first time I didn't ask. This time, may I?"

He shifted his gaze to her mouth and back to her eyes.

Her smile widened and she nodded, slightly out of breath.

He leaned closer and his free hand cradled the side of her face. His thumb brushed along the contours of her mouth before his lips descended.

She met him halfway. He tasted of warm chocolate and salty, buttery popcorn. She lingered over their kiss.

How much emotion could her heart handle without exploding? Or maybe fireworks were to be expected at a time like this?

Would it be too brazen to ask for a repeat of this kiss as her prize from dinner for knowing him so well?

She vaguely registered a gasp from the crowd around them and someone yelled to look out.

An instant later, pain ricocheted through her head with an explosion of stars and she fell into Joel's arms.

Chapter Fifteen

♥

J oel held Lauren to his chest and willed his heartbeat to slow.

Lauren's lips coated with the taste of chocolate were a potent combination.

Around him, others scuffled for something in the middle of the popcorn he'd dropped.

Joel blinked. Why was the grinning teenager to his left holding up a hockey puck?

In the stands?

Wait a minute. Hadn't someone yelled to look out?

So, why was Lauren still plastered against him?

With a mixture of fear and adrenaline rushing through his veins, he tilted her head enough to spot blood trickling down from a gash in her right temple along with tears leaking from her closed eyes.

His heart stopped, then beat double-time.

"Lauren? Talk to me."

Oh God. Please let her be okay.

She groaned and her eyelashes fluttered before scrunching shut. "Ow."

"Hold still."

"Not... going... anywhere."

His mind scrambled through everything he knew about head injuries. At a minimum, she might have a concussion.

Or worse.

If he hadn't been so distracted kissing the whipped cream from her lips, he might have been able to protect her. He should have blocked the puck or at least pulled her out of the way. And yet, he'd failed as a man because she lay injured in his arms.

His stomach churned.

It was up to him to take care of her.

He hugged her a little tighter as if he could absorb her pain while below them, the game resumed with a new puck.

With shaking fingers, he brushed her hair back from the blood running down the side of her face.

First things, first. Stop the bleeding. Put ice on the growing lump. Then probably have her checked at the emergency room.

Someone behind him tapped his shoulder. "Is she all right?"

"No." He glanced back to see a mom with a couple of children sharing a plastic tray of nachos. "Do you have any napkins?"

"A few." The woman handed them over.

He folded them in half to create a thicker pad and wiped the blood from Lauren's cheek before pressing the wad over the wound.

She moaned and tried to brush his hand away. "Stop. Too hard."

The balding man seated on the other side of Lauren turned away from the game.

His eyes widened as he noticed her injury. "Thought you two were just snuggling 'cuz she was scared. I'll get help."

"Thanks." He eased her back to sit in her own chair.

Lauren's neighbor worked his way past the others in their row and hurried up the concrete stairs.

Joel leaned across her body and lifted the bloodied napkins to peek at the cut. The bleeding seemed to be slowing down. "Can you hold this? It needs pressure but I don't want to hurt you worse."

Lauren nodded a bit, then winced. More tears leaked out beneath her dark eyelashes as she held the temporary bandage in place.

Now what?

Get her talking to assess her awareness.

He knelt where he could see her face. "Talk to me. Where are you? Do you remember what happened?"

If only she'd open her eyes, he'd feel better.

"Hockey... Date." She took a deep breath and barely opened her eyes as pink colored her face. "Kiss. Yelling. Then ow."

His shoulders relaxed.

No memory loss. That had to be a good sign.

Especially since she didn't forget their kiss.

Heat flooded his own face. Recalling that particular moment would keep him up late into the night.

As long as she was fine.

"How's the pain?" He rested a hand on her denim-clad knee.

"Like my skull's split open?"

The crowd roared around them and she closed her eyes again.

Now what? Was it safe to move her somewhere quieter?

Before he could decide, their neighbor was back with a yellow-jacketed security officer who cleared enough room for the trailing medic to reach Lauren's side.

The man pulled latex gloves and a package of gauze from his duffel bag of supplies. "How is she doing?"

Lauren opened her eyes. "How should I be?"

"My apologies, ma'am." The medic stared into her eyes for a few moments, then lifted the bandage and poked at the wound. "Security replayed the path into the stands—always do in case they have to settle arguments between fans—so they saw when you got hit in the head."

"Even without training, I know that hurts." The man grimaced. "I was already on my way before your friend over there started hollering in the hall."

Joel located their former seatmate watching them from where he sat on the stairs with the others who had been in their row. He pointed to the security officer and medic to make it clear. "Thank you."

The good Samaritan shrugged as if it wasn't a big deal, then refocused on the game.

"Did she lose consciousness at all?" The medic peeled tiny butterfly bandage strips from an open package and closed the edges of the gash.

Joel grasped Lauren's trembling hands. "I don't think so. She remembers what happened, though, if that helps."

The medic grunted. "Almost done here. This will hold it together for now, but the doctor may decide on stitches."

Lauren flinched.

Joel rubbed a thumb along the back of her hand. "What else?"

The medic taped a larger piece of gauze over the area. "With head injuries, we don't mess around. She might also have a concussion and therefore should be seen tonight. We can call an ambulance."

Lauren clutched his hand. "No. Joel can take me."

As if the thought of an ambulance brought back memories of different paramedics treating his father in the kitchen.

Which should affect him more than her, right?

Joel cleared his throat. "I'll take her."

The medic popped and shook an instant ice pack. "You can't have any pain killers until you've been evaluated, but this will help with the swelling."

Someone nudged Joel's side.

He pivoted to find the teenage boy beside him holding out the hockey puck. "I think she deserves this more than me."

"Thanks." Lauren's smile wobbled as she accepted the gift.

The teen grinned.

She was a charmer, but she was his.

His.

He'd examine that idea more later, but right now he needed to get Lauren to the car and on to the hospital.

The medic zipped his bag closed and stood. "Ma'am, can you walk?"

"I'm not sure, but I'll try." With one hand holding the ice pack in place and the other clutching the puck, Lauren scooted forward.

Joel wrapped an arm around her waist and helped her to stand. He relaxed his grip and she swayed. "Steady."

After easing her into her coat sleeves, he guided their shuffled trip down the now-vacant row to the stairs.

She rested a hand on the railing and sucked in a deep breath.

Enough of her bravery.

Time for him to be the hero.

"Hold on." He swept her up into his arms and adjusted his grip under her knees as she buried her head against his chest. "I've got you."

She sighed and tears dampened the front of his shirt.

He clenched his jaw and slowly carried her up the stairs behind the security officer while the medic followed.

Once into the corridor, another member of security waited with a wheelchair. "If you want to pull your car around closer, we'll take her down the elevator and wait for you by the door. We need a little information for the incident report but can get that on our way."

Joel settled Lauren into the chair then kissed her forehead. "I'll hurry."

"Bet we beat you."

He waggled his eyebrows. "And what do I get if I win?"

She blushed. "You'll think of something."

As he jogged toward the entrance, he overheard the security officer ask if they should take their time. Joel picked up the pace with a smile.

But by the time they wheeled her outside, Lauren's color had faded and tears snaked down her cheeks.

All thoughts of a victory kiss fled as he helped her into the car and buckled her seatbelt, desperately trying not to make things worse.

This might not be how he'd pictured their date ending, but he wasn't leaving her side.

Please, God, let her be okay.

Lauren winced at the bright light so close by, then closed her eyes.

"Sorry about that." A strange man's voice echoed near her right ear. "Let's stitch you up so you and your boyfriend can get out of here."

"Boyfriend? Do I have one of those?" She didn't use to. But somehow it felt like the truth.

Why did everything feel so blurry? Fuzzy? Pillow-y? Was that a word?

A woman giggled near Lauren's feet. "Honey, that man hasn't budged in an hour."

Someone squeezed her left hand. A deep chuckle came from that side. "Just what did you put in her IV before giving her the local?"

"You sound delicious." Lauren tried to roll her head in the man's direction but was stopped by pressure from a large hand across the top of her skull.

A skull that felt both too big and too small at the same time.

"Ouch."

The hand relaxed, then brushed hair from one side of her face, fingers trailing down her cheek.

While something—or someone—tugged on the other side.

Followed by what sounded like scissors near her eyeball. That couldn't be safe.

She lifted her free hand to push the nuisance away, only to find it trapped atop her chest.

"You have to hold still." Delicious Dude whispered in her left ear.

"Why? I just wanna..." She wanted to do something.

What was it again? Why was thinking so hard?

And why was her face numb? It was almost like the dentist's office getting a filling and having her lips fall asleep. And drooling everywhere.

"Gross."

Delicious Dude chuckled again. "What's gross?"

Lauren forced her eyes open a sliver, then slammed the lids shut again. But the brief glimpse was enough to recognize Joel and the fact she was in a medical facility.

Had he gotten hurt?

No. That didn't seem right. *She* was the one lying down with a doctor and nurse close by.

Why was Joel holding her hands and leaning in close enough to kiss?

Kiss.

A sweet image flashed across her mind. Standing with Joel in the storage room with his arm around her and then leaning in to press his lips against hers.

She frowned. No. That wasn't it.

"Hold on. Just one more stitch should do it." Rustling noises came from her right side as the doctor did something.

Something she didn't want to think about. Especially when she'd rather dream about kissing Joel.

Her lips tingled with anticipation. Or another memory?

She pursed her lips, then smacked them. "You kissed me."

Joel snorted, then coughed as if to cover it. "And that was gross?"

She started to shake her head, but was stopped again by his large hand on her scalp. "No. It was magical. I saw fireworks."

He squeezed her hands. "You're good for my ego, but while I'd like to take credit, that was the hockey puck."

Hockey puck?

She concentrated so hard it hurt, but the evening's events finally came into focus.

A date to watch hockey. Dinner beforehand. A game of questions that she'd won.

She risked another peek at Joel. "What prize did I pick for winning earlier?"

Worry drained from his eyes, then he winked. "Thank God you're coming back to reality again. But I insist you wait until you're not under the influence before you decide."

The nurse giggled. "The medicine should start wearing off pretty soon. But in the meantime, you wouldn't be the first to record a loved one in this condition just for blackmail or leverage later."

Lauren scowled. "That's mean."

Although she seemed to recall Greta or Julie doing something like that when Lauren had her wisdom teeth pulled.

Joel coughed. "I think we'll stick to over-the-counter painkillers from now on."

"Good idea." The doctor pushed aside the rolling stand with his tray of—tools?--and stood. "Mary here will bandage you up *nicely* and print out the discharge instructions for both the concussion and the stitches."

"Thank you." Joel rose and shook the man's hand.

"Yeah, thanks." Lauren echoed.

The nurse took the doctor's place by Lauren's head. Between dabbing something over the stitches and taping more gauze in place, she rambled on and on about keeping it dry. About sleeping. About pain. And about when to come back.

Like Lauren wanted more of this?

Hopefully Joel was taking notes.

Lauren let her eyes drift closed again. She'd much rather think about the fact Joel was here. With her.

As if he might truly care.

As long as he wasn't here out of guilt.

Lauren grabbed his hand. "This isn't your fault."

He flinched. "I should have been paying better attention."

"Blame that on me." She giggled and glanced at the nurse. "I think I must be a super-kisser. Or that kissing is my superpower."

Nurse Mary pressed her lips together as if hiding a smile.

Joel just shook his head.

As if blaming Lauren's words on the medication.

Should she be embarrassed? Or take advantage of the moment to speak another truth?

She hummed. "I'm the winner. And I've decided that dating you is my prize."

Joel choked.

The nurse scurried toward the door. "I'll be right back with a print-out of the instructions—"

"The usual for a concussion, right?" Joel seemed happy to change the subject. "No sports or strenuous activity, watch for new symptoms, and follow-up with her doctor to get the stitches out."

"Exactly." The nurse chuckled. "I'll also bring back a wheelchair if you want to get your girlfriend and her superpowers ready to go."

"Will do." Joel's laughter broke through his restraint as he retrieved Lauren's coat from a chair.

How had it gotten over there?

Ten minutes later, Joel buckled her into his car. Just like he had back at the hockey arena.

She rested her head back against the seat, then let it loll to the left so she could see his handsome profile. "You brought the car around faster than I got down the elevator earlier. What reward did you get for winning?"

He offered her an indulgent smile. "Just seeing you okay is enough."

"I'm not sure stitches are okay." Lauren tried to flip the mirror down to look, but could only see glimpses of the white bandage in the passing street lights.

She could only imagine the damage underneath. Or how ugly the bruise will be before it's done spreading.

"I hope it doesn't leave a scar." She gently ran her fingertips over the area between her eye and hairline.

"Doesn't change the fact you're beautiful." Joel made the statement as if it were an established truth.

"You said that earlier at the restaurant." Lauren grasped at the fleeting wisps as she tried to recall. "But you also said something about a memorable date... Or did you call it the strangest date? Because I think you were right."

He groaned, strangling the steering wheel as if it were a diner rag needing wringing out.

She snorted. Was it normal to crack yourself up?

Swallowing her laughter at her own expense, Lauren squeezed his elbow. "While I wouldn't change a thing, maybe our next date can be more normal?"

He darted a glance in her direction and a smile curved his kissable lips. "I'd like that."

Somewhere in the depths of her coat pocket, her phone alarm went off. She retrieved it only to find the reminder of tomorrow's plans.

Lauren groaned. "I really don't feel like moving tomorrow."

Joel chuckled. "Assuming you're still okay for church in the morning—"

"Don't see why I wouldn't be." She furrowed her brow.

"I'll drive you." He nodded. "Afterward, you only have to order me around and let me do all the heavy lifting."

"Can I ogle your muscles while you do?" She gasped.

Seemed the medication was still messing with her internal filter.

Either that or she'd gotten bolder with her former crush.

Joel's soft laughter filled the car and then they finished the drive in silence.

At her apartment complex, he escorted her to her door and waited until she'd twisted the keys in the lock.

"I'll be back in the morning. Sweet dreams, beautiful." After a too-brief brush of his lips across her forehead, Joel hurried away.

Once inside, Lauren leaned against the closed door for a minute.

Hours earlier, she'd feared that a date with Joel wouldn't live up to her imagination. And yet, despite how it had ended, she wouldn't change a thing.

A yawn almost split her jaw, triggering a stab of pain in her skull.

Maybe getting hurt was worth it for this level of attention from Joel? For however long it lasted.

Lauren forced herself upright, then staggered toward her bedroom with one hand on the furniture or the wall for support.

He'd promised to come back tomorrow and so she'd dream of that.

Dream he might someday choose to stay in her life.

And hope that dreams might come true for someone like her.

Chapter Sixteen

♥

"Just open the door." Joel glared at the young woman peering through the crack.

He had little patience for the delay.

Particularly when she was one of the trio who'd blindsided Lauren at work just a few days ago.

The girl stared back. "Who are you again?"

"Joel Dawson. Lauren's b—" Her boss, true but couldn't he claim to be more? "Boyfriend."

Yes. That felt right.

Just like it had last night at the emergency room when Lauren had been adorably loopy on the pain medication.

He'd have to make sure she actually agreed to the label today. Later. But first...

The woman barring the door pursed her lips. "She doesn't—"

Joel pressed a hand against the wood, forcing the crack to widen slightly. "We work together at the diner and I'm here to take her to church before helping her move."

"Good luck with that." The roommate stepped back to allow him entry into the apartment. "I'm pretty sure she's still asleep."

His heart clenched with a moment of panic, then eased with relief. "The doctor said she should sleep as much as she can."

If she was sleeping, no wonder she hadn't answered his call minutes ago.

"The doctor?" A second woman wandered into the living room clutching a coffee mug. "What story did she tell you this time?"

Joel gritted his teeth. "No story. She got beaned with a hockey puck last night and I drove her to the emergency room myself."

"Typical Lauren to be oblivious." The first girl laughed and exchanged glances with her friend.

Joel palmed the back of his neck. The sooner Lauren left the toxic pair behind, the better. "Which way to her room?"

"I'm sure she's fine, but if you insist on checking, it's the second door on the right just beyond the bathroom." The coffee drinker's eyes roamed over his torso as if evaluating the muscles beneath his shirt.

Enough.

He brushed past the duo, then stopped as the urge to defend Lauren overwhelmed his good sense. "Oh, and I'm afraid it's *my* fault she got hit. I wasn't paying attention. I mean, it's easy to get distracted when you're kissing someone as beautiful as her."

He continued down the hall to Lauren's room, tuning out their nervous giggles.

Her door was slightly ajar, so he tapped his knuckles on the wood. "Hey, sleepyhead, are you awake?"

No answer.

He nudged the door further open until he caught sight of Lauren, dressed in a giant green T-shirt and black athletic shorts, sprawled on her bed in a twisted nest of covers that mirrored the tangled curls across her pillow.

"Lauren?" He called into the room. "Can you wake up, please?"

Still no answer. Or movement.

Much as he hated to enter her room without permission, what if something was wrong? And no way was he going to trust one her roommates to act compassionately?

"I'm coming in." He stepped inside, then closed the distance until he was able to shake her shoulder. "Hey, Lauren. Wake up."

She mumbled something, proving she was at least alive.

The bandage had come loose during the night revealing a glimpse of the prickly stitches as well as a darkening purple blotch beneath her skin.

She was going to have quite the shiner. And the story to go with it.

The diner regulars were going to have a lot of fun teasing her.

Them. If the whole story got out.

His eyes dipped to her pink lips. Too much temptation.

Joel jostled her shoulder again, harder this time. "Lauren? Can you hear me?"

She moaned.

"Oops. Sorry." He stepped back.

As she finally began to stir and stretch, he retreated to the doorway and eyed the room.

Clothes still hung on hangers in the open closet and her unplugged phone sat atop the Bible on the nightstand, but a pile of boxes and the bare walls made it clear she was nearly packed and ready to move.

It shouldn't take more than one trip in their cars unless the furniture was coming too. But she hadn't said anything about needing a truck.

"Joel?" A sleepy voice drew his attention back to Lauren and her half-opened eyes. "I think I'm dreaming."

"No dream."

Except for the part of his heart that began to imagine waking her up every morning.

She started to push herself to a sitting position, but stopped with a groan as she closed her eyes and fingered the loosened bandage on her head.

Probably had a massive headache pounding in her skull.

That was one memory from his football career that he'd rather forget.

He glanced around the room again. "Do you have normal painkillers handy?"

Because she obviously couldn't handle anything stronger. Although her drugged ramblings had given him a lot to pray about during his drive home last night.

Her eyes flew open, the hazel color reflecting a deeper green from her shirt. "What are you doing in my bedroom?"

Joel held his hands up in surrender, staying clearly in the doorway. "I was only inside for a moment or two trying to wake you up. But I'm here to take you to church before helping you move. Like we planned."

She retrieved her phone from the nightstand, then groaned. "It's dead and I forgot to plug it in. No wonder I overslept."

"It's fine. The doctor did say you needed to sleep." He watched as she struggled into a sitting position.

A position that put her bare legs on display and allowed the loose neckline of her sleep shirt to dip lower.

He glanced away. "Did you still want to try to make it to church? Or maybe you'd rather rest..."

She groaned. "Since we're obviously going to be late, could we do the moving first and watch the sermon online later? I just need a few minutes in the bathroom, but maybe you can start taking some things out to our cars?"

"I'll do all the carrying since you're only supposed to do light activity."

"Is brushing my teeth light enough?" She gave him a half-smile.

"As long as you brace yourself against the counter and sit down if you feel dizzy." He lifted his palms again to stop her protest. "Just speaking from personal experience in my football days."

"Fine." She ran her hands through her curls, then stood slowly. "Let me grab a change of clothes, but everything else can go."

"Including the furniture?" Joel moved to steady her where she wobbled a bit on her feet.

"No, that stays." She yawned. "The sooner we get me moved out of here, the sooner I can take a nap."

By the time Lauren was cleaned up, rebandaged, and ready to leave, he had stripped the bed and loaded everything else into their cars.

After a quick walk through the rest of the apartment to confirm she wasn't leaving anything behind, Lauren left her key on the kitchen counter and led the way out the door.

He slammed it shut, then wrapped an arm around her waist in time to steady her before she fell down the stairs.

"Are you okay?" His grip tightened and she leaned against him.

"Just glad to be out of there. Did you see them staring?"

"Hard to miss." Her so-called friends had watched him carry everything out and seemed to pay particular attention to his backside.

Lauren clutched the railing as they descended to the parking lot, then peeked up at him. "I think they're jealous of me. One of them even asked me if you had any friends I could introduce them to."

"Wouldn't wish them on any of my friends." Although to their credit, at least the coffee-drinker had said she hoped Lauren felt better soon.

He turned them toward his car, making the quick decision that it wasn't safe for Lauren to drive yet.

He'd have his aunt shuttle him back over to get Lauren's loaded car later.

"Probably not on your enemies either." She took a deep breath and let it out slowly. "Well, I'm glad that chapter of my life is over."

"Me too."

And he was looking forward to the next chapter, especially to see what role he played.

Two hours later, her car was parked on one side of the driveway and the rest of her things were put away in his cousin Julie's room. The remainder of the day was devoted to her recovery.

And avoiding his aunt's smug approval at seeing them together as a couple.

Joel settled in beside Lauren on the couch. "Find a movie you want to watch as your prize from our questions game?"

"I did even though I'll probably sleep through it." Her wobbly smile tugged at his emotions. "Greta put my favorite Jane Austin classic in the DVD player before she headed to the grocery store but I can't reach the remote from here."

He grabbed it from the coffee table, started the movie, then placed the controller on the nearby TV tray next to Lauren's empty soup bowl. Aunt Greta's mothering skills reminded him of Mom taking care of Dad.

The opening music began to play and Lauren snuggled in beside him with a sigh, her curls tickling his jaw.

He smoothed them back and pressed a kiss to an uninjured spot on her forehead.

Love showed up in the simplest of ways from moving boxes to cooking soup to even enduring an Old English chick flick just so he could spend time with her.

It didn't matter where they were, as long as he was with Lauren, his heart felt at peace.

What was it that his parents had said about the kitchen being their paradise?

Memories of Lauren's laughter and teasing at the diner paraded across his mind, followed by that tender moment in the storage room when he had first kissed her.

A kiss he vowed to repeat—without apology and without hockey puck interruptions—very soon.

Lauren's breathing deepened as she fell asleep on his shoulder.

After years of college and seeking a high-powered job, he had found everything he was looking for right here.

About an hour into the Tuesday morning breakfast rush, Lauren stopped in front of the monitor and froze.

What was she supposed to do? Oh yeah. Enter the order.

She studied the notepad in her hand. Seat two. The usual.

The usual what?

With a sigh she returned to face off with what's-his-name from the newspaper. "Um, Kyle, right?"

"Right." He frowned, his gaze skipping from the notepad in her hand to the stitches in her forehead that now centered a lovely mixture of purples and yellows. "Having trouble remembering?"

"I know it's in there somewhere but getting it out feels like trudging through ankle deep mud."

"Two eggs over easy. Bacon. Whole wheat toast." He waited for her to write it down, then lifted his cup. "And coffee."

"Thanks." She finished the note.

"Are you sure you should be here?"

"As long as I don't get another headache, the doctor said I should be fine. Joel's making me take it easy." She waved at the stool he had brought from Greta's house. "I only get the counter folks today and if I need to take a short nap, there's a sleeping bag on the office floor."

As if she needed any more sleep after dozing most of Sunday and yesterday while Monica filled in for her thanks to a school holiday for President's Day.

"Well, take care of yourself. The diner just isn't the same without you."

"Thanks." She blinked back a few tears as she returned to the monitor to carefully enter the items on the screen.

Emotions close to the surface were yet another symptom of her mild concussion.

After sending the order to the kitchen, she took a seat on the stool to wait until she was needed. Across the dining room, Clarissa chatted with one table of customers and along the windows, Joel already cleaned up after another group.

From this angle, she had an unobstructed view of the muscles rippling under his shirt and the snug fit of his jeans as he leaned over to wipe off the tabletop.

Shame on her. Checking out his physique, just like her former friends had on Sunday. That was *her* right, not theirs.

Especially after their date. And the way she'd spent Sunday afternoon sleeping on his shoulder.

She turned her attention back to the customers seated at the counter.

The dentist at the far end raised his coffee cup then frowned as she stayed where she was.

She was missing something.

He stared at the brimming pots.

Oh. She scampered to her feet.

If only her brain would cooperate.

"I'm so sorry." She poured coffee into his cup. "Next time say something rather than let me sit there like an idiot."

"You're not an idiot. You're injured and actually doing quite fine considering. We're just spoiled to know how you normally are."

"Well, thanks for your patience." She replaced the pot to the warmer with a sigh of relief.

If people still liked her when she was at her worst, then maybe her normal was okay after all.

A middle-aged man took a seat at the counter and tugged on the cuffs on his jacket before studying the menu. She took a deep breath. This customer was a new face so she'd better not mess up.

The extra concentration required as she wrote down everything he said caused a slight twinge in her forehead. If she didn't relax, she'd have a headache for sure. She poured his coffee, then retreated to turn in his order and sit back down for another minute.

As she visually checked on her customers, she caught a flash of silver on the newest man's hand.

A silver ring, just like Mom was learning how to make.

She had finally reached her mom on the phone last night to tell her about the concussion and moving out of her apartment. In return, she learned that Mom had also moved; this time to another artist colony in

Arizona where she could learn silver-craft from a guy she met at a trade show.

Something Mom had said about investing in the man's enterprise triggered a buried memory of another argument between her parents about a business loan in default. Seemed Mom's curiosity had led to more than scattered hobbies, but abandoned businesses as well.

No wonder Dad had gotten frustrated with the toll on their family.

While Lauren still prayed she would eventually find her sweet spot and be able to stick with it, at least she had picked up a few sound financial management skills from her dad. She might be curious and love talking to people, but she knew how to live with a budget.

Not to mention that after working with Joel on the diner book-keeping from time to time, she had a new appreciation of risk and the importance of saving for emergencies.

As long as she learned to control her creative impulses or at least direct them wisely, she should eventually be able to regain Dad's trust.

The nearby monitor beeped with a flashing "C3" on the screen. Counter, seat three. It was her order ready to deliver.

She stood, printed the receipt, and approached the pass-through window to retrieve the reporter's food.

Four steps later, she set the plate in front of him. "One triple double, I mean, triple ripple." That wasn't right.

She took a deep breath. "I mean your double trouble. Argh. Here's your food."

Where were the right words when she needed them?

"Thanks for my *daily double*." Kyle laughed.

"Yeah. That." She blinked back a few tears again.

Warm hands settled onto her shoulders. "Everything okay here?"

She leaned back and soaked in Joel's warmth and strength.

"Yes. The food looks delicious as always." Kyle eyed the two of them.

"Good." Joel squeezed her shoulders, before moving past her to grab the coffee pot.

Kyle waggled his eyebrows. "He sure is taking care of you today."

She glanced at Joel's back and deflected. "He just feels guilty since he's the one who invited me to the hockey game in the first place."

"Nope. That boy feels more than guilt."

Hope stirred to life.

Could she take the risk?

Like their customers, Joel had already seen her at her worst and still liked her. Took her on a date. Kissed her. And watched over her while she slept.

Even if it sometimes felt like he was holding back, maybe she could trust him with her heart as well.

At least until he left for a different job.

Her stomach twisted.

Because that had always been his plan.

Chapter Seventeen

T hey were only a week into March but big decisions loomed ahead.
For all of them.

Joel walked beside his once-strong father as they exited the doctor's
office, unable to do more than hold the door while Dad leaned heavily
on his walker.

If today's simple trip for a check-up and the relatively short distance
to elevators taxed Dad's energy this much, a return to the diner's frantic
pace seemed impossible.

Inside the elevator, Joel pressed the button for the ground floor of
the medical building attached to the hospital.

Two months since Dad's open-heart surgery and—according to Dr.
Garrettson—at least another month until Dad would be cleared to resume any work at the diner.

Partially because of the physical strain of lifting pans or boxes of
produce with a healing incision site, but mostly because of his reduced
stamina. Although the prescribed physical therapy sessions three times a
week would help with both.

And then there was the long-term necessity of avoiding stress along
with better eating, exercise, and sleep habits.

The elevator dinged as they reached the bottom. The doors slid open
and Joel helped Dad out to the lobby. Snow swirled outside the glass wall.

"Looks like the storm is picking up." Joel zipped his coat. "Wait here
and I'll pull around under the overhang."

"Okay." Dad maneuvered the walker into position and sat facing the
windows.

Joel started to jog to the car but soon slowed to a quick walk after nearly falling. The slushy spots from earlier now held a layer of ice underneath. He turned up his collar and plunged ahead. March was usually the snowiest month in Colorado and the forecasters thought this storm could dump six to eight inches by evening.

The quicker he got Dad back home to where Mom slept off her head cold, the quicker he could get back to the diner. Hopefully he made it before their usual Friday lunch crowd started to trickle in, but Lauren had said they could handle it until he got back.

Lauren.

Other than a fading pink scar at her hairline and a vow to never watch hockey in person again, she'd fully recovered from their dating misadventure three weeks ago.

Three weeks in which he'd spent much of his spare time at Aunt Greta's house laughing with Lauren.

And sneaking kisses.

He grinned as he slid behind the steering wheel.

Another reason to hurry back to the diner.

By the time he got Dad settled in the passenger seat, the car's defroster blew semi-warm air across the windshield and Joel could see well enough to pull out onto the street.

Dad rubbed his chest in a now-familiar motion as if checking his scar for tenderness. "How is the diner?"

Joel resisted the urge to roll his eyes. "You saw it yourself two days ago when Mom brought you for coffee and pie."

"I've missed Greta's pie." Dad grinned.

Joel slowed down to leave more room between his bumper and the pickup truck in front of them.

Dad pivoted to face Joel. "I know you say it's fine now. But how was it back then? When I..."

Joel glanced over at the unspoken words that included so much fear and uncertainty the day Dad collapsed and almost lost his life.

He coughed to clear the emotion. "It was crazy."

Maybe Dad could handle bits of the truth even if Joel risked showing his personal incompetence at the time?

"How crazy?"

Joel stared out of the windshield at the blowing snow. "For example, we were so busy keeping up with everything until we could hire more help that we almost forgot the inventory. Ended up getting the next order a day late because of it, but since you always built in a cushion, we made it."

Close enough to the truth, right? No need to mention the extra trip to a grocery store with Lauren.

Dad grunted.

Joel cleared his throat. "Took me a little longer to figure out the payroll program but the checks still went out on time. Along with the quarterly tax payment."

"I'd much rather be in the kitchen than the office. Fewer mistakes there, but you're smarter than me."

Joel rolled his eyes. "If I was really smart, I'd have listened more. Especially after graduation when you asked me specifically to help with the business side of things."

"There wasn't time."

"But I could have made time on other visits. I was just too focused on my classes."

Too focused on his dream of corporate success and building an empire.

If he'd paid attention to the diner before, the sudden transition in leadership might have been easier. Except then he'd have missed the chance to work closely with Lauren and solve the problems together.

Dad shook his head. "It's as much my fault as yours. I knew how your Grandpa Harold died and so I should have planned ahead better. At least when I had to take over, everything was on paper instead of hiding in those newfangled computer programs."

Joel grinned. "But computers will do the math for you."

"Maybe." Dad frowned. "But I hate learning how to use them."

"You sound like Aunt Greta when it came to setting up the electronic order system. Then again, you're the one who bought it, even if Lauren had to dig the boxes out of the back room."

He folded his arms. "Our old one worked just fine."

The archaic spinning rack? Not really.

Joel kept his focus on the slick road. "On the plus side, Aunt Greta doesn't have to try to read my handwriting. And Trevor can also see what's needed without trying to look over her shoulder."

Dad grunted again. "I guess it was a good change after all."

Warmth began to spread in Joel's chest at the compliment. Someday he'd show his dad the data about what dishes were the most popular. And which could potentially be phased out.

"Speaking of the books, maybe you can bring home the ledger so I can see it."

Dread sliced through the warmth.

Even with small changes like swapping lasagna for meatloaf and selling more pie, he still had to keep a close eye on their cash flow. Especially when payroll included a salary for the absent owners.

No wonder Joel still wasn't taking much more than his tips.

Lauren would be furious if she knew.

So would Dad.

Even if his reasons involved building up an emergency financial cushion.

All the more reason to be glad he had integrated the paper ledger into the rest of the computerized bookkeeping programs. It was impossible to bring the office desktop home for an inspection.

Joel changed lanes and the subject as they neared their neighborhood.

A few minutes later, he helped his dad maneuver around the pile of boxes and bags in the entryway.

Over the past month, his mom had taken advantage of her extra time at home to clean out the attic and closets, discovering several forgotten treasures.

And a multitude of abandoned craft projects.

She'd never had much time for hobbies before, and now that Dad required less help, she'd jumped right in. To the point she spent more time cooking up soaps and lotions than food.

Meanwhile, he still needed to make time to haul the stuff in the hall away and donate it to charity.

Once Dad was settled in his recliner, Joel handed him the television remote. "Do you want me to put in that action movie I brought home from Aunt Greta's? Lauren thought you might enjoy it."

"If she said so." Dad nodded.

Mom stirred from her position under a blanket on the couch with a box of tissues nearby. "That Lauren's a good girl."

"She sure is." On that, they all agreed. Joel slid the disc into the player with a smile. "If you don't need anything more, I'm going to head back to the diner in time for the lunch rush."

Mom waved him out the door as the movie began. He hurried to his car.

Despite the snowy weather forecast, everything was right in the world and he'd soon see his girlfriend.

But more than a girlfriend, Lauren usually had good ideas. Like that weekly drawing for a free slice of pie and a say in the next featured flavor.

They'd need even more ideas to increase their income before Dad forced his hand to see the bank balance.

Joel swerved to avoid an accident with a sliding minivan and crept on toward the diner.

If only he knew the true secret to growing a successful business.

All his professors had talked about profit margins and dividends to investors, but in the real world of small business owners, success seemed to be making enough to pay the bills with a little left over for a rainy day.

Or to re-invest into building improvements and upgrades to equipment.

Joel pulled into the rear parking lot and soon slipped his way to the outside door, eager to find out what the day's old-timer topic had been.

He paused with his hand on the knob.

Had he really missed being a part of the community interactions as much as he'd missed seeing Lauren's smile?

When had the diner gotten under his skin?

Probably the first time the ladies group argued over yarn and told him they were praying for his dad.

Joel pushed open the door into the steamy kitchen and inhaled the beefy aroma of stew and yeasty rolls. He tossed his coat onto a hook and grabbed an apron. "Smells good in here, Aunt Greta."

"Back already? We hardly missed you." Aunt Greta winked over her shoulder before tipping her head toward the mountain of dirty dishes and turning back to the grill.

Trevor laughed as he slid several full plates under the heat lamps.

Joel shook his head. "I'll get right on them after I check on things out front."

Debbie poked her head out the cooler door. "Things? Or your girl?"

"Um, both?" He grinned as he pushed through the swinging door to the dining room.

Clarissa picked up the newly plated food while Lauren laughed with a group of customers across the room.

No better sound in the world.

And no place he'd rather be, as long as Lauren was by his side.

He knotted the apron strings at his waist.

If only they could come up with a way to boost their income enough to support his parents, the business, and all of the employees.

After all, his plans depended on earning more than tips, especially if he ever wanted to make Lauren a permanent part of his life.

Lauren slid her notepad into her pocket and turned toward the kitchen. Behind the counter, Joel lifted a full tub of dirty dishes.

She caught her breath and hurried forward.

He was back. And even in an apron, he radiated strength from the width of his shoulders to the chiseled set of his jaw.

The same jaw her fingers sometimes explored when they kissed.

Her face heated and she forced her thoughts back where they belonged. After all, customers came first. A task that came as easily as usual now that her brain was operating at full capacity again.

But as she rounded the end of the counter, he winked and she couldn't hold back her answering grin.

Joel disappeared into the kitchen and she stopped at the monitor to enter the orders from the group of local businessmen. Slow-cooked roast and stew seemed to be the favorites today. Must be the snow.

Speaking of the cold weather, they were going through the coffee faster than normal.

She checked their supply, started another batch, and made the refill round starting with Greta's admirer Clay at the counter. By the time she'd emptied the pot, Joel worked to restock the tub of rolled silverware and Clarissa delivered food to a construction crew swapping jokes.

Joel wrapped a gummed paper strip around each bundle. "I've made a dent in the pile of dishes back there. How can I help out here?"

Lauren surveyed the room. "We'll finish up the current customers, but as they leave, you can take over the new ones in your usual section."

"My section." He sighed.

She glanced up at his expression to find a mixture of pride and satisfaction as if he claimed ownership to more than a few tables. Yet wrinkles creased his forehead.

"How's your dad?"

Joel turned with a tender look in his eyes. "Doc said he's on track. But Dad's obviously disgruntled to hear there's another month of rehab before he can even think about coming back."

Meaning she had at least a month more as Joel's girlfriend before he could start looking elsewhere again?

His smile faded. "I'm starting to face the reality that he might not return here full time."

Was he sad for Frank? Or for himself?

Joel straightened. "In the meantime, I need to find a way to increase the business' profit margin enough to support all of us."

She nodded.

After helping Joel with some of the bookkeeping as an excuse to spend more time together, she knew he was proud of the small emergency reserve he'd set aside as their profits slowly increased.

Joel was working as hard at the diner as his dad did in physical therapy. Every gain was precious, since the price of beef was going up. And chicken and sugar and...

If only there was a way to help bridge the gap.

"I'll think about it." She squeezed his arm, then turned to load a tray with full plates.

By the time she had delivered food to the table of businessmen, she was the closest to seat a small family at the vacant booth near the door. Their young boy wore an Eagles hockey jersey, bringing back memories of a treat-seeking youngster in front of them at the game.

Lauren backtracked a few steps to grab a coloring page and bag of crayons from a drawer in Hope's buffet. Maybe instead of simply cutting apart dollar store books she could also find sports-themed pages to print for the boys?

Back at their table, she pulled out her notepad and focused on the youngest guest. "Are you an Eagles fan?"

The boy bounced on the vinyl bench seat and launched into a monologue naming all his favorite players and a play-by-play description of a game he'd seen.

Lauren looked at his parents across the table. "Guess that was a dumb question."

The dad grinned. "He's been a bit obsessed ever since I took him."

The mom chuckled. "A bit?"

"What can I get you all to drink?" Lauren took their order and retreated behind the lunch counter where Joel added the last bundles of silverware to the full tub.

She pulled over a cork-lined drink tray. "I should have given you that batch. The little boy's a true hockey fan. Even knew all their names."

Joel replaced the extra napkins and other supplies on their shelf. "Did you tell him about your puck signed by the team?"

"I should."

The autographed puck was only part of the sorry-you-got-hurt package sent by the organization.

She poured a small glass of milk for the boy before adding ice to the larger glasses for soda. "You do realize that if you'd taken me to a basketball game instead, I wouldn't have had a black eye for over a week."

Joel's gaze swept over her face, lingering first at her lips before settling on a spot to the right of her eyes. "And no battle scars to be the topic of conversation."

"Never mind that. I'd like the absence of drama in my life for a while." She topped off the glasses and moved on to deliver the family's drinks and take their food order.

As she went through the familiar dining room activity, thoughts of how to increase business mingled with hockey images until the two melded. Other restaurants ran specials linked to the local team's performance. Could they?

She stopped to help Joel clear a table. "What if we started a sports special like if the Eagles make a certain number of goals in a game, then the next day customers who mention the score would get fifty percent off their meal or something? That would raise interest in the local team and might bring more guests in here."

Joel stacked the dirty dishes into the tub. "That's more fun than a regular coupon and should save the printing or delivery costs."

She squirted the tabletop with disinfectant spray for him to wipe down. "But would a deal like that really make us money?"

"I'll have to run the numbers to know for sure. But if people are getting their food for half-price, they might be willing to buy dessert. Or drinks. And those are our true money makers."

She stepped to the side as he finished cleaning the tabletop. "Or we could invite members of the team here to sign autographs? If the word got around, people would come and it wouldn't cost us anything aside from maybe a little advertising to announce the event."

"I like how you're thinking."

"Hmm. That's hockey but baseball is around the corner. What if we sponsored a local high school or little league team?"

"Good idea. Keep 'em coming." He winked at her before heading back toward the counter.

Her pulse skittered. Nothing quite beat Joel treating her like a true partner.

Things were certainly looking up.

God, please bless us with Your wisdom.

A few minutes later, she picked up the order for the hockey fan's family and headed across the room.

Along the way, she passed an elderly couple brushing snow off their coats and taking seats at a small table. "I'll be right with you."

She sidestepped a trio of businessmen preparing to leave and delivered her armload of plates to the appropriate members of the family.

Straightening, she eyed the row of windows facing the street and the accumulating snow outside. If she suggested hot chocolate to the non-coffee drinkers, that might make a little more money today.

She spotted an older woman with a walker struggling to navigate the drifts in the street's crosswalk. The woman slipped and fell.

Lauren gasped.

A horn blared as a large pickup swerved to avoid the fallen woman.

Time slowed as the truck's new path aimed straight toward the diner's windows.

Lauren stared at the driver's wide eyes and wider mouth.

"Look out!" She snatched the little sports fan from his seat and swiveled away from the window.

She'd only managed to take a single step before the truck crashed through the fragile barrier with a whirlwind of noise from the honking horn and shattering glass mingled with screams as diners realized what was happening.

Painful shards embedded in her back as a whoosh of frigid air and snow swirled around her.

Lauren staggered forward and sucked in a breath before opening her eyes.

Joel ran out from behind the counter. Probably should have grabbed the first aid kit since he'd been closest.

Half the dining room stared in shock while the construction guys jumped to their feet and joined Joel's rush toward them.

Several people pulled out cell phones and someone yelled they were calling 9-1-1.

The boy in her arms started crying and she looked down to assess the damage. There didn't appear to be any blood. Hopefully, he was just scared.

And he wasn't the only one.

How were his parents?

Her heart raced as she turned her head toward the booth. One wheel of the truck rested where the boy had been sitting and his parents crawled over the glass-sprinkled table to reach her.

To the right, the rest of the truck's front end occupied most of table two, just vacated by the businessmen.

A minute earlier, and there would have been people trapped under the vehicle.

Or dead.

She swayed on her feet.

Dear God, that was too close.

Chapter Eighteen

♥

J oel's heartbeat thundered in his ears, almost drowning out the
crunching of glass shards under his shoes as he ran toward Lauren.

For as long as he lived, he'd never forget the wide-eyed look on her
pale face as she'd turned away from the impact.

She'd been right there and could have been killed by the truck now
sitting half-inside the diner.

Along with the screaming child in her arms.

He reached her side and wrapped an arm around her shaking shoulders.

The splinters of glass on her back pierced his skin as she leaned against
him. Once the immediate shock wore off, she'd be in incredible pain.

"Dylan. You're all right." The boy's mother ran her hands over his
body before pulling him into her arms with a shushing sound that
calmed his cries.

The father embraced his family and met Joel's gaze with tears in his
eyes.

The man had almost lost his son.

Just like he could have lost the woman in his arms.

Life and the diner wouldn't be the same without her.

He tucked Lauren against his chest to absorb her trembling and
raised his voice to be heard over the panic, wind, and snow. "Everyone
look around you. Aside from glass cuts, is everybody okay?"

Joel glanced down at Lauren's back and winced at the sight of blood
oozing through her shirt, before looking away to assess the room. "How
many are hurt? How's the driver?"

Beside the truck, the trio of orange-vested construction workers in Clarissa's section had pried open the door and one leaned halfway into the cab.

One of the crew stuck a thumb out to one side. "Bleeding but conscious."

Thank You, Lord.

Behind him, a woman's voice carried above the wind. "I'm on the phone with 9-1-1 and an ambulance and the police are on their way."

Joel nodded. "Thank you."

Clarissa reached them. "What happened? I mean why did…"

Lauren looked up. "A woman fell in the crosswalk and he swerved to miss her. Must have slid on the ice."

The information skittered through the dining room as groups of customers huddled as far as they could get from the broken windows. Snow swirled inside and drifted down onto half-eaten plates of food.

Aunt Greta stared through the pass-through window with her mouth hanging open.

Exactly how he felt.

Lord, I'm supposed to be in charge but I don't know what to do. Give me wisdom. I could use all the help I can get.

He closed his eyes for a moment and rested his chin on top of Lauren's head. Icy flakes blew in his face and he shifted his position to shield her from the cold.

As part of their accident investigation, the police should call a tow truck.

And once they moved the crashed vehicle, he'd need to patch up the broken wall to keep the weather out. Only then could they clean up the mess and figure out what to do next.

Customers pulled on their coats while approaching sirens echoed above the wind.

First things first.

Make sure the injured were taken care of, starting with Lauren.

The bells clattered as an officer came through the front door and stopped. His eyes swept over the scene as he spoke into the radio on his shoulder.

Someone else was in charge for the moment, but Joel could still do his part.

He guided Lauren toward a less-windy corner on the other side of the main door. Soon she was joined by an elderly couple with numerous cuts and a few others including the snow-covered woman who had fallen outside as customers created a space for the arriving paramedics to work.

Within minutes, Lauren was seated backward in a chair with her head on their clasped hands while a female paramedic removed the pieces of glass sticking out through her bloodied shirt.

The woman patted Lauren's shoulder. "Do you mind if I cut open the back here to remove the rest of these? I can see if you'll need stitches instead of just butterfly bandages on the deepest spots. I assume you have a coat here?"

Lauren nodded, then peeked in his direction as a blush stained her cheeks.

Right. She was about to lose her shirt in a public place.

He cleared his throat. "I have something in my locker you can borrow."

Joel loosened his grip, retreated to the office, and put on his own jacket before hurrying back. He handed Lauren a sweatshirt from his college days. "It might be a little big."

She clutched it under her chin and smiled. "It's—"

She winced as the paramedic did something to her back. Her voice wobbled. "It's perfect."

He carefully brushed a hand over her hair, wincing at the tiny splinters of glass hiding there, then stepped aside to give her privacy as the paramedic ripped the T-shirt fabric.

Trying to ignore the discussion about butterfly bandages and possible stitches behind him, he focused instead on the police officer taking pictures of the damage as other officers interviewed the witnesses.

A fire truck blocked the street as a swarm of first responders processed the scene outside the building.

A lunch regular who had been seated at the counter approached. "I'm a carpenter and would like to help out."

Joel turned his attention to the flannel-clad man who did not appear much older than himself. "What's your name again?"

"Matt Simpson." Matt tipped his bearded chin toward the shattered window. "I have plywood and plastic sheeting at my shop so I can screw together a covering. If I leave now, I could be back and ready to work once the tow truck gets the vehicle out of here. That would at least stop more snow from coming inside."

Tension eased from Joel's shoulders as one worry took care of itself. "Thanks. I'd appreciate it."

"No problem. I'd hate to see that buffet suffer water damage." Matt pointed toward the door and the antique furniture that had been Grandma Hope's.

It had sat in her dining room for most of Joel's childhood. At least until his uncle had died and Aunt Greta's life had upended, forcing change.

Felt a bit like now with the ripple effect of problems hitting one after the other.

Carpenter or not, concern about an antique seemed wrong when there was a gaping hole and shattered table eight feet away.

Joel tilted his head toward the bigger issue. "In addition to blocking the wind, is there any way you can help out with the rest of it too?"

"I'd be happy to work up an estimate. We can talk more when I return, but I can already tell you replacing that size window is going to cost at least a grand just for the glass. And that's assuming the one next to it isn't also damaged when they pull the truck out." Matt pulled keys from his coat pocket and headed for the door.

Joel sank onto a nearby chair and ran a hand over his face.

That was some very expensive glass.

As if the diner had enough money in the account to pay for this level of repairs, although insurance should help after their deductible. Then again maybe the truck driver's policy would cover it so he didn't need to touch their emergency fund.

But how long until they could reopen?

He was a businessman without a working business. A business that depended heavily on daily cash flow...

One of the construction workers stopped beside him. "Who should we pay for our meals?"

"You shouldn't have to pay for a ruined meal." Joel stood and waved to where the injured man had been put on a stretcher and wheeled out. "Besides, you went out of your way to help the driver. It's on the house."

"Thank you." The man dipped his head in appreciation before leaving with his friends.

Leaving Joel's mind scrambling down another path.

While the customers shouldn't have to pay for meals they didn't eat, they had a kitchen full of food prepared for the rest of the expected lunch crowd.

Food that would not get sold today.

Was there a shelter that would like the stew on such a snowy day?

Maybe they could feed the officers and paramedics a little something as a thank you? At least offer them coffee since their fingers had to be freezing.

Like his were.

And probably Lauren's.

He glanced over his shoulder to where she sat slumped over the back of the chair now wearing his sweatshirt.

The paramedic had moved on to bandage cuts on another injured customer.

In two steps, he was crouched beside her. "How are you?"

She lifted her head and offered a weak smile. "Just giving thanks. It could have been so much worse."

Joel leaned forward and kissed her gently. "But it wasn't."

He brushed a fingertip down her cold cheek.

A shiver wracked her body and she winced as if the movement irritated her injuries.

"Would you like some coffee to warm you up?"

Her smile wobbled. "Warmth would be good."

"Stay here and rest." He stood and hurried to where Clarissa cleared half-eaten food and abandoned dishes from a table littered with broken glass. "We can take care of this later. Why don't you put on your coat and then see if anyone wants coffee?"

She rubbed her hands over her arms. "That sounds good. I didn't have any idea where to start."

"I know the feeling." He moved on toward the kitchen. "Aunt Greta, what do you think about—"

"Calling the homeless shelter?" She raised an eyebrow. "Already done. They'll be sending someone in about an hour to pick up whatever leftovers we want to donate."

Joel nodded. "Great. Now what do you think about offering hot stew or pie to the officers and workers out there?"

Aunt Greta wrapped an arm around his waist. "That's the Dawson's Diner way."

He leaned into her embrace. "I'm learning."

Lauren peeked in through the pass-through window. "We can set up a station at the lunch counter since this end didn't get damaged."

"Didn't the paramedic tell you to take it easy?" He moved closer to face his serve-even-if-it-hurt-her girlfriend.

She blinked slowly. "She did. But I only came over here because it's warmer near the kitchen."

He wasn't buying her innocent act and lowered his gaze to her hands. Bingo. "So, what are you doing trying to lift a crate of coffee cups?"

She bit her lip and released her grip. "Waiting for you?"

Lauren added the last framed photo to the stack in her arms, then crossed to the tables grouped together in the middle of the dining room.

Maybe she could talk Joel into redecorating beyond the fresh paint. Cut down on the number of pictures on the walls or at least organize them into clusters.

Could even leverage the fact he'd put her in charge of the dining room to take some of the burden off Joel's already weary shoulders.

But first she had to know what she had to work with.

Ignoring the itching tug of the healing wounds on her back, she sorted the collection into categories, putting scenery, townspeople, family photos, and old newspaper articles in different areas.

A cool breeze filtered through the room and she pulled down the sleeves of Joel's sweatshirt. She'd planned to give it back today, but Matt and his helper had taken the plastic barriers down to prepare for the arrival of the new glass later.

She'd overheard the carpenter talking to Joel earlier about a rush order and framing the edges. And something about patching drywall before replacing brick and trim. Not to mention the paint inside.

Which had led to their current plan to paint everything else while they had the chance.

Even so, it was all hands on deck if they were going to reopen in under a week.

Which was why Joel had called a staff meeting.

And why Greta was baking a small batch of cinnamon rolls as incentive.

Lauren inhaled deeply. As bribes went, Greta knew their weaknesses.

Joel set two steaming coffee cups onto a free table beside his ever-present notebook and a stack of papers. "She said they'd be done soon."

Lauren grinned. "Perfect. Now what did you find out about the upholstery?"

Other than the obviously shattered window and crushed table, the back-to-back bench seats between the two booths had taken the brunt of the damage and would need to be rebuilt and reupholstered.

He pulled out a chair. "They said they can't match the color—even if we were willing to wait—so we'll have to go with black or something else."

She tried to imagine black alongside the existing burgundy and failed. "What if..."

Maybe it would help to be standing in the area as they talked?

Instead of sitting, Lauren picked up her coffee and wandered closer to where Matt and his helper worked.

To where they measured and hammered and chatted about Matt's old house that he was apparently renovating piece by piece as he could afford it.

Normally, she'd be jumping into that conversation eager to learn.

But she'd been trying to rein in her natural curiosity and focus on the diner's problems for a change.

Lauren blew across the top of her coffee, then took a cautious sip as she eyed the space formerly occupied by the back-to-back bench. She skimmed her gaze toward the front door.

There had to be an easier solution to their seating problem.

"I know it's not ideal, but you got something against black upholstery?" Joel stood on her right side cradling his own coffee.

Lauren pointed at the single bench where the boy's parents had sat near the door. "If we slid that over, it would make a complete booth that matches the rest of what we already have. And then we could cancel the order for a new table."

And save some money in the process.

Joel gestured to her left. "But even when we get Grandma Hope's buffet back, that still leaves a gap of wasted space. And one less spot for paying customers."

She sipped her coffee again as she studied the area where the piece of antique furniture had been.

In the immediate flurry of activity to remove the intruding truck from the diner without causing more structural damage to the wall, the buffet had been shoved aside by overeager helpers.

Resulting in a cracked and wobbly leg to complement the water spots from melted snow.

After being present during the insurance adjustor's walkthrough yesterday, Matt had taken the damaged piece with him. He would bill the diner for the window and structural repairs, but wanted to take on the woodworking project as a personal challenge.

He'd said something about using it in his portfolio.

But in the meantime, Joel was right. It was a waste of the diner's limited space.

Unless...

"What about adding a few chairs for a waiting area instead?" She faced him. "They'd be much cheaper than replacing a table and upholstered booth."

He pursed his lips. "So they'll sit and wait rather than sit and eat? We've never really needed a waiting area before. Except we might if we have one less table overall."

"What if we started offering to-go or delivery pick-up orders? Or had a bakery display case for takeout? That way we could sell meals or even whole pies and we'd still make income from that spot. Meanwhile the turnover would be higher than sit-down guests."

"You're never going to let me forget my 'get 'em in, get 'em fed, get 'em out' model, are you?" He winked.

She grinned. "I might, if..."

"If?" He glanced at her lips before meeting her eyes again with a growing smile.

"If you let me help paint this afternoon."

"Are you sure?" His smile faded.

"I'll be fine." She hid her smile behind her half-empty coffee cup.

Especially since Joel's overprotective nature would be keeping tabs on her every movement.

She shrugged, feeling it in her tight shoulders. "If it hurts, I'll stop and watch everyone else. However, back to the topic of our wasted space. Without Hope's buffet, we'll need some sort of temporary shelves or a counter for those pick-up orders."

"Excuse me." Matt approached them. "Couldn't help but overhear. I have a finished piece that might work in that spot."

"What would that cost?" Joel was always concerned about the bottom line.

Matt brushed the question aside. "Consider it a loan until I fix the buffet. But since I'm trying to build up the furniture side of my business, what if I left my card on it for advertising?"

"That sounds like a perfect win-win situation." Lauren elbowed Joel's ribs, willing him to agree.

Before Joel could answer, the bells clattered and a middle-aged man in a suit entered.

Lauren frowned. "We're closed."

Couldn't he see the sign on the door? They'd only left it unlocked so Matt had easy access to his tools in the truck parked outside.

The stranger looked down his nose as he scanned the chaos. "Where is the owner?"

Her muscles tensed.

The intruder's lips lifted in a smile that felt anything but friendly. "Because we need to talk."

Chapter Nineteen

♥

L auren glanced from the smug stranger to Joel and back.

Anyone already familiar with the diner knew Frank was still recovering, so what new trouble was about to land on Joel's shoulders?

Joel pushed past her to stop the intruder near the door. "I'm as good as you're going to get today."

The man eyed Joel's T-shirt and jeans. "If you insist."

Joel propped one hand on his hip and casually sipped his coffee.

As if he had all the time in the world while waiting for the man to get to the point.

Lauren rolled her lips inward to stop her laughter. Seemed Joel was going to do just fine against this unwelcome adversary.

Beside her, Matt's chest shook until he coughed. But he didn't step away. Just stood there silently offering support and backing Joel up.

And watching the stranger very carefully.

As if he knew something they didn't.

Lauren narrowed her eyes, not wanting to miss a thing.

The newcomer tugged on his lapels, then flicked an invisible speck of dust from his sleeve. "I was in the area finalizing a contract on the old barbershop down the block and saw your broken window."

Joel stood still. And waited.

Finally, the man removed a slim silver box from the pocket of his suit jacket, flipped it open to reveal a stack of business cards, and held one out.

Joel took it, but only gave it a glance before shoving it into his back pocket. And taking another sip of his coffee. "And...?"

The man affected a casual shrug as if Joel's reaction didn't matter, but his shrewd eyes appeared to be measuring the walls.

There was no hiding the gleam of interest that sent prickles up Lauren's spine.

The man sniffed, his lips twitching. "I know that profits are always tightest in the food industry and this damage has to have hit the bottom line. Hard. So just tell the owner that I'm willing to take this mess off his hands."

Mess?

Joel stiffened and Lauren could already imagine his frown.

Matt's hand on her arm stopped her progress before she realized she'd been stepping forward to defend the diner.

Defend the Dawsons.

She huffed out a breath.

The wanna-be buyer waved a too-manicured hand toward the north. "Could give him a fair price for that vacant space next door too if that helps."

"We're not for sale." Joel raised his voice and pointed at the door. "Please see yourself out."

The man muttered something, then smirked before exiting.

Joel twisted the lock with a firm click, then turned with blazing anger in his eyes and a vein ticking along his jawline.

"What did he say at the end?" Lauren held her breath.

"That one way or another, he guaranteed we'd change our minds." Joel fished the business card from his back pocket and glared at it as if it was a venomous snake about to strike.

"That was Brock Ridge from Rocky Ridge Development, right?" Matt practically growled beside her.

Joel looked up. "Unfortunately. What do you know about him?"

"That's right." Lauren faced their carpenter. "It seemed like you knew him."

Matt crossed his arms over his chest. "Just rumors around the construction community since he seems to be starting several new projects lately. Sounds like he imagines himself to be some sort of up-and-coming developer. But he's also right in the middle of the downtown revitalization efforts including ties to that proposal for a parking garage."

Lauren rolled her eyes. "As if we need one of those here."

"Not now, for sure. But if he *revitalizes* downtown too much, that could change." Matt shook his head. "Other than that speculation, I've heard plenty of whispers in general about how he cuts corners on quality and is pretty ruthless with vendor contracts. It's not how I conduct business."

"That figures." Joel crumpled the business card and tossed it aside. "Now, what were we talking about before being interrupted?"

Lauren could only blink.

Matt rocked back on the heels of his boots. "I just finished restoring an old pie safe and can bring it round tomorrow or the next day to fill in while I work on the buffet."

Right. A new display area for extra pies or to-go orders.

To sit just inches from the wadded-up cardstock.

If Joel could pretend he wasn't rattled by the man, so could she.

As the men shook hands to finalize the deal then drifted toward the windows to check on progress there, Lauren heard voices from the kitchen.

Might as well finish sorting the last of the photos before their meeting started. Would give her a better idea what to keep and what to replace in terms of decorations.

Assuming Joel let her take the lead after all.

Abandoning her coffee by a seat at the main table near Joel's papers, she meandered to the collection of family photos, then arranged them by generation or family group.

With a stack for all the sports teams Joel had played on including a diner-sponsored little league team with Joel in the front row and a proud Frank posed by the coach.

Leaving Joel's generation behind, she trailed her fingers over a photograph of a much-younger Hope with her husband Harold. From all she'd heard, they'd poured years of their lives into this business.

"What do you have there?" Joel stopped near her elbow and eyed the pictures over the rim of his coffee.

"I was just thinking that your Grandma Hope would hate seeing the diner like this."

"For sure." Joel looked around. "I know it was hard for Dad to see the damage. It doesn't look like Dawson's Diner this way."

Greta approached with a platter of rolls. "It actually looks like it did back in my grandparents' day when we didn't have all those pictures hanging up."

Fewer pictures sounded good, as long as she could get Joel to agree.

When Greta detoured to give Matt and his helper a treat, it was the perfect chance to present her idea.

"After we paint, I'd like permission to hang bigger scenic prints on the walls instead of all these small frames. They make the room feel cluttered."

She could already see the changes and felt a burst of energy. "Wish we could afford a stunning Callahan print or three from the gallery across the street, but I know I can create a similar feel with posters from Rocky Mountain National Park or enlargements of photos of Lake Loveland. Buy affordable matching frames from a hobby store."

"We should have a little budget left over from the insurance check..." Joel drained the last of his coffee. "Sure. As long as it's nothing too extreme."

She set the photo of Hope and Harold down next to one of Hope's parents posed in front of the building. "You can trust me. And I'd still keep a section of family history by the front door."

Nearby were a couple articles about floods in the Big Thompson canyon. One pictured Joel as a teen with a childish Julie. But the other?

It was hard to imagine Hope that young or Frank that small.

Those would be great additions to the history wall with their mixture of Dawson family memories and landmark community events.

She looked closer at the caption about Hope's family's café. Café? Not diner?

Joel clapped his hands. "Now that everyone's here, help yourself to a roll and we'll get started."

Lauren quickly sat by her now-cooled coffee and grabbed an extra-gooey treat, forcing Trevor to pick a different one.

Meanwhile Debbie guarded two more for her twins who were coming in later to help tape around the trim before they painted.

The only person missing was Clarissa. But with the diner closed anyway, she had asked for the time off to spend with her brothers since they were off school for Spring Break.

As Lauren washed down bites of warm cinnamon roll with her remaining swigs of coffee, Joel recapped their timeline for reopening.

The insurance company had approved a claim for close to ten thousand dollars of repair costs and were issuing payment soon before seeking reimbursement from the driver's company. Joel was still negotiating with the agents hoping to get paid back for the spoiled ingredients in the cooler.

But nothing would make up for a week's worth of lost income for each of the staff.

While Joel promised compensation for the hours they each spent during the cleanup, that was still fewer than a normal workweek. Not to mention her loss of tips.

At least her medical bills were being covered by the driver's insurance, especially so soon after the hockey accident. She was gaining a reputation at the doctor's office.

Joel tapped his pen atop his collection of papers. "However, on the topic of insurance, we need to create a detailed inventory of all the equipment so that our policy is up to date. And they can likely charge us more."

Lauren sighed. Just what they needed.

Joel turned toward his aunt. "So, Aunt Greta, if you guys can list everything in the kitchen down to the last plate and spoon, Lauren and I can tally the tables, chairs, service counter, and coffee cups."

Her eyes widened. That was a lot of counting, but better out here than in the kitchen.

Trevor reached for another cinnamon roll. "I need to fuel up before that job. Maybe we can celebrate with pie?"

"I agree. Especially if you'll make Grandma Hope's apple crumb." Joel grinned. "Like she always said, nothing a slice of pie can't fix, right?"

Greta chuckled. "Truthfully, it was *my* grandmother who used to say that. And it was *her* mother's original recipe."

Lauren turned to Trevor and Debbie. "In case you missed the family connections, Frank and Greta's mom was named Hope and her family were the original founders. Which is actually all the more reason to honor their history, even if I'd like to confine it to one wall."

She gave a quick summary of her plan to condense the clutter and update the pictures for the other walls.

Debbie nodded. "Definitely pick the best ones, but there's no reason you can't put the discards into a photo album or scrapbook to keep there at the front in case any of the regulars want to revisit history. Or any new customers are curious."

"I like that idea." Greta settled back in her chair with a wistful smile.

"And there's that scrapbooking and stationary store just a couple of doors down. But, speaking of diner history..." Lauren retrieved the article she'd just read. "Was this ever Hope's Café?"

Greta shook her head. "It used to be the Heartland Café back like 70 plus years ago, then switched to Dawson's Diner around the time Frank and I were born since that was our last name. Never was officially Hope's Café although that's what Dad always called it." She smirked. "Mostly when things weren't going well or he wanted to give her a hard time."

"Hope's Café has a nice ring to it." Lauren glanced at Joel.

He held up his hands. "That's a decision for Dad to make, not me. I'm just the manager."

He might think that, but every day and every decision had him more deeply invested in the business.

If given the choice, would he still want to leave?

"But back to the subject of baked goods..." Joel shuffled his papers. "Our profit margin per cinnamon roll is high. Same for pie." He nodded toward Lauren, then briefed the others about her suggested takeout and bakery area. "I think there's a way to bake more—"

"Sorry. Don't have time." Greta grimaced. "Not even pie can fix that."

"We could put that slogan on a T-shirt and sell them. Or wear them." Lauren licked the last of the icing off her fingers as Greta protested.

Joel held up his hands. "You'll be happy to know that uniforms—even the T-shirt variety—are not in the budget... For now." He smirked as his aunt sputtered and the others laughed.

Maybe shirts were out of the question, but she could still make a pretty sign for their new front shelves.

Trevor raised a hand. "If I might offer a suggestion. Mom's chemo is close to done and her doctor is optimistic."

"That's a relief." Greta patted his arm. "Hope things can settle down for you."

He nodded. "The kitchen has been a welcome distraction, but I'm ready for more. Have more bandwidth and more familiarity here. What do you think about this: Greta and I swap places? I've got the training to take over the lead, Debbie could move up to assist, and Greta can do more midday baking?"

After a moment of stunned silence, Greta nodded. "I'd welcome that change. I was glad to step into Frank's shoes when we needed it, but other than a return to the dining room and the tips I've been missing out on, baking is my happy place."

Just like her mother Hope before her.

And Julie who was off becoming a pastry chef.

Joel glanced between the two kitchen staff and nodded. "Consider it done."

Trevor leaned forward. "Now that Greta's in position to meet the demand for more baked goods, I have another suggestion. What if I take the cost-analysis menu planning we'd talked about one step further and create a chef's special of the day. It could add some variety to the menu on a small scale but also help use up produce that's close to expiring."

Joel tilted his head and frowned. "Would that make money?"

Trevor nodded. "Doesn't have to be a discounted deal. Just something new. Could try out a few healthier or fresh options that some customers might appreciate. Down the road, perhaps we can scale back the menu to the most cost-effective choices or at least those where the ingredients are less likely to be wasted."

"I like where you're headed." Joel's smile returned.

Trevor's smile grew to match. "Not that I think we should raise prices in this economy, but we can still cut our costs to maintain the profit margin. All while making it easier on the kitchen staff at the same time."

The man had obviously put a lot of thought into his suggestion.

Joel flipped to a new page in his notebook and made a note about menu changes under the heading *Ideas for Later*. He added a column for *Things to Do Before Monday*.

Paint, pictures, moving the booth, chairs for the waiting area, Matt's loaned pie safe, and the insurance inventory were added. Along with cleaning out the cooler and placing a food order that accounted for the extra baking to come.

"If we have more pies or rolls than we can sell here..." Debbie finally spoke up. "Maybe there's a nearby coffee shop or gas station or a caterer that would like baked goods? We could reach out to them now before the dining room reopens."

"That's a definite possibility, but I don't want to get ahead of ourselves until I know what we actually have to work with." Trevor looked Joel in the eye. "If we can get to work back there, I'm sure we'll come up with even more ideas to make up for the lost revenue."

At Joel's nod, Trevor stood and led his team to the kitchen.

With all of them working together, they'd be ready to reopen even stronger than before the crash. Except how would people know to return?

Lauren pointed to Joel's notebook. "Add calling Kyle to your list."

"Kyle?"

"Our early morning regular reporter who covered the accident initially. He might like to do an update story and oh, happen to mention that we're thrilled to be able to reopen on Monday."

Joel made the note. "Free advertising? I like how you think."

"Free is important, right?"

"You know how tight the bank account is." He tossed the pen onto the paper. "Once we're open again, even with a to-go area, a chef's special, and more baked goods, we need ways to encourage more people to stop by."

She leaned back in her chair, then adjusted her position to keep the slats off the most tender spots. "Before the crash, we were talking about doing something sports related like a Meet-The-Eagles hockey day or having a discount tied to the number of goals scored."

"That's right." He turned to a new page and started taking notes.

"Maybe we could have a first-responder appreciation day? After all, we certainly have reason to appreciate the police, paramedics, and firemen."

He smirked. "And we could also include that in the interview for Kyle's article?"

"Why not?" She shrugged. "Going forward there's always something going on in Loveland from Valentines Day that's obviously already passed by to fireworks over the lake and sculpture shows this summer to the Corn Roast Festival and the County Fair this fall. Those are prime opportunities to hand out coupons for a special deal."

"Slow down." He kept writing.

At least he didn't criticize her wild ideas. Or maybe he was only indulging her because of her injuries.

She let her mind wander and recalled another family picture. "But before all of that, little league baseball teams have sponsors with banners on the field."

Except all of those ideas were centered outside the diner walls.

Could they do anything closer to home to get their current customers to come back more often?

She eyed the empty spot near the door, ignoring the crumpled-up business card. "We could put up a community bulletin board advertising local events so people have a reason to stop by. And if we collect a fishbowl of business cards, we could not only draw a name for a free meal but feature the weekly winner on the board as extra advertising for them."

She grinned as Joel flipped back to the first page and made a note.

It felt good to do something to help the diner survive.

And spending more time with Joel didn't hurt either.

"We already have coloring pages for the kids. What if we had a contest and the winner got a free kid's meal? That would bring the family back to eat."

"You can stop now."

"Hey." Lauren propped her hands on her hips. "I thought you liked my ideas."

He held up his hands in surrender. "I'm getting a cramp from all the writing."

The noise from the street faded as Matt and his helper secured a new sheet of glass into place.

The sooner the wall was enclosed so they could start painting, the sooner they'd be putting the rest of Joel's list into action.

Joel reached over to grasp her hands. "I wasn't sure we'd be free or not, but maybe this weekend we can..."

"We can what?"

"There's a hospitality industry conference and trade show in Denver."

"That sounds interesting." Her breath caught as his thumbs rubbed circles on the backs of her hands.

"Maybe they'll have more ideas for us."

Us.

She could only hope and pray there was an *us* when the dust settled.

Her gaze drifted back to the heart of the reconstruction, catching on the business card mocking her from the tiled floor.

A chill ran up her spine.

That assumed they still had a diner to run.

God, I'll do whatever it takes to keep our doors open.

Chapter Twenty

♥

Their day at the expo had hardly begun and already Joel was developing a headache.

Mostly because of the disappointment on Lauren's face every time he had to bring up their limited budget.

A pauper's pittance if he were being honest about the true state of the diner's finances.

No wonder Dad's health had suffered under the weight of constant stress.

Joel clasped Lauren's hand and tugged her away from a booth laden with a rainbow of expensive linen napkins and tablecloths. "We use paper, remember?"

"I know." She glanced back at the display. "But other than our first date, this is the closest I've been to a fancy restaurant in years."

He winced a bit at the memory. Thank God they'd gotten past the stilted conversation stage of their romantic relationship.

But then his mind flashed back to college when Desiree's preference for expensive dinners led to their breakup.

Joel squeezed Lauren's hand. "We'll have to change that."

Assuming he could begin paying himself all he'd earned instead of just tips. Otherwise he'd be tempted to dip into his seed-the-dream savings.

"Really?" Lauren's hazel eyes shone.

"I promise." They passed by more booths full of similar linens. "However, in the interest of time, maybe we should focus on the vendors that actually sell something we can use?"

Not that they had the money to buy anything.

They were window-shopping for ideas. And ideas only.

"Party pooper." She stuck out her lower lip in a pout but the twinkle in her eye gave her away.

Unable to resist her allure and eager for a distraction, he dropped a quick kiss on her upturned nose.

"You missed." Her lips spread into a grin.

"Didn't miss the chance to spend time with my girl, did I?"

"Your girl." She sighed. "You're forgiven."

"Whew."

Hand-in-hand, they wound their way through the trade show crowd and past displays featuring industrial appliances.

Maybe someday there would be time or money for kitchen upgrades.

Just not anytime soon.

Especially since they needed the insurance check to arrive so they could pay Matt's bill for the repairs.

His phone chimed with an incoming text. He'd been in a texting loop with both Trevor and Aunt Greta ahead of Monday's reopening.

Who knew handing over the spatula in favor of more pie would cause so many questions.

Or require so many reassurances.

Instead it was a message from Desiree with a link to yet another opening at her company. Seemed she had heard on the news about the truck hitting the diner and since he would apparently need a new job...

He immediately deleted the text and briefly considered blocking her number completely.

The persistent woman could not figure out that a broken window did not mean a permanent closure. And even if it did, only an idiot would start a job search by asking his ex-girlfriend for help.

Not with Lauren in his life now.

He shoved the phone into his back pocket again as they rounded the corner into a new aisle featuring a section of food vendors, many with sample-laden trays.

Joel's stomach growled.

Lauren laughed. "Sounds like this is something we can use."

"Hey."

His protest fell on deaf ears as she pulled away and reached for a toothpick kabob of cheese.

"For me?"

She removed a cube of pepper jack and popped it in her mouth. "Get your own."

They wandered from booth to booth accumulating nibbles of fresh guacamole on corn chips, bacon-wrapped mushrooms, and sun-dried tomato hummus with sliced pita bread.

The last two were tasty enough but not something he'd ever see the diner crowd appreciating.

Near the end of the row, Joel spotted the supply vendor they used and approached the balding man behind the table. "I'm Joel Dawson from Dawson's Diner in Loveland."

"I'm Tom." He reached out with a firm handshake. "You must be Frank's boy."

"I am." Joel nodded. Connections mattered in any industry.

"Was sorry to hear about the truck crashing into your place. Saw the pictures on the news."

Lauren shook her head. "That was an unforgettable day."

Joel wrapped an arm around Lauren's waist and gazed down at her. "It could have been a whole lot worse if not for you."

The memory of her clutching the screaming boy still interrupted his sleep.

She blushed, then turned back toward Tom. "We're on track to reopen Monday."

Tom eyed the two of them and smiled. "That's great. Oh, by the way, we're piloting an online ordering system with a few of our clients."

He picked up a brochure and indicated a spot inside before handing it to Joel. "Just redid our website to include this program and you're welcome to try it out. There's even a place to input your inventory and set thresholds."

Lauren leaned in to study the screenshot image on the brochure. Her hair tickled his cheek and he inhaled the fruity scent of her shampoo.

"Hey." She pointed at one spot. "That looks like our inventory sheets."

Joel half-listened as the man described specific features of the program. About how it was free to use during the piloting process as they worked out the bugs, but would eventually be a paid feature.

Depending on how much that cost, he might follow Dad's example to stick with what was already working.

Beside him, a wide-eyed Lauren practically bounced with energy. All over a normally boring aspect of their business.

Then again, taking inventory together in the storeroom had led to their first kiss. And a whole lot more.

Would recording it on a website change that?

He eyed her pink glossy lips as they moved and smiled. If only they were somewhere else so he could act on his impulse.

With a gentle tug, he pulled the brochure from Lauren's fingers. "We already got our restocking order delivered yesterday ahead of reopening, but will certainly take a closer look."

Tom smiled. "It's a pleasure doing business with you both."

"Likewise." Joel shook the man's hand again.

"Thanks." Lauren took the brochure back and tucked it away in the complimentary tote bag hanging over her shoulder.

A few booths later, she clutched his arm beside a display of menu boards with removable black letters that snapped into white grooves. "What do you think about one of those?"

"Where would we put it?" Between the walls of windows, restroom entrances, serving station behind the lunch counter, and access to the kitchen, the only possible wall space was now occupied.

He should know since they'd just painted every inch and hung a tasteful selection of Colorado scenery, a historical montage, and Lauren's suggested bulletin board.

"Doesn't really fit with our new decor anyway. But it would be easier to update than the laminated cards we have now." She pursed her lips. "Speaking of which, many of ours are pretty beat up. How hard is it to make new ones?"

He shrugged. "Not too hard. I found a formatted file on the computer and any office store could print and laminate them for us. However, Trevor and I should sit down with Dad and re-evaluate the menu offerings and prices before we print anything."

She got closer to read the price tag, then backed away with wide eyes. "I understand you're supposed to spend money to make money, but that's ridiculous."

He choked back his laughter at her shocked expression. "We might not have a lot of cash lying around, but thanks to you we're learning to be creative."

"Since this is not one of those booths we can put to use right now, let's go." She tugged on his arm.

He chuckled. "Lead on."

As they continued their tour of the vendor showroom, Lauren collected samples of printed menus and stuffed them into her bag along with a brochure from a table and chair supplier.

If they didn't have money to buy a menu board, they certainly couldn't afford new tables.

Honestly they didn't even have enough to print a few new laminated menu cards. Not after the diner had been closed for a week and they'd needed to restock the spoiled produce.

And that was just the diner's bills.

What about his parents paying their personal bills?

Hopefully a grand reopening with everyone's collective strategies would pull off the miraculous. Just a few good weeks without new disasters and he could breathe a bit easier.

Then he'd treat Lauren to a special dinner at a fancy restaurant.

She stopped beside a booth selling glass-sided pie display cases. "Ooo. One of these would look great in our new to-go area."

"Whoa. Let's reopen first before we start buying."

The sparkle faded from her eyes.

He cupped her elbow. "Forgive my practicality. Pick up a brochure for when—by faith—we can use it."

"It never hurts to dream." She nodded as if convincing herself of something, then added the display case information to her tote bag.

More dreams were added before she stopped again at a table featuring online college courses, recommended books on restaurant management, and cutting-edge software.

Who got excited about school?

He already had an expensive degree... and a crash course in diner management.

Would he have been more excited about certain classes if he'd seen the practical application beyond delegating from behind a polished mahogany desk? But when hearing lectures about advanced financial management, he'd never pictured himself wearing an apron, frying bacon, and pouring coffee.

Lauren handed him a flier about an ordering program. "Isn't this what we have?"

He glanced at the name. "It is."

She tapped the bulleted points. "This says we can use it to track and tailor our daily specials—"

"To optimize profits." He scanned the other listed features.

After getting the touch screen ordering system running, he'd only skimmed the surface of possibilities when it came to calculating profit margins.

In fact, the program beat his manual spreadsheets by a long mile. Trevor would love—

She nudged his side. "I think I found a booth we can use."

"You sure did." He gave her a sideways hug and continued reading while she browsed the rest of the display.

His mind spun with possibilities. What should he implement first?

Using these report settings, they could tweak what they were already doing to make a bigger profit. Then Lauren's days-long brainstorm of ideas to bring in new customers would take them even further.

Far enough to easily meet the full payroll, rebuild their emergency fund, and eventually set money aside for a few improvements like those dreams in her tote bag.

Lauren's passion was contagious and, since she'd made the diner her little piece of heaven, there was no place he'd rather be.

Especially if she was there beside him.

Like she was right now.

Thank You, God, for Lauren and all her ideas. I couldn't have made it this far without her.

The buzz of conversation around them faded until all he saw was her beaming face as she clutched a handful of brochures under her chin.

He tugged her away from the table and into his arms.

Her gaze drifted over his face and her expression switched from joy to longing.

She made him feel powerful and strong and...

Successful.

He lowered his head and, in the middle of a ballroom swarming with vendors, poured out his heart in a lingering kiss.

The only thing sweeter than Joel's lips was the dawning realization that she'd finally found a place to shine.

She eased back and gazed into his blue eyes.

The intense look in his eyes stirred her confidence.

He believed in her and thought she was something special. Not just as fun girlfriend material but maybe as a partner with input about the diner business.

"Never seen anybody get that worked up about computer software before."

Lauren glanced at the heavyset man running the booth. She should be embarrassed, but then again, Joel was the one who had started the kiss.

She giggled. "He gets a little excited about maximizing profits."

Joel cleared his throat. "Yeah, what she said."

He steered her further away from the booth before leaning down to whisper in her ear. "It's you I get excited about."

She peered up with a smile. "I know the feeling."

Some might think it was fast, but she'd moved past crush-status fully into love.

He gave her a quick kiss that sent her heart racing again.

As they continued down the aisle, she remembered her handful of brochures about online business degree programs and a collection of other random courses. Finally, something she wanted to learn and information she could immediately apply in her favorite place.

She stuffed them into her bag to examine later. But for now, there was still plenty to see and no one she'd rather see it with.

That evening, after a fast-food dinner on the drive back north, she waved goodbye to Joel and let herself into Greta's house.

Greta sprawled in her recliner with her phone pressed to her ear. "Isn't there a show on Broadway you'd like to see for your birthday?"

Seemed she was still trying to convince Julie to get away from the culinary school campus and see more of New York City.

"Say 'hi' for me." Lauren wiggled her fingers at Greta and continued down the hall to Julie's old room. She slipped off her shoes, draped her coat on the back of the desk chair, and padded over to the bed.

After propping herself up with pillows, she spilled the day's collection of brochures onto the comforter and sorted them into two piles. Useful now or future dreams.

Her heart raced with renewed enthusiasm as she found the educational ones and studied the available options. Some offered hospitality management associate or bachelor's degrees while others focused only on running a restaurant.

With an online program—like the one Clarissa was finishing up—she'd be able to plan her classes around her longer hours at the diner. She really could have both.

She leaned back against the pillows and stared at the decorations on the walls, some childish and some more sophisticated.

Julie was in New York making her dream come true.

Now it was Lauren's turn.

Some programs ran year-round. So all she needed was to apply and come up with the money.

Her chest tightened.

Dad would still pay her tuition, wouldn't he?

He'd been so mad that she'd dropped her classes after Frank's heart attack and surgery. So, he should be happy that she was going back to school again, even if it was online. Right?

Only one way to find out.

Besides, what was the worst he could do?

Say no? Belittle her choices? He'd already done both when he'd basically walked out of her life.

Her stomach rolled because it was the rejection she feared the most.

She took a deep breath and with a trembling hand picked up her phone.

Within seconds the ringing tone echoed in her ear and all she could do was wait.

Chapter Twenty-One

♥

L auren hugged her knees to her chest, rocking slightly on the bed as she waited breathlessly for her call to connect.

Was it really possible God had led her to this moment?

Led her to the numerous possibilities she'd discovered among the hospitality expo booths?

She gripped the phone tightly with numb fingertips.

Or were the colorful brochures scattered across the comforter just more wishful thinking?

After all, who was she to hope that God's plan for her future could take her in a different direction from the rest of her family? From her successful sisters?

A click was her only warning before Dad answered. "Finally came to your senses and are ready to apologize for quitting?"

Lauren's stomach churned. "Hello to you, too, Dad."

"Is there a reason you called?"

Did a girl need a reason to talk to her father?

She clutched a pillow to herself and dug deep for courage. "I was calling to tell you that this time away from school has been very enlightening. And I've officially found my true passion."

"Passion? Not with some boy, I hope." Dad growled in her ear.

The memory of Joel's kisses distracted her for only a moment, but she focused on the brochures once again.

On the hope of what could be.

She squared her shoulders. "I've discovered the ideal place to use my talents, help people, stretch my creativity to overcome the challenges, and still enjoy what I'm doing."

"And what might that be?" His skepticism shook her confidence.

Lauren imagined standing in the middle of the dining room. Hearing the chatter of happy regulars and the strident debate of the old-timers at the lunch counter.

There was no ignoring the obvious truth anymore.

"My dream is to work at the diner." Hopefully for the rest of her life. Her dad coughed. "The w-w-what?"

She lifted her chin. "I've decided not to go back to the university in the fall."

"Hold on—"

"Instead, I'd like to take online business classes in the area of hospitality management." She blurted the words out in a rush.

"You've got to be kidding." He barked a laugh that ricocheted to her heart.

"Totally serious." She fanned out a few brochures. "I already found several reputable programs and that's without doing a lot of research into my options."

"You've changed interests so many times I don't see how this is any different."

She winced at that unfortunate truth.

"Give it another month or two and you'll be off doing something else."

"Not this time." Lauren shook her head even though he couldn't see her.

"It's just food and there are diners on every corner."

"Yes, everyone needs to eat. But the global hospitality industry ranks right up there with retail, energy, and tech. Why? Because taking care of people and meeting their needs matters."

She squeezed the pillow tighter. "You know I've been working at Dawson's Diner for years and I love it there. And since Frank's heart attack, the more I get a glimpse into the business side of things, the more I'm invested."

"Some investment. What have you got to show for it?"

"Friendship. Satisfaction. Pride in a job well done."

A family. Peace. The approval in Joel's eyes.

The reminder that Greta said she had a gift.

"But no money."

She sighed. "Maybe not as much as you'd like me to earn, but money can't buy happiness."

"But it helps when you have some." Dad huffed. "You're just like your mother."

Tears stung her eyes. "Perhaps. But she finds joy in doing what she loves instead of bending herself over backward trying to fit your mold of expectations."

Had she really just said that to her own dad?

Lauren held her breath.

He snorted. "Is that what you think happened?"

"That's how it felt." Her voice cracked. "How it feels now."

"That's ridiculous."

"Maybe to you." She blinked back the tears and visualized Joel standing beside her at the diner. "I've found where I belong and there's nothing that will make me change my mind."

"We'll see about that." Her dad disconnected the call.

Leaving those ominous words echoing in her ear like a threat.

Lauren sagged against the headboard, cradling the pillow and wishing Joel was there to comfort her.

She might have just lost her father's love.

And yet, truth be told, his approval had always been something out of reach. Something she'd turned herself inside out to get, while ignoring—and losing—her unique self in the process.

No more.

Dad might truly reject her for speaking her mind. Cut her off financially for charting her own course.

But there was no denying the burden that had lifted from her shoulders simply by acknowledging where she belonged.

Where she was created to serve.

A place where she had only her Heavenly Father to please.

And now, more than ever, she needed to do all she could to help the diner succeed. Because it was her only family now.

·♥·♥·♥·♥·♥·

A week after their grand re-opening, Lauren approached the new waiting area near the front door and scanned the faces for the right one. "Scott?"

The man with a John Deere hat stood and she handed him the plastic bag containing several take-out boxes. "Chicken-fried steak with mashed potatoes, side salad with ranch dressing, and a slice of apple pie. Your receipt is in the bag. Thank you for stopping by."

He peeked inside. "I picked up a cinnamon roll at the gas station last week and thought I should check out more of the menu."

"We appreciate the business." Lauren smiled.

Greta would love to know that her extra baking was paying off in more ways than one.

He exited, letting in a swirl of fresh almost-spring air. It could snow again tomorrow—that was Colorado weather even in late March—but for now, things were looking up.

Lauren surveyed the diner's fresh paint, sparkling windows, and the new bulletin board on the wall near the door. Colorful St. Patrick's Day pictures by last week's young artists were being voted on by other customers using multi-colored stars.

So many ideas had merged together in the past week, and based on the packed dining room—and many compliments on their new look—business was booming to the point they might need to hire that seventh crew member after all.

And with baseball season around the corner, it wouldn't be long before their team sponsorship created more awareness. Which reminded her they needed to create and deliver the diner logo for the banner.

Across the room, Joel deposited a handful of cleared dishes into the tub beneath the counter, then with cleaning supplies in hand, he paused to chat with a lunch regular.

In just a few hours, they'd be working on bookkeeping tasks instead of serving customers.

Her heart raced at the thought of potential kisses in the office.

No place she'd rather be than wherever Joel was.

The bells over the door clattered.

Lauren turned to greet the newcomers with a smile, but spotted her dad instead.

Her smile froze.

He'd never been here before.

In fact, she couldn't remember the last time he'd been back in town. Why now?

Unless he was here to make good on his threat to change her mind. But would he stoop to creating an embarrassing scene right here where she worked?

With dragging feet as if wading through a vat of mashed potatoes, Lauren moved toward the door.

He raised an eyebrow as his gaze swept over her.

She resisted the urge to swipe at the food specks on her apron. Her casual T-shirt and blue jeans fit the atmosphere better than his expensive suit and polished shoes.

"Welcome to Dawson's Diner." She fought to keep a light tone. "If you're dining alone, will a spot at the lunch counter be okay?"

They preferred saving the tables for larger groups whenever possible. He eyed the crowded room. "I guess that will do."

"Right this way." She concentrated on not tripping, even though she could almost feel his stare between her newly healed shoulder blades.

Tense conversations on the phone were one thing, but face to face brought new challenges. How was she supposed to honor her father when he thought her dream was a waste of time?

She passed Joel carrying a rag and spray bottle. Hopefully her face didn't show her stress.

Pretend Dad was just another customer. On just another Monday. If only it was that easy.

With gritted teeth, she led him to a stool near one end, then continued on behind the counter before facing him again.

She handed him a menu from the condiment rack. "Today's featured item is chicken fried steak, mashed potatoes, and either soup or salad. The soup-of-the-day is vegetable beef. Joel will be taking care of you, but can I start you with something to drink while you decide? Coffee or iced tea?"

"Water." He ignored the menu and swiveled to study the dining room instead.

Why did it matter what he thought?

Would he even know how much time she had spent helping fix it up after the accident or how many of her ideas had been used?

Never mind. She had other customers to serve.

She filled a glass with ice water and set it in front of him.

"We need to talk." Dad's voice rang with familiar authority.

"About what? My plans or your plans for me?" She winced.

Had she truly said that out loud?

"About your *lack* of plans and my plan to help get you on the right track."

She folded her arms and lowered her voice. "You can't make me change my mind about this. I'm not like you. I've tried for years to find a *respectable* degree and career you'd approve of, but they all bored me to tears. This—hospitality—is where I belong."

She gestured around the diner to where Clarissa laughed with an older man and Joel stretched over a table with a rag in his hand.

A true smile curved her lips. "I love interacting with people and brightening their days. Plus this is both mentally challenging and physical work, and since I've been doing this since I was in high school, I already know it won't get boring like the rest of the things I've tried."

Dad opened his mouth as if to interrupt.

She held up her hand. "You might think I'm a misfit, but I *fit* here. And this place is like a family."

"You have a family." He frowned.

"Not like this one. At least they didn't leave me behind." Her voice cracked. "Why can't you just love me for who I am?"

Dad blinked as if shocked by what she said, then his eyes narrowed.

She braced herself for the coming lecture.

"Hey, Lauren." Joel scooted behind her and tossed the rag and spray bottle onto their shelf. "Just seated a party of four at table twelve."

"Thanks." She relaxed.

Saved by the boss and the demands of a full dining room.

"Excuse me, young man, but—"

She pasted on a smile. "Joel, this is my father, Hugh Graham, who apparently stopped by to surprise me. Dad, this is Joel Dawson. He's using his MBA to manage his parents' business."

Take that, Dad, since you're so hung up on impressive degrees.

Joel reached out a muscular arm to shake hands. "Nice to meet you, sir."

Her dad's assessing gaze swept over Joel as he returned the handshake.

If Joel wasn't embarrassed to be working at the diner or feel the need to make excuses for wearing jeans to work, then neither should she.

"If you'll excuse me, I have customers to help." She hurried toward table twelve, but couldn't avoid the feeling she left unfinished business behind.

Was it wrong to be glad that the counter was part of Joel's section?

"Have you decided what you want?" Joel searched the man's face for similarities with his daughter.

Maybe they had the same eyes or mouth, except it was hard to tell with Mr. Graham's frown.

"I want my daughter to—"

"Did she tell you about the daily special?" Joel deliberately interrupted whatever the man was going to say.

He remembered enough of their previous talks about her past to know that the stress he'd just seen on her face was due to the man in front of him.

The man scowled and picked up the menu.

As he studied the options, Joel noticed the outward signs of financial success from the man's designer suit and silk tie to the expensive gold watch. Bet he had Italian leather shoes on his feet.

This man had the look Joel used to crave. The status symbols Desiree wanted for him. But the very thought now pinched his toes.

He was quite comfortable right where he stood, especially in the athletic shoes from the back of his closet.

Joel might not look like a successful businessman, but thanks to the article in the paper and the rest of their reopening ideas involving the community, profits over the past week were noticeably improved.

Looked like it was possible to succeed in business with a small-town mentality after all.

Mr. Graham set the menu aside. "I'll have a Reuben sandwich. With the soup of the day instead of fries."

"Coming right up." Joel retreated to input the order on the computer.

He'd barely hit send when his phone vibrated with an incoming text from Matt.

Have your invoice ready for whenever the insurance check arrives. In the meantime, I found something interesting in that antique buffet and will bring it by in the next day or two.

Seemed like a good-news-bad-news text.

Hopefully whatever Matt had found would erase the sting from the financial hit.

Then again, coloring pages and napkins storage didn't qualify as *interesting* in his book. Joel thought they'd emptied out the drawers before Matt hauled it away, but maybe they'd missed something?

Joel typed out a quick response. ***Way to be mysterious. Can't wait to see what you found.***

As he delivered food and processed a payment for other customers along the counter, his mind drifted between Matt's discovery and the way Mr. Graham kept watching Lauren.

And frowning as if he was disappointed in her.

What was the man's problem?

Was he letting his pursuit of financial success rob him of a relationship with his own daughter?

Joel grabbed a pitcher of ice water and moved down to start a conversation while he refilled the man's glass. "What brings you to town?"

"I've got meetings with potential clients over the next few days." Mr. Graham's narrowed eyes swept over Joel's T-shirt and jeans. "Do you really have an MBA or did she make that up?"

"Fresh off the press. I graduated in December and came home to help out."

"Oh yeah. My daughter said something about the owner getting sick." He laughed. "Bet you can't wait to get out of here so you can actually use what you learned. You're wasting your degree just like my daughter is wasting her life."

Joel shook his head. "That's what I used to think, but it's not true."

"What? You can't be serious."

"Very." He looked around the diner. "I've learned more here about running a business than in all my classes and internships combined."

"Here?" Mr. Graham's eyebrows rose. "That's crazy."

Joel heard the sliding of a plate along the pass-through window's ledge and turned to collect the meal and his thoughts. As long as the other customers in his section were okay for now, he had time to talk.

He delivered Mr. Graham's meal and a bundle of silverware. "In the corporate world, many of the aspects of business become fragmented into separate departments that end up fighting each other for additional resources and lose sight of the big picture. But here, the diner has all the essential pieces under one roof."

"Like what?" Mr. Graham dipped his spoon into the soup and blew away the steam.

"We procure raw materials at the best wholesale price available and arrange delivery to our storage facility—the cooler, freezer, and storeroom in the back." He jerked a thumb back over his shoulder toward the kitchen. "We also have a production facility where the raw ingredients are processed and assembled into a finished product along with a bit of quality control, also known as taste-testing."

Joel rubbed a hand over his stomach and licked his lips. "That's one of my favorite parts."

Mr. Graham swallowed a bite of his sandwich and smiled. "I think I see what you mean. This is delicious."

"But having a superior product at a low cost per serving doesn't mean anything without a sales team and distribution system." He pointed to where Clarissa wrote down orders at one table and Lauren carried an armload of filled plates.

Mr. Graham followed Joel's finger and his eyes widened before he nodded.

"There's marketing through the daily specials, an article in the paper, a coloring contest, or selling our cinnamon rolls at a local gas station. Human resources department to hire new help. Payroll. Facility maintenance and janitorial services. And the usual financial reporting like profit margins, taxes, accounts receivable, and accounts payable." Joel ticked the points off on his fingers.

Lauren's dad just stared.

Joel folded his arms over his chest. "We do it all. And while profit margins are historically slim for the food industry, I've enjoyed the challenge of making small improvements."

His heart beat double time. He'd set out to defend the diner and just proved to himself that he was in charge of a real business. The whole thing.

No way could he go back to focusing on only one aspect.

And he wouldn't be where he was now without Lauren's help.

Or the additional creativity of the rest of his staff.

This place had truly become a home away from home with a family he enjoyed spending time with.

Joel studied the man chewing slowly as if lost in thought about the merits of a diner as a legitimate business.

Time to close the deal and get the man to stop frowning at his daughter.

Joel propped his hands on the edge of the counter. "Lauren said you're in sales."

Her dad straightened on the stool. "Was. I'm the new Deputy Chief Financial Officer." He rattled off the name of a prestigious software company Joel would have bent over backward to get hired by a few months ago.

"Then you know firsthand that the financial success of the company depends as much on creating a quality, groundbreaking product as it does on a dynamic sales force. But the heart of good business is always customer service, right?"

"Of course." Mr. Graham wiped his mouth with his napkin.

"Take another look at your daughter." He pointed to a nearby booth where Lauren visited with two older couples.

She leaned over to point out something on one of the menus, said something that made the women chuckle, and jotted a note on her pad.

"Does that look like good customer service to you?"

The man watched the interaction for a moment, a look of pride dawning on his face. "It does."

"She's the best salesperson we've got. Not only that. She's a marketing genius. Most of our reopening ideas were hers. She was made for this and I couldn't run the diner without her."

The hint of a smile played around Mr. Graham's lips. "You seem to know my daughter quite well. Anything else I should know about?"

"About her work here?"

Or something more personal like how she preferred classic movies, was addicted to caffeine, or could devour ice cream for any and all occasions. Or maybe that she had hilariously adorable reactions to prescription pain medication?

Her dad smirked. "Like your intentions?"

Joel's heart skipped a beat. Because he definitely had some.

Not only to turn the diner business around and someday run it for himself, but also to claim Lauren as his own.

But he'd just met the man.

Was it too soon to chase those dreams?

Or just too soon to tell her father?

Chapter Twenty-Two

♥

Exhausted and yet energized after such a strange Monday at the diner, Joel had barely stepped over the threshold into his parents' house when his mom stumbled through the doorway of the kitchen.

She stared at the floor rather than making eye contact, her hands fisted, white knuckled, in her red-plaid apron.

An uneasy feeling settled in his gut.

He toed off his tennis shoes and left them in the entryway before padding closer. "Is something wrong with dad?"

She shook her head. "He's resting after his therapy session. Dinner should be ready in about half an hour."

"Okay..." He inhaled the aroma of Italian seasonings with heavy garlic overtones.

A combination that usually made his mouth water in anticipation of her manicotti. A dish she normally reserved for his birthday. Or...

Joel raised his eyebrows. "Are you trying to butter me up?"

Mom lifted glassy eyes to stare somewhere behind him. "There's something we need to discuss as a family."

Tension knotted between his shoulder blades, but he knew better than to push for answers before they were ready to talk.

His parents were masters at presenting a united front. And if Mom had made his favorite meal, they obviously had a strategy in place for the coming conversation.

He'd have to be patient. Or at least try.

Joel forced a smile to his lips. "I'll just take a quick shower and be back to help set the table."

Mom nodded, then retreated to the kitchen.

Leaving Joel with a racing pulse as he headed down the hall to his room for a change of clean clothes.

What on earth did they need to talk about?

Dad had been getting stronger and could even be cleared next week to come back part-time. Then again, Mom had implied Dad wasn't the issue.

And while the business finances had been tight enough to cause Joel sleepless nights, they'd definitely turned a corner after last week's reopening.

Joel was reaching for the soap when a different idea struck.

His parents probably wanted him to take over the diner in a more official capacity for the long term and thought he'd argue.

Didn't they know his feelings toward the diner had changed?

He smiled as he stood under the hot water.

Inheriting the family legacy was better than simply having his own business someday. Even more so if he could run the diner with Lauren by his side and pass it on to their children.

He imagined a dark-haired boy with Lauren's smile and the pressure around his heart increased until he felt he might explode with anticipation.

At their current income projections, he could finally collect a full paycheck next week and start looking for a ring.

Once dressed, he headed back to the kitchen, setting the table while his mom slid a tray of buttered bread under the broiler.

Dad shuffled into the room with his cane and took a seat.

Joel turned from the sink with a pitcher of ice water in time to catch his mom's glance between Joel and his dad before she turned away, brushing at her cheek.

His heart stuttered.

Mom had implied otherwise, but did Dad have a bad doctor's appointment after all?

Once the meal was on the table and everyone seated, Joel bowed his head.

"God, thank you for this food." Dad's voice cracked. "Please provide for our needs and give us wisdom in the days ahead. Amen."

Joel glanced up to see tears running down Dad's cheeks. And Mom's.

God? What's going on here?

Soon Joel had a plate of cheese-stuffed pasta and garlic bread. He picked up his fork and took a bite, but his favorite flavors could not soothe the tension building in the room.

Knowing the truth had to be better than imagining some awful new diagnosis.

He swallowed hard. "Whatever you wanted to talk about seems bad. Just cut to the chase."

Mom cleared her throat. "We're going to have to sell the diner."

"What?" Joel dropped his fork. Anything but that. "Why?"

His gaze darted between his parents who now held hands on top of the table.

"It's time to admit the truth." Mom stiffened her shoulders.

Shoulders that had borne too many burdens lately.

Dad avoided eye contact. "The doctors said the stress was killing me, so I'm not going to be able to run the business, at least the way I used to."

Joel shook his head. "But, I can keep running it for you."

Please, God, don't let them take away the diner.

"Your dad is trying to make the best of this." Mom squeezed Dad's hand. "While we hope he can find another type of work in the future and be independent enough that I can get a job too, we need both a regular income and—"

Joel pushed his plate aside. "If this is about your salaries, we can keep paying them."

Mom pinned him to his seat with her frown. "I accidentally opened your bank statement. We know you're not paying yourself what you've earned and that's got to stop."

"I hoped you wouldn't find out. Considered it my room and board to be paying you instead." He glanced between the two of them. "But we've had an uptick in foot traffic over the last week and now not only can I rebuild the rainy-day fund but pay myself too."

Dad took a deep breath and raised red-rimmed eyes. "If it was only our salaries, we might be able to hold on. But without a tenant in the other half of the building, we're losing more on taxes and insurance. And now there's a mountain of medical bills coming due."

"Isn't that what health insurance is for?"

Dad snorted. "We've got a super-high deductible plan because that's all we could afford to carry. And not everything was covered or in-network. Plus they only cover a certain number of therapy appointments. I reached the end of those weeks ago, but since my doctor insists I keep going for a while, we're paying full price in addition to outrageous prescription costs."

Mom huffed. "He's on four different heart medications and even with insurance, they're running at least two hundred dollars a month. But therapy's almost a hundred a visit."

Joel nodded slowly. "How much are the other bills?"

Dad hung his head. "We need fifteen thousand dollars in three weeks or else they'll send it to collections. And we've already tapped into most of our emergency savings for therapy and medicine."

The bleak picture came into focus. "So you truly need a lump sum now, but why sell the diner? Why not sell—"

Dad reached into his pocket and pulled out a business card with a familiar logo.

But unlike the crumpled version Joel had left on the floor after Matt's warning, this one was pristine.

Joel's stomach churned, stealing more of his appetite.

Dad sighed. "This guy showed up here at the house just over a week ago. I'd been meaning to talk Greta into selling our uncle's side of the building somehow, but Mr. Ridge wants the whole thing."

Letting go of the vacant half was a good option, but Joel had no idea if the property title could be split without hiring a lawyer whose hourly rate they'd never afford.

But wouldn't that be better than losing the diner too?

Dad reached for Mom's hand. "Unfortunately, it's time for this chapter to close. I'm still getting stronger so I plan on going back to work somewhere. Somehow. But we need the money now."

The brutal truth slammed Joel between the eyes.

Other than their house and the tiny retirement account he'd pestered them into opening a few years ago, everything else was tied up in the diner business and the building.

Dad stared down at his plate in defeat.

Joel's mind scrambled for ideas, even ones he'd normally avoid. "What about a loan? Couldn't you borrow against—"

"We thought about it." Mom grasped Joel's arm as if pleading for him to understand. "We can't borrow against the building without putting Greta's share at risk. We've also considered getting a second mortgage on this house or a loan against the business in order to pay off the medical bills, but no matter what collateral we use, there's still the problem of making those payments on top of our normal living expenses."

Dad wrapped an arm around his wife. "Even if the hospital agreed to a payment plan instead of us taking out a personal loan, that's still another five hundred dollars a month on top of everything else."

The harsh reality of their budget came into focus. There always had to be income to offset expenses.

Joel picked up his fork and poked at the cooling food on his plate.

A meal he'd thought held so much promise served only to destroy his dreams.

They ate in silence for a few minutes.

At last, Dad wiped his face with his napkin and sat back. "I have to think about the future. I'm not getting any younger and all of our money is tied to that building and the diner equipment. We could try to sell just the business itself, but if we sell it all, we can pay the bills and have enough left over for a fresh start."

Real estate transactions were fairly straight-forward, but selling a business was more complicated.

Joel's mind spun as he tried to calculate the business' net worth and potential valuation for a sale.

His parents owned all of the equipment and most of the building—which eliminated a rent expense—but they also legally owned the liabilities of other business expenses including utilities, insurance, food deliveries, employee payroll, and taxes.

Stoves were worth money. But so was the customer base.

Joel took a long drink of water and tried to settle his thoughts.

The best outcome would be a lump sum from selling the business plus ongoing income from renting the building... that could still be sold at some point in the future.

But either way the diner would change hands.

Mom stacked their empty plates. "We hate to undo all of your hard work keeping the diner running this year, but we're thankful because it wouldn't be worth as much if it had fallen apart."

All of his long hours with nothing to show for it. Guess he should have paid himself after all.

Regret wound bitter tentacles around his heart.

He shook his head. No, he had done this for his parents. To honor them.

Even if he walked away with nothing.

Lord, help me continue to honor them. Even in this.

Mom scooted back from the table and stood. "We wanted to tell you our decision before telling Greta."

Joel straightened. "Wait a minute. Doesn't she have a say in this? After all her parents ran the diner too."

Dad grunted. "I bought the assets years ago by myself. Greta inherited half of the vacant side when Mom's brother died without heirs. But the diner side of the building is all mine while Greta got Mom's house."

Mom sat back down. "Greta's emotionally invested and could lose her job if the new owner doesn't keep the staff, but legally it's our decision to make."

He winced.

Not just Greta, but Lauren and the others were about to lose their jobs, too.

Was it too late to do anything to stop this train wreck?

Joel propped his elbows on the table. "Have you already contacted a business broker or Realtor? Or are you just going to give it all to that shady developer guy? Because I don't see him keeping a restaurant in that space."

Not with what Matt had shared about the man's reputation. Or the man's own words about profits.

"We're not taking the first offer if that's what you mean. But yes." Mom glanced at Dad whose shoulders slumped as if making their decision official had killed him inside. "A Realtor will stop by to take a closer look at the property either tomorrow or the day after."

"So soon?" Joel buried his face in his hands as his dream slipped further away.

Dad folded his arms over his stomach. "The sooner it's listed, the sooner we can find a buyer, and the sooner we can close."

"I wish I could buy it." Joel's voice broke.

It was a truth he'd acknowledged too late.

Tears filled Mom's eyes. "We wish we could give it to you since it would be part of your inheritance anyway, but we can't."

Joel eyed them both, willing to beg if necessary. "Can you put it all off—including telling Aunt Greta—for a few days just to see what I can come up with?"

His mom's smile faded, as if he was a fool for ever thinking it was possible.

Joel glanced at Dad. Was that a spark of hope in his eye?

Or maybe a tear.

Hard to tell with his own emotions swirling like a tornado.

"Excuse me." Joel pushed away from the table with dinner sitting like rancid bacon in his stomach.

He needed space to process the horrible news, and thinking came best while running. After changing into workout gear, he slipped out the front door, leaving his parents still talking in the kitchen.

His feet pounded the pavement as thoughts pummeled his brain.

People's jobs were on the line. Their livelihood. Customers would lose their favorite spot to meet friends over pie and coffee. So much history within those walls, including a few stolen and not-so-stolen kisses in the storage room.

His great-grandparents' legacy passed down to his grandparents and on to his father... and now sold to the highest bidder.

It wasn't right.

Then again, his parents never saw the heart attack coming either.

Their future had drowned under a mountain of medical bills and they must put their business on the market before it cost their home as well. Because if the bills ended up in collections, those sharks didn't play around with compounding interest and late fees.

Blood rushed through his body and brain.

What about him? What about his dreams?

If only he could come up with the money somehow.

Depending on the valuation, he'd still have to qualify for a loan that size without collateral... and then spend years paying off the debt. It would always be touch-and-go to make payments from the diner profits without cutting into his living expenses too much. Or sacrificing a future family.

He turned toward home. He needed a computer to do the research and number crunching.

What would his professors have said about investing in a business right now?

They'd say he was crazy to be thinking about it and encourage him to pursue a real job with a six-figure income.

His pace slowed.

If he landed the kind of position he'd been searching for in January, he could earn enough to pay back a loan in a reasonable amount of time and leave Lauren in charge to manage the diner in his absence.

While he couldn't imagine being apart every day, it might save the day temporarily.

But, until he knew for sure, he couldn't let her know her job might end.

Not if he had a chance to save it.

Lauren placed the coffee pot on the warmer and nudged Joel's ribs. "Maybe we should charge Roy and Dennis for a pot rather than a cup."

Joel mumbled something and stepped away to pick up the cleaning rag.

In fact, he had avoided close contact most of the morning.

"What's your problem?" She leaned closer.

He scrubbed the already clean counter. "What are you talking about?"

"You're a grump."

"I didn't get much sleep last night." He fought a yawn.

"Is that why you were here so early?"

"How can you know what time I arrived? You weren't even here yet." His joke fell flat and his eyes seemed sad before he glanced around as if looking for a reason to escape.

"Whatever." She rolled her eyes. Oh no. His attitude was catching. "When you're ready to tell the truth about what's bugging you, you know where to find me."

"Yes, I came in early to do some stuff on the computer. But there's nothing for you to worry about."

"But plenty for you to carry alone?" She shook her head before trying for a semi-dramatic exit. Except she had nowhere to go.

Not that she wanted to get away from him anyway.

She just wished he trusted her enough to share his burdens.

Lauren blinked back unexpected tears.

After her dad's surprise visit to the diner yesterday, she could have used Joel's support and encouragement. Then again, maybe Dad had said something to turn Joel against her.

Maybe even reminded him of all the more lucrative opportunities Joel sacrificed by working at the diner.

Well, two could play the avoidance game.

Several tiring hours later, she flipped the sign to closed and began the daily cleaning and stocking routine while Joel disappeared through the kitchen doors with the money tray and receipts.

Good riddance.

Still, by the time she gave Clarissa the okay to leave, Lauren wanted to reconnect.

Her heart rebelled at the awkward distance between them.

God only knew what Joel's problem was, but at least she could be a supportive girlfriend while giving him space to think about whatever had distracted him all day.

She entered the kitchen to find the delivery man wheeling a dolly load of boxes in through the open back door under Joel's supervision.

Somehow she'd managed to forget the day of the week.

Lauren reached for the clipboard holding the invoice so she could check off the arriving items while the other staff started putting things away.

Like they usually did.

Except Joel moved the clipboard out of reach. "I've got this. Why don't you finish preparing the deposit instead?"

Lauren stepped back in shock. "Alone?"

They usually did that together, too.

"Why not? I trust you."

He trusted her with the money, but not his problems?

She swallowed her hurt and turned away.

Across the kitchen, Greta watched them with a puzzled frown.

Escaping into the office, Lauren shut the door before sitting in Joel's chair behind the desk. Mentally reviewing the checklist of things she and Joel did—together—every afternoon, she tried to pick up where he'd left off.

First, she needed to see what, if anything, had been entered into the ledger. She wiggled the mouse to awaken the computer monitor and the screen came to life.

But instead of the accounting program, she found an email inbox. For Joel's personal address rather than messages for the diner.

Sliding the mouse toward the red X in the corner to close the window, she caught a glimpse of a familiar picture in the signature line of the open message.

Her breath caught in her throat.

Why was Joel reading an email from his ex-girlfriend?

Was he cheating? Hoping for a second chance with his past?

No. This was from the woman's professional account.

Which could only mean...

Nausea churned as Lauren began to read.

Chapter Twenty-Three

♥

L auren's hand shook as she scrolled through the email displayed on the diner's computer screen.

She should feel guilty for reading Joel's private messages—and maybe she would later—but for now she could only register shock.

And horror.

For there in black and white was his ex-girlfriend's blatant glee at learning he was requesting consideration for her company's next round of interviews.

An ache grew in the back of her throat.

Lauren started to close the message, hoping to erase the truth.

Only to see the open window beneath it with a message from her dad's company.

She clicked to that window, then struggled to draw in a full breath as she read the words acknowledging the receipt of Joel's resume.

It was mostly a form letter response.

Except for the mention of a possible recommendation from Mr. Graham.

Was Dad helping Joel find a job? Was that Dad's twisted way to remove the diner's added appeal for her?

Lauren didn't recognize the name in the signature line, but that didn't change the facts.

Coupled with the still-visible picture of his ex-girlfriend at the end of her email, Joel was seriously job-shopping.

He'd be leaving.

No wonder he'd been avoiding her.

A wave of nausea cramped her midsection.

Was that why Joel wanted her to do the bookwork today? Because he'd be gone and she'd need to take over?

Had he meant for her to find this open email? After all, he'd been the one to send her in here to work on the deposit.

Could this be his way of breaking the news without having to actually say the words?

Just like her dad, slipping away in the night and leaving Mom to make the announcement.

She shook her head. "Joel, you're a coward."

"I'm a what?"

Lauren pulled her gaze from the screen to find the traitor standing in the doorway. Lost in thought, she hadn't heard the door open.

And now he'd heard something she never should have said aloud. Except...

"When were you going to tell me?" She waved a trembling hand at the screen.

"Tell you what?" His eyes widened as he glanced from her to the computer. "If this is about the payroll, I can explain—"

"Payroll?" She tilted her head.

He blinked several times.

She narrowed her eyes. "What else have you been keeping from me?"

"Look, I know I promised you that I'd pay myself a full wage, but things were tight, so..."

Her stomach rolled. "You lied to me. And now you're quitting."

How much more could she take before losing control?

"Quitting? Never." He shook his head as he approached the desk. "You're being ridiculous."

She could have laughed off his assessment last month, but now that she knew he had lied...

Her battered heart ripped in half.

No doubt about what he really thought of her.

Just a silly diversion to pass the time before he left.

She forced air into her lungs. "I knew better than to hope you could truly care about me. This was never going to work between us, was it?"

He stopped at the edge of the desk and silently stared at her.

Probably searching for another lie to offer.

"Whatever's wrong, I'm sure I can explain—"

"Never mind, I'll save you the trouble." She stood and headed to her locker to claim her purse. "It's been fun while it lasted, but now it's back to the real world. Right, Boss?"

"Where do you think you're going?"

"Home." Except that she had no home to call her own either.

"But, we still have work to do."

"Do it yourself." She avoided his outstretched hand and skirted out the doorway, holding back the rising tears until she reached the parking lot.

Seemed she'd be looking for a new job herself.

Too many memories here.

Joel stared at the empty doorway.

What just happened?

He ran a hand through his hair as he tried to recall the scene.

The woman he loved had called him a quitting coward and walked away with a look in her eye that shouted how much he'd let her down.

True, he'd kept his small paycheck a secret from her, but she'd been mad earlier in the day. Because he'd been quieter than usual?

That's what he got for trying to protect her.

What should he have said? 'Good morning, beautiful. By the way, we're all about to lose our jobs.'

Or 'Let's put away this order together so we can kiss in the closet one last time for old times' sake before Dad sells the diner.'

He dropped the clipboard onto the desktop beside the cash drawer she obviously hadn't finished processing.

What exactly had she been doing while he checked in the delivery?

And who said she got to leave him with all the work? To think she'd accused him of carrying it alone, then walked out when he needed her help.

He gritted his teeth.

Maybe a fresh start would be a good thing for his health... and his bank account.

He rounded the end of the desk and spotted the computer monitor with his email account open on the screen. Instead of inputting receipts, he'd been reading email when the delivery guy knocked on the back door.

And the main message on the screen...

A groan rose from his toes as he plopped into the chair and stared at the incriminating words. If he had Mr. Graham's personal recommendation, they looked forward to working with him in the future.

He buried his face in his hands.

She was right. He hadn't trusted her with the truth, so now she logically thought he couldn't wait to leave and that he might use her dad as his golden ticket.

The same man who had hurt her before.

And beneath that email was the very visible face of his ex-girlfriend in the signature line from her company's human resources department.

Then Joel had stupidly brought up the payroll lie that she hadn't even known about.

No wonder she'd stormed out of here.

So, how would she react when it came out that he'd known she would lose her job and didn't tell her?

Joel massaged his temples. "I'm an idiot."

"What did you do this time?"

He stared at Aunt Greta in the doorway.

The teasing twinkle in her eyes faded into concern. "And why did Lauren bolt out of here?"

"You'd better take a seat." He sighed as he slumped back in the chair.

"That bad?" Aunt Greta pulled over another chair.

He took a deep breath. "I asked Mom and Dad for a few days to come with a solution before they told you, but—"

"You're leaving." She folded her arms over her chest. "No wonder—"

"Hold on." He held up his hands to stop her.

Couldn't anyone see that he'd had a change of heart and wanted to stay? Yet, that was the least of their problems.

He sighed. "There's no easy way to say this. Mom and Dad said they are going to sell the diner."

"The what?" Color faded from Aunt Greta's face as her hands dropped to her sides.

"The diner. The business and all the equipment and maybe even the building too." He rubbed a hand over his face.

"Why?" She groaned. "Let me guess. Medical bills. I wondered how they were doing but Frank refused to talk about it."

"I didn't know either. Then again, I was so busy keeping us in the black here that I never got around to asking."

If only he'd known, he might have been able to...

To what? Know he'd failed earlier? Not gotten so attached to this place?

He studied the room that held so many teenage memories of his father behind the desk and more recently working with Lauren.

Change hurt.

"I assume they've—" Aunt Greta's voice cracked.

"Considered all their options. Yes." He cleared his throat. "Even if they got a loan or worked out a plan to pay off the medical bills, they'd still need extra income to make those payments. And Dad's not ready to take on a second job when he hasn't been able to do the first. No matter how you look at it, this place is their primary asset."

Aunt Greta's shoulders slumped. "So, you told Lauren?"

"Not exactly." He pressed fingers against his tired eyes. "I spent half the night trying to come up with ways to borrow enough to buy it myself. Even considered getting a different job that pays more while Lauren runs things for me here."

He waved one hand toward the computer monitor. "She found a couple emails I forgot to close from earlier and knows I'm looking elsewhere."

"And probably thinks you're walking out just like her dad. Poor girl." Aunt Greta shook her head and mumbled something he couldn't understand.

Poor girl? Lauren didn't even give him enough credit to believe he wouldn't leave her.

Then again, why should she stay?

Couldn't get the diner profitable enough to support his parents and *all* the employees including himself. Hadn't saved enough money during college so he'd have a sizeable nest egg to invest, and couldn't qualify for a personal loan without collateral.

His family's legacy would be eliminated with the sale of the diner. People would lose their jobs. And there was nothing he could do to stop it.

To top it off, his girlfriend walked out because she thought he was a quitting coward, even while he tried to save their future.

Except she didn't know the truth because he hadn't trusted her enough to tell her.

Joel slouched in the chair. "Like I said, I'm an idiot. I let her down just like everyone else around here. I can't manage everything anymore."

"When I am weak, He is strong." Aunt Greta's voice trembled as she quoted the familiar scripture and her shoulders straightened. "God's got this covered."

"What?"

"Did you pray about a solution or are you still trying to do it all by yourself?" She stood. "You know, it's okay to ask for help when you need it. Unless you're enjoying this pity party, you might want to try something new. And you've only failed when you stop trying."

What he really wanted was to go for a run and leave this whole mess far behind.

Lauren stumbled in the door of Greta's house and headed for the kitchen with her carton of ice cream.

She needed a spoon and then the chocolate therapy could begin.

She'd gotten her hopes up and started dreaming about a future running the diner with Joel... while he'd still been dreaming about a real job somewhere else.

Did he think she'd give up her dream to follow him?

Would he have asked?

No, he couldn't trust her. After all this time, he still saw her as a giggling girl with a hopeless crush on a guy out of her league.

You're being ridiculous.

She grabbed a spoon, slammed the drawer shut, and sank to the linoleum floor before removing the paper lid and licking off the sweet residue.

Her creativity and curiosity were too much for him and he couldn't take her seriously.

The wooden cabinet doors bit into her back as she dug into the frozen lump of chocolate.

After all her sacrifices and hard work, she had nothing. She'd even dropped out of her boring college classes to spend more time at the diner.

Thought she had finally found her place and set boundaries with her dad... but only set herself up for more rejection.

The icy treat melted on her tongue while tears flooded her eyes.

Now she really was ridiculous. Who cried over a boy who wasn't worth it?

Except, Joel was amazing and funny and handsome and everything her heart longed for.

Until he decided to leave.

She scooped another bite, pulled out her phone, and called Julie.

Every pity party needed another ear.

But when Julie answered, Lauren let her best friend chat for a while about all she was learning in her classes. And about breaking up with her boyfriend but already spending time with another.

Julie sighed over the line. "There could be complications, but then again, I might not be here long enough to find out."

Lauren swallowed her latest scoop and winced at the brain freeze. "What? Why would you quit?"

"Not voluntarily, for sure. Mom's worried about my tuition if they don't get a new tenant for the old drugstore soon. Right now she's not making tips at the diner either."

Oh. Maybe Lauren should insist on paying more to rent Julie's room.

"Enough about me. How was *your* day?" Julie sounded extra cheerful, almost like she was faking it. Or glad for a subject change.

Lauren dropped her spoon into the much-reduced container. "What if I told you I'm curled up on your mom's kitchen floor with a quart of triple chocolate fudge ripple between my knees?"

"That bad, huh? What did he do?"

Lauren snorted.

Julie knew her well enough to know that only boy problems warranted triple ripple therapy. They'd shared several break-up splurges through the years, but nothing compared to the betrayal she felt now.

Lauren adjusted her position against the uncomfortable cabinets. "I found a couple email messages on the computer at work. He's asking about job openings in Denver and somehow got my dad to vouch for him. And he even applied at the same company where his glamorous ex-girlfriend works and she's super-excited to see him again."

"Ouch."

"He's leaving." Her voice cracked.

So much for love and happily-ever-afters.

"Did you ask him to explain? There has to be a reason." Julie sounded as confused as Lauren felt.

"No. He'd been quiet all day like he was hiding something. Once I figured it out, I headed straight for the ice cream." She took another bite but it soured in her mouth.

"Hmm. So you left first?"

"I didn't want to get hurt, but it's too late for that." She set the half-eaten carton on the floor beside her.

Should she have handled things differently?

Except it seemed he'd also lied to her about the payroll for weeks.

"Is he worth fighting for?" Julie's sigh whispered through the phone.

"Only if he thought *I'm* worth fighting for. But no, he thinks I'm being ridiculous."

"Uh-oh. The r-word." Julie paused. "How many times do I have to tell you that you're not a misfit. You're creative and spontaneous."

"Some call that flighty and immature."

"And friendly."

"Chatty." Lauren stuck her tongue out at the phone as if Julie could see her.

"Stop. You are fearfully and wonderfully made by God's design. It's not an accident or a mistake."

"I know." Lauren leaned her head back against the cabinets and closed her eyes.

When all else failed, her faith remained. And if God had a plan for her life, then He had made her this way on purpose.

Even if she didn't understand why.

And even if the people she loved rejected her because of it.

"Do you?"

Tears welled behind Lauren's eyelids. "I'm trying to believe it."

"Try harder."

She laughed at her friend's blunt tone. "Okay. My creativity is a gift. I am unique—"

"And valuable and lovable just as you are."

"So, don't change a thing?" She bit her lower lip.

"Nope. Embrace who you are... and someday someone special will embrace it too." Julie sounded wistful as if she hoped the same for herself.

Lauren choked back a sob.

She thought she'd found that special someone in Joel.

And that glimpse of all that could have been only made her current heartbreak that much worse.

Enough to have her picking up the carton once again.

Chapter Twenty-Four

♥

With muscles burning and lungs screaming, Joel's feet slapped against the pavement as he kept trying to outrun his scrambled emotions.

Left foot, right foot.

Left, right.

He was a failure.

A coward.

A quitter.

A weakling who couldn't help his parents save their diner.

He brushed the sweat from his forehead and turned onto the path that wound through the neighborhood park.

All those years of college education had met the real world and fallen into a heap of trash like a mountain of rotting potato peelings.

And by hiding the truth from Lauren—by trying to be the hero sweeping in to save the day—he'd hurt her.

Reminded her of her father's rejection.

As if she didn't matter.

As if she couldn't help him with real problems.

But what could she do besides listen to him rant about being a failure when all he'd ever wanted was success?

Puffing for breath, he slowed his pace a bit.

The only one hearing him rant now was God.

"God I can't do this. I could have had my dream, but now it's all going to disappear."

All of it?

No, he'd still have his family and his parents would still have their home.

He'd still have the practical knowledge he'd gained from his months of work.

Topped by everything he'd learned about serving from Lauren.

Lauren.

The ache inside reached deeper than his devastation over losing the diner.

Her fun, spontaneous and fresh way of looking at life made every day an adventure, and he needed her in his life, especially to balance out his obsession with numbers.

He'd give anything to go back and redo the last twenty-four hours.

To figure out a way to succeed.

What was it Lauren had said about success? Doing what he was uniquely created to do and serving others in the process.

And serving certainly wasn't the dirty job he used to think. After all Jesus, the King of Kings, washed feet and that had to be worse than chopping onions and washing dishes.

And wasn't there another verse somewhere that said whatever he did for others was like doing it for God?

That meant providing their customers with a friendly oasis in a stress-filled world mattered. And serving God that way also meant trusting Him to provide for his needs and that of the future family he'd started dreaming of.

The pounding on the pavement found a new rhythm.

Joel was made to run a business and every day he kept the diner open was a success.

But even if his gifts for the task came from God, he still needed direction.

I could use some divine wisdom about now. All I see are closing doors but I know You've got a plan in all this. Plans for hope and a future. So show me what to do. And help me fix things with Lauren.

If only he hadn't left his phone at home, he'd call her right now. Explain his thinking, apologize for not trusting her with the truth of his insecurities, and beg for her forgiveness.

Beg for her help.

If he could ask God for wisdom, surely he could ask Lauren to help carry his burden, just like she'd offered to earlier.

Then they could face their uncertain future together.

Feeling stronger, he turned for home.

Lauren had a gift for the people-side of the business. Maybe they could brainstorm ideas and solutions together like they had after the truck accident?

Maybe she had a better idea than his random scheme to work somewhere else for a while as a way to buy the diner.

But wherever they ended up when the dust settled, he was better off with her beside him than alone with his pride for trying to succeed by himself.

Aunt Greta's earlier words came flooding back. God had it covered, because when Joel was weak, then God showed Himself strong.

A few steps later, another layer of truth filtered through his cluttered thinking.

If he was going to sacrifice long hours working for the diner, he'd rather it be *at* the diner and *not* for another company.

Peace settled around his heart.

He wouldn't look for another job until no other options remained.

If he were a gambler, one could say he was going all in. Pushing all his chips to the center of the table.

Spotting the last turn for home ahead, Joel picked up the pace again.

He had started his run feeling like a failure, but like Aunt Greta said, he hadn't really failed unless he quit.

God, I'm going to keep serving at the diner until the end, but I sure could use a few ideas.

Lauren swirled her spoon in the melting mass of ice cream as she mentally replayed her conversation with Julie.

Why had she let her insecurities assume the worst about the best guy who'd ever come into her life?

Maybe he hadn't been making fun of her or trying to get rid of her.

Maybe he had a good reason for not telling her he'd talked to her dad about a new job.

Not that any such reason existed on the planet, but she should at least have made him say it plainly instead of running away to pout.

Better to know the truth than to wonder.

And hadn't he offered to explain?

She picked up her phone, then heard the garage door open. Talking to Joel would be difficult enough without his aunt around to eavesdrop.

Lauren rose to her feet and stuck her melting ice cream in the freezer.

Greta came through the door with a sack of groceries, then pulled the same flavor of chocolate therapy out of the bag.

Lauren moved away from the freezer. "Did you get that for me? Did Joel tell you—"

"He told me all right." Greta went to the cabinets for a bowl and a spoon. "And this is for me."

Lauren froze in place. "You? Why are you upset that Joel and I had a fight?"

"Because I stuck around long enough to find out that Frank and Nancy are planning to sell the diner."

"They what!" Lauren slapped a hand across her chest and collapsed against the counter. "They can't. They wouldn't."

Surely she had misunderstood.

Greta lifted a scoop of ice cream toward the bowl, paused, detoured the bite into her mouth, then left the empty bowl behind as she headed for the kitchen table.

It must be true.

Julie's mom never ate out of the carton.

Lauren sank onto a chair across from Greta.

"After I left work, I called Nancy myself." Greta swallowed another bite. "They need the cash to pay the medical bills—both now and ongoing—and are making tough decisions about their future. It's not an easy place to be. I should know."

True. After her husband's accident, coma, and eventual death, the mountain of debts had forced Greta to sell her house and move her and Julie in with Hope.

Forcing her to go back to work while her retired mother kept an eye on a teenager.

And even Greta's later inheritances didn't guarantee financial security, not if Julie was worried she'd have to quit school.

Poor Greta had lost her husband, her home, her freedom. Eventually her mother. And now?

She was about to lose her job.

Because Frank and Nancy's tough decision was to close the place they loved.

That *she* loved.

"So Joel knew and didn't say anything?" Lauren rubbed her temples as the potential consequences swirled in her mind.

"He found out last night and tried to adjust to the news himself."

"Guess he couldn't bear to tell us."

After the hours they had invested to keep the diner going and then reopened, he would know how upset everyone would be. How disappointed she would be.

A weight settled on Lauren's chest. "No wonder he was so quiet today."

Greta speared her with a stare. "He had some hair-brained thought to get another job somewhere else so he could make enough to buy it himself."

At least she wasn't the only one with crazy ideas.

The rest of Greta's words sank in.

Joel wanted to tie himself to the diner for good. That didn't sound like someone wanting to leave after all. And he certainly wasn't a quitter if he was willing to work even harder to keep the diner.

Guess he had a very good reason to look for another job after all.

Which also meant he hadn't rejected her. Yet.

But he could. Still might after the way she'd reacted.

Overreacted.

She groaned. "I'm an idiot."

Greta laughed. "That's what he said about himself. You two are quite the pair."

A twinge of hope flickered around her heart then faded. They had been a pair... until she destroyed his trust.

Now, she needed to come up with a way to help him. To compensate for her lack of tact and for walking out today when there was still work to be done.

But first, an apology.

Lauren pulled out her phone and tried to call him. It rang through to voicemail and she lost her nerve, hanging up before leaving a message.

Her mind spun, but landed once again on the obvious when it came to her livelihood. Her financial future.

She slouched in her chair. "If they sell the diner, we'll lose our jobs."

"Maybe. If someone buys the restaurant business, they'll need help." Greta scooped another bite. "But if no one steps up soon, they'll have to sell off the equipment instead and try to find a new tenant for the building. Or even sell the building…"

Lauren's stomach churned as she imagined the dining room full of office furniture or retail shelves.

Or worse being destroyed and turned into a parking garage or apartments.

Greta scraped the sides of her ice cream container. "If we end up needing new jobs, there are a lot of restaurants in town that could use experienced waitresses."

Lauren recalled the hospitality conference and the feeling she was made for the serving industry. "If not here, somewhere."

Greta sighed. "I just hate to see my mom and dad's business close."

"Is there any other way? Do we have to give in without a fight?"

Oh God, is there any other way out for them?

A glint sparked in Greta's eyes. "If their medical bills were paid, that would take the immediate pressure off. But they'll still need to come up with a long-term income solution since their monthly expenses have gone up plus Frank's health might force an early retirement or a difficult career change."

Lauren sat up straight. "So, we focus on the current bills first. How much do they need?"

"How much money do you have saved? Because I'm already maxed out paying Julie's tuition without tips or rental income."

"Tell me. How much?"

"Nancy told me fifteen grand is due in the next few weeks, but they'll need an extra thousand a month after that."

Lauren winced. That was a lot.

She didn't have much of her own, and Dad held the purse strings for her college fund. If he wouldn't pay for online hospitality classes, he'd never agree for her simply to give some away.

Greta dropped her spoon on the tabletop and leaned back in her chair. "We've got another problem too. While Frank's heart attack and surgery forced him to accept physical help, he's always hated the idea of charity."

Lauren frowned. "Except I know that he's given a lot to the community. Sandwiches and coffee for firefighters battling the forest fires a year or so ago. And I saw the articles about flood relief in the past. What about his donations to the food bank?"

"It's easier for him to give than to receive." Greta rolled her eyes. "But even if my brother would agree, we don't bring in enough—including tips—to make much of a difference."

The germ of an idea grew. "Remember that jar we had out the week Frank collapsed?"

"What jar?"

"Oh yeah, you were in the kitchen. I put a jar by the cash register and people wrote notes or dropped in cash. I know they used the money because Nancy told me how much it helped with cafeteria meals while she spent time at the hospital."

"Honey, it will take a whole lot more than a jar on the counter, but it's a start."

Lauren pushed back from the table and began to pace.

If God had made her a creative-thinking people-person, perhaps it was for such a time as this. Time to be herself and fight on her terms to save the diner or at least help the Dawsons as much as she could.

She would not go down without trying.

And she wasn't giving up on Joel either.

He had liked her before and she could hopefully make him trust her again.

But first things first.

"We need a bigger jar." Lauren crossed the kitchen to grab the notepad and pen from beside Greta's telephone. "In fact, how about an online jar that anyone can access easily and that even takes credit cards? Haven't you seen those private fundraiser pages? A lot of them have to do with medical bills, too."

Greta leaned forward, propping her elbows on the tabletop. "If it's going to work, we need to get this ball rolling. Time is running out."

"I will create the page since I'm better at tech than you are."

Greta shook her head. "Too true."

Lauren tapped the pen on the paper. "Then, once it's set up, we can start sending the link to all our friends and family through email or social media."

"We could make a poster or sign for the window so customers and regulars know where to look."

Lauren wrote it down. "What about a bake-sale or something?" She shook her head. "Never mind, you're already baking enough for the diner's regular business."

"Write it down anyway. I can do a little and others might want to step up." Greta tapped her fingers on the tabletop. "What about an after-hours dinner where we charge by the plate—more than we usually do—and have some sort of program?"

"Maybe a talent show for the regulars?"

"Or a silent auction? We could always set things up in the vacant half of the building and not interfere with the dining room during business hours."

Lauren scribbled their ideas down.

Was it just a couple weeks ago that Joel was the one getting the hand cramp of her burst of ideas?

She eyed her list. "That should give us plenty to start with. If you can run to the store for poster board and markers, I'll help you make a few signs. After I get the fundraiser page set up."

Greta carried her spoon to the sink, then tossed the empty container into the trash. "Feels good to be doing something other than worry. But I sure hope Frank doesn't fuss about accepting whatever we can raise."

"He probably will, but I'll take the blame for this. After I remind him he'll be back to giving to others soon enough." She snapped her fingers and made another note. "Oh. And I'll call Kyle at the paper."

But as Lauren went to her room to grab her computer, she couldn't ignore the nagging feeling that she was missing something.

Something important.

Something she'd have to figure out later once their plans were in motion.

It wasn't until nearly midnight when she was falling into bed that Lauren finally saw she'd missed multiple calls from Joel.

Along with a series of text messages sent hours earlier.

Call me.

Are you ignoring me on purpose?

And lastly... **Please come a half hour early tomorrow. We need to talk.**

Her stomach churned.

Instead of apologizing like she'd planned to, she'd accidentally given him the silent treatment. And it was much too late to fix her mistake tonight.

Lauren pressed her cell phone to her chest and buried her face in her pillow.

She'd had the chance to make things right, and instead...

Instead, she was being forced to wait until morning.

Oh God, please let Joel forgive me.

Chapter Twenty-Five

♥

J oel flipped on the lights and surveyed the kitchen with a sense of resolve.

Until there was a new owner to kick him out, he was here to stay.

But staying would be easier once—if—he cleared the air with Lauren.

His calls yesterday had kicked straight to voicemail. Or else rang and rang as if she'd been ignoring him. Making him afraid to just show up at his aunt's house.

At least his text messages had eventually been marked as read.

Hopefully Lauren came in early so they could talk without an audience.

Lord, give me wisdom today. First with Lauren. And then about the diner as I crunch more numbers.

Joel hung his jacket on a hook and went to start the coffee.

As he pushed through the swinging doors from the dining room, a yawning Lauren stumbled in the back door.

It was all he could do not to wrap his arms around her and never let go.

But first, they needed to talk.

Joel gripped the edge of the steel worktable. "Good morning, beautiful."

"Morning to you, too." She bit her lip. "I need to—"

"I'm sorry I—"

"What?"

"Go ahead." He eyed the dark circles under her eyes.

"No, you first."

Unable to bear the distance for a moment longer, Joel pulled her close and nestled her against his chest. "If I could do yesterday over again, I would. I have to tell you—"

"It's okay. Greta filled me in about your parents' decision to sell. And the extreme lengths you'd go to buy it yourself." She squeezed her arms around his waist.

And his fears released their hold on his heart.

If she knew all that and still hugged him back, their relationship would survive even if the diner didn't.

Tension drained from his shoulders. "I should have told you right away, but I was still in shock and trying to find a solution. I really wish I could buy it... for us."

"Us?" She eased back, her wide eyes shining with something like hope.

Or was that love?

His pulse raced. "Yes. Us."

He stared into her eyes trying to let her know how much he loved her.

How much he wished to make her a permanent part of his life.

But there were still other issues to resolve first.

He took a deep breath. "I'm sorry I lied to you about my paychecks even if I thought it would help keep us afloat. You deserved to know the truth but... You were right. I was a coward."

Even if she thought less of him, she deserved nothing but brutal honesty.

She blinked several times. "But you're not a quitter."

Joy welled up at her firm declaration.

"I promise that I'm not going anywhere." He lifted her chin and kissed her. "Especially not away from right here."

He kissed her again.

"My turn." She trapped his face between her hands and stared into his eyes. "I'm sorry I ran away yesterday. It was silly and immature to over-react like I did and I'm sorry that I didn't trust you more. Forgive me?"

"Absolutely. Forgive me?"

"Forgiven." She pulled him down for a lingering kiss that sizzled like bacon in a hot pan.

The load was lifted completely from his shoulders.

She winked. "Now, we'd better get to work."

"I already started the coffee."

"Good, 'cuz I was up way-too-late last night making phone calls and on the computer."

"What have you done?" A burst of energy pulsed through his veins. Was it love... or hope?

"Greta and I decided we're not going down without a fight either." She tapped a finger on his chest. "Prince Charming, you aren't the only one full of noble ideas to ride in and save the day."

"But I like my white horse." Joel grinned at her playful description. Except there was little they could do to change the bleak reality.

Before Lauren could explain what she meant, the back door opened and the rest of the staff filtered in. Soon they were engaged in the routine prep work, allowing Joel's mind to wander back to the issue at hand.

Even if he drained his personal savings, it was nowhere near enough for a down payment on the business. Assuming he could find someone willing to loan him the remainder.

And was it selfish to want to reserve some of his savings for a future with the woman of his dreams?

Joel was in the middle of transferring the latest batch of bacon to the holding tray when the conversation behind him pulled him from his spiraling concerns.

"How many extra pies are you planning to bake?" Trevor's question seemed like a fair one.

After all, the demand had picked up since their re-opening.

Not that a rising profit margin would do much good going forward.

Aunt Greta hummed. "If I set up the tables today, I'm hoping to contribute a dozen a day if I can use the ovens here."

Joel glanced back at the others.

There wasn't room for more tables in the dining room. And they sold three times that many pies a day already.

What had he missed by zoning out the usual chatter?

Debbie's knife clanged against a metal bowl as she scraped something from her cutting board. "I can make a grocery store run and then come back for an hour or two to help."

Joel slapped fresh slices onto the hot surface.

It seemed like they were talking about the diner's ovens. But not their ingredients.

Almost like it was personal baking. Except who needed a dozen pies a day?

"Hey, Aunt Greta?" Joel pivoted so he could still check on the bacon. "Did your oven at home break or something? And why would you need that many pies anyway?"

She stared back. "They're for the bake sale to benefit the Frank Dawson Medical Relief Fund so we can hopefully save the diner."

"The what?" His jaw dropped. There was so much to unpack in that statement.

Aunt Greta turned to where Lauren chopped bell peppers. "Didn't you tell him?"

A dark pink bloomed across Lauren's face. "We covered other topics first, but then you got here and we started the prep like always."

Since when was kissing and making up a topic?

Although they never had gotten around to discussing her reference to Prince Charming...

Joel raised an eyebrow, then turned down the burner under the bacon. "Somebody had better catch me up and start at the beginning."

Aunt Greta continued kneading dough in a giant metal bowl. "We're family and what affects one of us, affects us all. Our jobs are on the line."

"So, you told more than just Lauren about..." His shoulders slumped. "I'd rather that wasn't common knowledge outside this room."

Debbie jutted her chin. "We all know that your parents have a lot of bills and they may need to sell the diner. We should have seen it coming sooner."

Trevor nodded. "With my mom's cancer, I'm feeling the pressure myself and know there aren't any easy choices. So while I don't have anything to donate to the cause, I'll do my absolute best to boost our revenue here... assuming we get to stay open."

"We'll all do what we can to help," Clarissa said.

"Thank you." Joel folded his arms. "But what's this about a medical fund?"

Lauren abandoned her cutting board and crossed the kitchen to his side. "Your parents have given so much to this community, I—we—believe others might want the opportunity to give back. Like having an online donation jar."

He recalled Lauren's note and tip jar after Dad's heart attack.

The notes had helped encourage his mom and eventually his dad.

It was a great idea. But... "Can that pay all their bills?"

"Maybe. Maybe not. We'll never know unless we try." She wrapped an arm around his waist.

Hope rose in his chest and then sank. "They need fifteen thousand right away and more after that."

Lauren pulled out her phone and tapped the screen with her thumb. "And we've already raised almost two thousand since I started the fund last night."

"That much?" He leaned closer and stared at the number on the screen.

"That much." Lauren grinned as she bounced on her toes. "I can't wait to see how much it grows today."

His mind spun with possibilities. "If we find a way to pay their urgent bills, that will buy us time to work out a long-term solution to keep the doors open and ownership in the family."

And all the hours he'd spent last night working up an accurate business valuation would come in handy.

"Exactly." Lauren's smile faded as her eyes widened. "Oh, Greta, I forgot our signs in my car. Be right back."

She rushed out and he turned back to the sizzling bacon.

Long-term solutions.

If the multitude of additional fundraising ideas currently being debated behind him worked, his dreams might have a chance after all.

A slim chance, but a chance.

Please, God.

Soon after they unlocked the front door, Lauren found him in the kitchen. "I called Kyle, but he wants a quote or two from you."

"About what? More free advertising?" Joel left the pans soaking in the sink of soapy water and followed her out into the dining room.

Lauren moved on to serve the other morning regulars.

At the counter, Kyle patted the stool beside him and pulled a small recorder from his pocket.

"How can I help you?" Joel joined the reporter and summoned a smile.

"Lauren's already given me all the particulars about why she started the fundraiser page. What I need from you is an official comment to clarify where the money is going, especially so soon after that truck crashed into the diner and forced you to close for a week."

"The driver's insurance company is paying for all those repairs plus our loss of income." Or at least most of it. "Any events or specials that customers have seen since we reopened have been solely creative marketing efforts to boost our profit margin without needing to raise prices."

Kyle tapped his fingertips on the counter beside the recorder. "Fair enough. But where specifically is this additional money going?"

"The fundraising efforts are to pay down my dad's medical bills. The co-insurance portion above their deductible added up quickly. Also, his ongoing physical therapy is necessary but no longer covered and isn't cheap. All money raised will go to ease their personal financial burden."

"So the diner is not involved, even though the staff are spearheading the fundraiser?"

Joel cleared his throat. "We're a family around here, even if all the employees are not related to my dad... Frank. Who better to help than those closest to him?"

Kyle lowered his voice. "Lauren said something last night about the diner may be sold."

"Off the record?"

The reporter switched off the recorder.

"Honestly, my parents are considering that possibility in order to raise what they need both now for Dad's medical bills but also down the road as Dad continues his recovery." His voice cracked.

Kyle slowly nodded, a flash of deeper understanding in his eyes.

Joel swallowed hard. "But our hope is that by getting help for their immediate needs, we will find a way to eliminate that option and no one else will have to know that it was ever considered."

Kyle narrowed his eyes. "In a way this fundraiser helps keep the diner open."

Joel stared down the reporter's accusation. "Whether the diner stays open or not, my parents still have a mountain of bills to pay and we'd like to help them rest a little easier at night."

"I understand. I just have to ask the hard questions so I have answers when my boss criticizes the slant." The reporter held out a hand for Joel to shake. "Thank you for your time. I wish you the best."

Joel retreated to the kitchen with a sour taste in his mouth.

As much as he hoped for a positive outcome for the diner and his future, the fact was they were asking for other people's help.

Something his dad had been too proud to do.

Something his aunt had pointed out as a flaw in Joel's character too.

Well, as long as he was eating humble pie, Joel might as well dish up another serving and ask for a little help of his own.

He stored the clean bowls and pans away before finding Lauren by the coffee machine. "Is your dad still in town?"

"I think he said he'd be here for a couple days." She frowned. "Is this about what I saw in your email?"

"No." He slid his hand from her shoulder down to her elbow. "I really do need to explain about that when we have time, but for now..."

Was he wrong to think the man could help?

Was he asking too much of Lauren?

Her shoulders slumped. "What do you need?"

Joel squeezed her arm. "I—we—need some practical business advice from someone with an objective opinion."

She pursed her lips. "I'm not sure how objective he can be."

True. The man had strong opinions when it came to his daughter and her future.

But as they said, beggars couldn't be choosers.

He exhaled slowly. "Could you call him? Or give me his number? I'd like to see if he could stop by the diner after we close today."

"For what?" Her voice wavered a bit.

If only he could reassure her. Ease her fears.

Joel released her elbow and wrapped her arm around her waist instead and lowered his voice, ignoring Kyle's curious stare from two stools away. "If—when—the fundraiser works, that's still just the first step. My brain is spinning and I need help sorting out which ideas are even possible. Not to mention I could be overlooking something obvious."

"That is something Dad would be good at." Lauren leaned into his side. "If you can keep an eye on things out here for a few minutes, I'll give him a call."

She straightened and moments later had disappeared into the kitchen. Was probably headed to the office for a little privacy in case the conversation got heated.

Dear God, please let her find favor.

As Joel went through the familiar motions of serving the customers in both his and Lauren's sections, he debated how best to present the facts.

Could he find the emotional distance to treat their situation as if it were just another case study from his college program? If so, he'd need to organize not only his arguments but the financial numbers.

He was scribbling a few notes onto a blank page in his order pad when Lauren returned.

There was tension around her eyes, but a smile curved her lips. "Dad said he'll be here."

"Great." Joel blew out the breath he'd been holding. "Now I just need to get my parents on board."

He pulled out his phone and leaned against the end of the counter as he waited for his mom to answer.

"What's going on?" Mom's voice rose. "You never call this early. Did something happen at the diner—?"

"Calm down. I just need a favor and wanted to ask before I forgot." Joel eyed the colorful posters by the front door.

Something had happened at the diner, but it was nothing like she feared.

"What kind of favor?" Mom's panic faded into wariness.

"I hoped you could bring Dad by after closing today."

"That shouldn't be a problem. We were already going to meet the Realtor this afternoon—"

"No!" Joel glanced around at the too-curious customers, then lowered his voice. "You said you were going to give me a day or two before you did anything."

"Right. We did say that." Mom's sigh was loud in his ear. "I'll cancel our appointment."

"Thank you."

"So what should I tell your dad this is about? You know he's going to want to know."

"You can either tell him we have a surprise waiting—"

"You know how much he hates surprises."

Joel smirked. "Just tell him I have a few ideas to run past both of you and it can't wait until tonight. But between the two of us, I'm calling everyone together for help brainstorming."

Joel sidestepped as Lauren passed by holding two breakfast specials.

"Everyone?" Mom's voice faded.

"Like it or not, we're all in this together."

Together.

For better or for worse.

He watched as Lauren delivered the meals, then pointed another customer to the sign she'd hung by the front door.

It was up to him to prepare for the meeting as if his future—their future—depended on it.

Because it did.

Chapter Twenty-Six

♥

J oel twisted the lock on the diner's front door, the click of the tumblers nearly drowned out by the rumbling engine of a car pulling to a stop at the curb.

His parents' car.

Arriving as if they were visitors instead of owners.

Joel's stomach did a slow roll and he wiped sweaty hands on his jeans.

In the next hour, he'd know whether the diner could ever be his. Or if his future led somewhere else.

Either way, the rest of the staff had agreed to postpone their end-of-day cleaning in order to meet.

Dad paused on the sidewalk outside and leaned on his cane as his gaze swept over the building. Almost as if he memorized it before saying goodbye.

Joel unlocked and pushed open the door. "Glad you could make it."

Mom linked arms with Dad as they entered. "Not sure what ideas—"

"Frank!" Lauren rushed forward to greet them with distracting hugs. "It's always good to see you out and about again. And Nancy, I hope he isn't giving you too much trouble."

"No more than usual." Mom looked around the entryway. "When are you getting Hope's buffet back?"

Joel rocked back on his heels. "Our carpenter friend Matt was able to repair the leg but ran into a hiccup matching the stain. He's having to refinish the entire piece. But now that you mention it, he texted me a few days ago saying he'd found something interesting that he'll bring by."

"Really?" Lauren's eyebrows rose. "I love a good mystery. Why didn't you say anything?"

"Well, there's a lot that's happened since then so it slipped my mind." Joel shrugged, then gestured toward the center of the room where they'd pushed two tables together. "Mom and Dad? Can I get you something to—"

"What's that for?" Dad pointed a finger at the posters on the new community board. One featured a pocket full of small slips of paper with the donation website printed on them.

"The Frank Dawson Medical Relief Fund?" Mom's voice quavered. "Is this your surprise?"

Joel held his breath.

If his parents rebelled at this part of the plan, the rest of the coming discussion might be a waste of time.

"That's just one of the reasons we wanted to meet today." Lauren pulled out a chair for his dad. "You've done your share of helping this community and people want to give back."

Dad frowned. "We're not beggars asking for a handout."

Lauren patted his shoulder. "Absolutely not. We've just let people know there is a need and provided a way for them to pitch in if they want to help."

Mom paused by Joel's side. "We appreciate the thought, but this still won't change—"

"I'm praying it will." Out the window, he spotted Lauren's dad approaching. "If you'll excuse me, we have one more guest."

Joel reached the door in time to hold it open. "Thanks for coming, sir."

Mr. Graham nodded. "I have to admit I'm more than curious about this meeting, but I couldn't say no to my daughter. Not after the last few days."

Joel twisted the lock on the door, then turned toward the center of the room where Aunt Greta and Trevor greeted Joel's parents and introduced them to the newest members of the diner staff.

Joel led the way with Mr. Graham close behind. "Everyone, this is Mr. Graham. Lauren's dad."

"Please, call me Hugh." The man shrugged out of his suit coat. "I feel a little overdressed."

"You're fine." Lauren hurried forward to take his coat and was pulled into a hug instead. Her eyes widened with surprise, then closed as she wrapped her arms around her dad.

A long moment later, she stepped back and motioned him toward an empty chair. With a voice clogged with emotion, she said, "Can I get you something to drink?"

"Maybe something cold with caffeine?" Her dad draped his coat over the back of the chair and loosened his tie.

"Coming right up. Anyone else?" With a list of requests, Lauren retreated toward the counter.

Leaving Joel to make the rest of the introductions.

"Mr. Graham—Hugh—this is my dad, Frank Dawson. Dad ran this diner for years after taking it over when my grandpa died."

Using the table for leverage, Dad stood and reached out a hand. "Nice to meet you. You have a great daughter."

Hugh shook Dad's hand, then turned to watch Lauren. "She is. Thank you."

They both sat and Joel breathed a sigh of relief.

So far, so good.

Lauren returned with a tray of drinks and after passing them out, took her seat beside him.

Joel eyed the legal pad and stack of papers he'd spent hours compiling, then cleared his throat. "Let's begin with prayer."

He took a deep breath. "God, we come together as the Dawson's Diner family and ask for Your divine wisdom and provision. Thank You for saving Dad's life and bringing him this far in his recovery. As my Grandma Hope loved to remind me, our family has weathered many storms by relying on our faith. And each other. So I'm asking that You give us fresh ideas so we can meet my parents' financial needs and still keep the diner in the family. Amen."

Lauren squeezed his hand and he felt a burst of courage.

He turned to his parents first. "Mom and Dad, I've asked Lauren's dad to be here for his objective business advice since we're so emotionally close to the situation. He's the new Deputy Chief Financial Officer at his company and might have some creative solutions of his own to offer."

Beside him, Lauren straightened and smiled at her dad.

"For the sake of Mr. Graham—Hugh—I'd like to start by review-ing our situation."

Dad squirmed a bit as if he hated being the center of discussion.

"Before Dad's heart attack and open-heart surgery, he and Mom planned to operate this diner for years to come. They privately own three-quarters of this entire building from an inheritance, with my aunt owning the remaining twenty-five percent. Basically half of the vacant storefront next door." He nodded toward Aunt Greta.

"Therefore the business itself technically lists only the equipment and furnishings as assets. That said, there are also years of history to consider along with a loyal customer base. Correct?"

Dad nodded with a slight smile.

Joel glanced at the bullet points on his notepad. "Sticking to the facts, since the start of the year, the business account has logged a profit even with our adventure when a truck came to lunch."

A few of the others chuckled as he tipped his head at the new window.

Mom cleared her throat. "But you haven't paid yourself enough, so that's not exactly accurate."

Joel avoided the other stares and looked at Hugh instead. "Ever since Dad was hospitalized, the diner has continued to pay my parents their salary. Not just to live on but because as owners they should receive income from the business. However, while being cautious with our cash flow, I decided to only collect my tips temporarily, and let the rest of my wages go toward their salary. Considered it paying for my room and board."

Hugh whistled. "That's some creative-but-still-ethical accounting on their behalf. I assume the rest of the liabilities are taken care of?"

Joel nodded. "They have, sir. And the truth is, I could have paid myself full wages weeks ago except I was setting most of the profits aside to build a business rainy day fund. The same fund that has kept us in the black while we rebuilt and now wait for the insurance check."

He referred to the stack of papers on the table. "However, for the sake of this discussion, I've pulled together all the numbers you might need in addition to a copy of the equipment inventory and valuation our insurance guy wanted."

Joel pushed the stack toward Hugh. "You can see our sales and expense averages over the past three months, plus fresh projections based on our increased foot traffic since we reopened."

"Exactly." Lauren ran a finger through the condensation on her glass. "All our marketing ideas should be able to sustain that momentum, too."

Joel smiled. "Bottom line? The business itself is on solid ground."

Hugh scanned the top sheet listing a monthly budget. "Now, if I understand it correctly, the business does not have a rental expense because the owners also own the building."

How had he neglected that on the list?

Joel swallowed hard. "True."

Hugh reached behind him to pull a pen from his suit coat pocket, then took Joel's legal pad as well. "If you had to move the diner assets to a different location, what would you expect to pay in rent?"

Aunt Greta leaned forward. "Nobody said anything about moving anything."

Hugh held up a hand. "I'm just collecting all the relevant facts."

"I suppose it would be similar to what we charge for the other half of this building when it's under lease. Neither side is all that big." She frowned, then looked to her brother.

Dad named a figure and Hugh wrote it down.

Joel folded his arms on the table. "With the business numbers in place, let's turn our attention to the current situation. As I see it, my parents have three needs: immediate medical bills to pay, a regular monthly income source, and ideally a nest egg for the future."

He waited for their nods. "And you think that means selling the business and possibly the building in order to pay the urgent bills and have something to live off while Dad seeks to get back into the workforce somewhere in some capacity."

Dad wrapped an arm around Mom. "That's the gist of it."

Hugh made a note on the pad, then continued flipping through the various pages Joel had compiled during his breaks earlier.

Aunt Greta turned to face his parents. "Selling is a logical solution. Except we all might need new jobs when it's over. Not to say we can't find work somewhere else, but we love working here, especially with our history. Not to mention—and I think I speak for most of us when I say—serving the regulars is a sort of ministry opportunity. A chance to love on people and brighten their days."

A quick glance around the table showed Trevor, Debbie, and Clarissa nodding.

Aunt Greta's gaze shifted from his parents to Lauren and she raised an eyebrow.

Lauren turned to his parents. "We all agree that you two need to do what is best for your future, but you don't have to rush into any decisions."

She pulled out her phone and swiped her thumb across the screen. "You saw the posters for the medical relief fund when you came in. Well, you can blame me for that, but the donation site has already collected almost five thousand in less than a day."

"Five... thousand?" Dad's jaw dropped.

"That's amazing." Mom blinked back tears. "And so generous."

Lauren put her phone down and linked her hand around Joel's bicep. "And that's just word of mouth before Kyle's article hits the paper tomorrow."

Trevor chuckled. "Or we auction all the extra pies Greta volunteered to make for the bake sale."

"Bake sale?" Dad grunted. "Where on earth—"

Aunt Greta held up a hand. "I own half of that side of the building. It's still empty so there's no reason not to use it for something useful in the meantime." She smirked. "My phone's been ringing nonstop and I'm meeting Beatrice Jenkins this evening about letting the church ladies' aid group set up the bake sale and a craft fair to benefit the medical fund."

"A craft fair?" Mom sat up taller. "What kind of things would they sell?"

"You can look but you can't buy anything." Aunt Greta wagged a finger. "We're trying to put money in your pocket and not the other way around."

Several people laughed at his mom's blush-and-sputter reaction to the blunt truth.

Clarissa spun her half-empty glass of water in her hands. "We're also holding a silent auction so others can donate services. In fact, while I was home with my brothers over Spring Break—the week we ended up being closed anyway—I took the plunge and started a side gig."

How did he not know that about one of their employees?

"You're majoring in graphic design, right?" Lauren tilted her head. "So what kind of work will you do?"

"I was going to start small with logos, but I'm already landing clients faster than I'd dreamed. And a few of them are wanting business-level branding that includes website banners and other promotional materials which then is morphing into basic website design." Clarissa shifted in her chair, her attention darting between Joel and Lauren. "So while I'm donating a logo package for the auction, I'm..."

"Please don't say you're quitting?" Lauren sounded shocked that anyone would consider such a thing.

Even though others including his own cousin Julie had semi-recently done the same in order to pursue their dreams.

Clarissa flinched. "Not right away since I'm still getting my business off the ground. And I would never leave you in the lurch or anything because I've loved being a server here. But by summer, I'm going to need more flexibility to work around my brothers' schedules. And like I said when I interviewed way back in January, my family will always come first."

It couldn't be easy taking on guardianship for younger siblings. Especially those who couldn't drive.

Aunt Greta reached across Debbie to squeeze Clarissa's arm. "You'll be missed. But change isn't always a bad thing. We know God's got a plan for your life... and while He'll take care of you, He'll also bring us the right person for the job in His time."

Clarissa offered a small smile in return.

Joel cleared his throat. "So, between the online donations and all the other stuff planned, is it fair to say the medical bills should be covered over the next few weeks?"

"Absolutely." Lauren slapped her hand onto the table, then giggled at her own dramatics. "Consider it done."

His parents nodded, their smiles growing.

Joel's shoulders relaxed. "Now for the issue of a regular income..."

God, please let this work.

Hugh looked up from the papers he'd been studying. "Frank, how likely are you to work again?"

Joel winced and Lauren sucked in a breath.

Dad clasped Mom's hand. "More than if you'd asked a few weeks ago. In fact, I have an appointment next week with my doctor where he should clear me. My biggest challenges are still stamina and reducing stress. But with Joel handling the financial side of things here, I hope I might contribute in the kitchen again."

Trevor folded his arms on the table. "What do you think that would look like?"

"I wouldn't dream of taking away the place of our only trained chef even if I could handle the longer hours." Dad shook his head. "I would need to start slow anyway. Plus I've kinda gotten used to sleeping in a little."

Joel's mom chuckled. "We both have. But if Frank's coming back to work, I could also—"

"Hush. One thing at a time." Aunt Greta nodded to Trevor, her silver hair swinging with the movement. "As head of the kitchen staff, what do you think about Frank working from like eight to noon as a prep and support person behind you and Debbie? That would free me up for just baking or helping in the dining room again."

With Clarissa's thoughts of leaving, he and Lauren could use the extra help in the dining room.

Trevor leaned back in his chair. "I'd say the kitchen would be fully staffed and in good hands." He glanced at Joel. "And between Greta and possibly hiring another waitress—even before Clarissa leaves—you'd have more time for washing dishes."

Lauren snorted and elbowed him in the ribs. "Three servers at a time is ideal, but a designated busboy would be a perk."

Joel just shook his head. "I wouldn't know what to do with all the extra time."

Trevor smirked. "You could do some of your number-crunching while the doors are still open instead of only after hours."

That had possibilities. Even if he lost his excuse to spend that time with Lauren.

Time enough to think through the ripple effect later.

Joel faced his parents. "Seriously, it would be good to see you back in the kitchen again. Mom, too, if she wants—"

"She doesn't." Aunt Greta stared his mom into silence before looking his way. "I know for a fact she'd rather spend her free time away from my brother lost in a craft project or enjoying coffee with church friends. Or even hearing about her brother's latest travels."

"It's true." Mom shrugged. "But there's no way we can accept a full salary if Frank is only working part-time."

"If I might interject." Hugh referred to his notes, then leaned back with a sigh. "Even if Frank is able to return full time eventually, in my opinion, you still need to sell the business."

Joel gasped as if the floor had dropped out from under his chair taking his dreams with it.

Chapter Twenty-Seven

♥

They still needed to sell the business?

Rocked to her core, tears flooded her eyes, and Lauren squeezed Joel's hand painfully tight.

Surely he regretted inviting her dad to the meeting and asking for his so-called objective opinion.

But they'd make it through this somehow. Together.

Her dad looked around the table at the other devastated faces and grimaced. "It's not the end of the world."

"It feels like it." Joel swallowed hard, then rubbed his thumb over the back of her hand. "I want nothing more than to keep the diner in the family for years to come. And hoped to eventually be able to buy it from my parents."

I really wish I could buy it... for us.

Us.

She was more than ready to make that status official.

Some might say it was fast, but she'd fallen in love with him weeks ago. Probably even before he'd carried her up the stairs at the hockey game.

"Let me explain." Her dad gestured to the legal pad filled with numbers. "There are a couple ways to place a value on a business. One is to go off book value or rather what all the equipment costs minus the debts to vendors. As in what you'd pocket if you liquidated it all."

Dad waved a hand toward the cluster of family photos she'd re-hung near the entrance. "But that ignores all the history and loyal customer base. So the alternative is to multiply the annual profits by a factor of two or four. Or better yet is a combination of the two to arrive at a fair valuation."

All this financial stuff hovered beyond her expertise.

Lauren nudged her dad's side. "Plain English, please."

Dad turned to a fresh sheet of paper and wrote a six-figure number across the top. "This is my best estimate of the value—a sale price, if you will—based on the equipment inventory and current income and expense projections."

Wow. One hundred eighty thousand dollars.

That would take care of Frank and Nancy for quite a while.

But there was no way Joel could come up with that much on a server's wages.

Tears pricked her eyes.

No wonder he'd considered a high paying job elsewhere.

Maybe he still should.

Dad looked at the older Dawsons. "If you were to sell the business—to your son or to anyone else—you could potentially accept a down payment and receive the remainder as say seventy-five percent of the profits over time until the balance was repaid."

Dad turned to Joel. "That's assuming twenty-five percent is enough of a cushion to put back into the business."

"It should be." Joel's voice cracked as he continued to stare at the big number on the page.

Did he feel as hopeless as she did?

After all, that number was as daunting to scale as the Rocky Mountains nearby.

"That's what I thought. Now, in addition to receiving a profit-sharing payment for the business assets, the Dawsons could also receive monthly rent." Dad wrote another number halfway down the page.

The same number Frank and Greta had given him earlier in the discussion.

Dad turned to Frank and Nancy. "In fact, I'd make a long-term lease agreement a requirement of the purchase deal. Probably with a fixed rate or with capped yearly increases. Either way, that guarantees the diner would stay in this location while you continue getting regular income."

"Wait a minute." Lauren grabbed the stack of papers and shuffled through them until she came to the payroll expenses.

Yes. Just like she'd thought.

She turned to her dad with wide eyes. "That rent payment is less than Frank and Nancy's current salary."

Joel sat up taller.

Dad grinned. "Exactly. By paying rent instead of a salary, the business profits should increase." He scanned the faces around the table. "Meanwhile the Dawsons collect that amount in addition to whatever Frank earns from his hourly wages like any other employee. That shouldn't affect them too much month to month. Because..."

Her dad tapped the big number at the top of the page. "They'd also have this much coming in over time to invest. Plus they still own the real estate and their share of the vacant space next door with that potential rental income when another lease is signed."

"I see what you're saying." Joel cleared his throat. "Selling the business gives them everything they need."

Frank leaned forward. "I agree. So is there any reason Joel can't buy it? If Nancy and I will have enough to pay our bills, I don't care how long it takes for him to repay the purchase price."

Joel's eyes glistened as he faced her dad. "Can you help us figure out a way?"

A wave of hope stole Lauren's breath.

Please, God?

Dad pursed his lips as if thinking. Or weighing his words.

After another moment, he stared at Joel. "Do you have any savings to use as a down payment? I mean, Lauren said you just graduated. And you admitted you haven't been taking home a full wage for a while..."

Joel shifted on his chair, looking from her dad to his parents and back to her.

How embarrassing to be put on the hot seat so bluntly.

So publicly.

Down the way, Trevor also squirmed while Debbie and Clarissa exchanged pained looks.

Could she openly admit her meager bank balance even if those gathered were as close to being family as her own father?

Joel blew out a breath as if coming to some sort of decision. "I have been saving as much as I could all along through college. Had planned to add more to it so that years from now I could start or buy a business."

He shook his head. "Never dreamed I'd need it this soon. Or that I'd even want to use it here."

Frank, Nancy, and Greta all laughed.

And Lauren couldn't help but join in as she remembered his obvious disgust over bacon grease burns and the mountain of dirty pans.

Joel nodded toward the notepad and the visible number at the top. "It's not anywhere close to that scary amount of debt. And while I'd still like to keep a little back for emergencies and other personal needs..." He glanced at her. "I'm willing to put almost everything I have on the line here. And then do all I can to build our profits so I can pay the remainder down faster."

"I know you would." Frank's voice broke even as his smile grew. "And nothing says we have to charge that exact amount of rent either. At least the first year."

Lauren eyed the other staff around the table.

Judging by all the wide eyes, it seemed they were figuring out the diner might be saved after all.

They'd—she'd—do everything possible to help by continuing to cut costs.

Even if it meant staying shorthanded in the dining room for a while. Or sending a few people home early.

She shook her head. It was too soon to worry about staffing issues when the future of the diner still hung in the balance.

Her dad drew a circle near the top of the page and slid the notepad to Joel. "Give me your best estimate for a down payment."

Joel pulled out his phone and she caught a glimpse of his banking app before turning her head to give him a bit of privacy. Because there was no reason to intrude on his personal finances.

But turning her head, put Dad in her line of sight.

She still couldn't believe he'd come to help them fight to keep the diner. But was he there for her... or because of Joel?

The feel of Dad's arms around her earlier still warmed her heart. He hadn't hugged her since before the divorce. What had changed?

She stared at Joel. What exactly had the two of them talked about two days ago?

If only she could believe the best.

Joel wrote down a five-figure number, then pushed the notepad back to her dad before taking Lauren's hand in his again.

As if he needed the confirmation of her support in this critical moment.

She interlaced their fingers. After all, he was trying to buy the diner. For them.

For us.

"Please, Dad," she whispered. "Please let that be enough to let us stay here."

Her dad hummed, then looked at Joel. "Are you open to a partnership? Because an additional influx of cash into the deal helps your parents even more now while reducing the remaining balance due. And I know you'd be good for your share through sweat equity and hard work."

She held her breath.

Could Joel work with her father as an investor? And how much say would he want in the day-to-day operations?

"Um..." Joel released her hand and wiped his palms on his legs. "I'd have to think about it, but it would definitely depend on who was investing and how much voice they wanted in decision-making."

Beside her, Dad tapped his pen on the paper. "You'd certainly stay the majority owner. But while you think about that, are you open to working as a consultant?"

She sucked in a quick breath.

Here it came.

The job offer to steal Joel away.

"Only on the side because the diner comes first." Joel squeezed her elbow. "But, for curiosity's sake, what did you have in mind?"

"If you can slip away for a day now and then, I would love to see you kick my sales force into gear with a pep talk comparing business basics to the diner like you did with me a couple days ago. Actually, we have a leadership retreat next weekend and could use another speaker. We do pay well."

Wow. So Joel had convinced her dad that a diner was a real business after all.

And he could be paid to do the same for others?

Joel looked at her with a hopeful gleam in his eye before turning his attention toward her dad. "We have a couple part-timers who might be able to pitch in occasionally. And I know Lauren can manage things here every bit as well as I can."

"I'll do my best." She sat back in her chair. With Joel's outspoken belief in her abilities, she felt like a true partner in the business.

Joel stared her dad in the eye. "And if consulting work and speaking fees will help me pay down the balance that much faster, I'd request that any partnership agreement also includes a buy-out clause."

Lauren held her breath.

He was so smart. Perhaps even more so because he'd asked for God's help at the start of their meeting.

"Fair enough if you decide you can't get along." Her dad chuckled as he turned to a fresh page in the legal pad. "So while I'd insist a lawyer draw up formal agreements to be signed in front of a notary in order to protect all the parties involved—and before any money changes hands—can we agree on the essential terms now?"

Within minutes, he'd written up a basic long-term lease agreement for the next fifteen years with a specified rent per month with a maximum annual percentage increase.

And a purchase agreement spelling out the agreed-upon business valuation, a blank line for the down payment amount to be added, and terms of seventy-five percent net profits above any additional principal payments until the total valuation had been repaid.

It might take years to pay it off, but knowing the diner would be in Joel's capable hands was worth the sacrifice.

Frank signed both pages with a wide smile before passing them to Joel. "There's no one I'd rather see take over Dawson's Diner than you."

"And no place I'd rather be." Joel signed with a flourish, then turned to her dad. "Now for the partnership agreement so I know how much of a down payment I'll eventually need to repay when I'm able to exercise the buyout clause."

"If you insist." Dad started listing out the terms on a fresh page.

Joel leaned across Lauren so he could see the proposed agreement as it developed.

In exchange for—her eyes widened at the amount—Partner A would own thirty percent of the business. Partner B would assume the remaining liability of the purchase agreement as majority shareholder.

Her dad paused and looked up "Is that enough ownership for you?"

"It is." Joel reached to take the pen as if ready to sign.

"Not so fast." Dad added a line about how to dissolve the partnership should the business fail or they decided to part ways before the majority owner could buy back ownership. He then turned to Lauren and stared as if lost in thought.

Her heart sank. What additional terms would he ask for now?

"I believe Partner A should have a voice in business-related decisions." Dad tilted his head. "Is it too much to ask for naming rights?"

"What?" She gasped. "Why? You said family history is important to the valuation, so how would an outsider know what's appropriate or not?"

Her heart pounded in her chest and tears blurred her vision.

Why would her dad sabotage the deal when it was this close to being completed?

Chapter Twenty-Eight

♥

L auren held her breath, waiting for her dad's explanation.

Instead he shrugged. "You're right. An outsider wouldn't know a thing."

She tasted bile in the back of her throat, his neutral response a punch to her gut.

How could Dad be so callous? So impersonal when the Dawson legacy hung in the balance?

No way would she let Joel form a legal partnership with her dad.

Even if it would save the diner, it was too risky.

She grasped Joel's arm. "I can't believe I'm saying this, but—"

"Stop. I'm not done." Dad fingered through the papers spread before him until he found one in particular and slid it toward her. "Personally, I have no desire to own a bunch of tables and ovens. But *you* might."

"Me?" She eyed the paper, finally registering the list of business assets.

All the equipment inside this very room.

Tables. Chairs. Coffee machines. And so much more.

And Dad thought she wanted them? As if she had the money to consider buying any of it?

"What are you saying?" She looked up from the list, almost choking on the hope rising in her chest.

Dad's gaze slid to something—or someone—beyond her, then back to her. "I've been thinking about what you said on the phone. Even more since Monday when I stopped by and saw you in action."

A warm hand landed on her shoulder.

Grateful that Joel had her back—literally and figuratively—Lauren braced herself for whatever Dad had to say next.

"Lauren?" Dad cleared his throat. "You were right."

"I... What?" She blinked.

Across the table, Greta chuckled.

Dad gestured broadly, the motion starting with the booths by the windows and ending at the lunch counter. "I may have let the past consequences of your mother's artistic urges blind me, but here your creativity is an asset."

"Really?"

He nodded. "You belong here more than in a college classroom getting a degree you won't use. And so I was open to the online program you tried to tell me about. However..."

Her stomach cramped. "What changed?"

"This." He tapped a finger on the in-progress partnership agreement. "I still have money set aside for your education. But I believe you'd rather use it for something else. Like a solid investment opportunity you believed in that would give you on-the-job training."

Was he really saying what she thought he meant?

She must have looked as shocked as she felt, because Dad nudged her chin upward.

A smile spread on his face. "What do you think about becoming Partner A?"

She looked from her dad to the handwritten agreement.

To the dollar amount invested.

And a thirty percent ownership stake in the place she loved like home.

She rested a hand over her pounding heart. "Really? But why?"

Dad's gaze shifted from her to Joel. "It only took a single lunch here to know that this diner deserves to stay in business. Deserves to continue serving the community the way your family has for years. And I believe that you can do that. Together."

Happy tears flooded her eyes as a buzz of excited voices rose around the joined tables.

The Dawsons and the other diner staff had been thrilled to see Joel get his chance to buy the business and lease the building. And now it seemed they were even happier to see Joel in a partnership with someone they already knew.

As for her. Ecstatic didn't begin to describe her emotions.

Mostly because Dad hadn't rejected her for standing up to him. Because he fully supported her decision to forge a different career path.

"Thank you." Lauren wrapped her arms around her dad, her heart about to explode in her chest.

Oh, to be in a right relationship with her father.

A father who did not think she was a misfit after all, but believed she was capable of investing in a business.

And not just any business, but this one.

"So, I could really help Joel buy the diner?" She whispered the question mostly to herself. As if saying it out loud would make it real.

Lauren Graham as co-owner of Dawson's Diner.

What would the previous generations of owners think?

Actually, she could almost imagine precious Hope smiling as her family gathered around the tables in what was basically her café.

Dad gave Lauren a final squeeze before pulling away from their embrace. "I guess this means you want to be Partner A."

"Absolutely." She glanced at the paperwork. And the dollar amount listed there. "Except for one change."

"Naming rights?" Dad grinned. "Or something else."

"Hold on." Joel stood and pulled her to her feet, their chairs scraping the tile behind them. "If you'd all excuse us for a minute?"

He tugged her along as he speed-walked toward the kitchen.

What was he upset about?

Joel had been about to sign the partnership agreement based on the assumption it was her dad investing, so what had changed?

Was it her? Was *she* the problem?

Lauren tripped at the thought, but Joel was there with a steadying hand.

No. She'd jumped to conclusions before.

Had doubted instead of trusting.

Whatever he had to say, she owed him the chance to explain.

Joel led Lauren through the swinging doors into the kitchen and stopped beside the still-cluttered prep counter.

Had that just happened?

He'd spent the last two days praying and planning and crunching numbers and praying even more. All in hopes he could somehow figure out a way to buy his parents' diner for himself.

For Lauren.

For their future.

He'd just never believed it could actually happen.

Leave it to God to come through in such an unexpected way.

Joel wiped a sweaty palm on his jeans, then cupped Lauren's cheek, staring into her eyes. "What are you thinking?"

She offered a wobbly smile. "It's all a bit blurry back there. Am I dreaming? Did my dad really say he'd give me the money to invest?"

"He did." He tucked a strand of wayward curls behind her ear. "But don't make any hasty decisions on my account. Running a diner is a lot of hard work."

"I know. I've been doing it as long as you have." She smirked, then glanced around the messy kitchen. "There's no place I'd rather be than here."

"I agree." Especially with her in his arms.

Her eyes widened. "Unless you'd rather not be partners with me? I know—"

Joel pressed a finger against her mouth. "I'd much rather be partners with you than your dad any day. And not just because you know and love this place as much as I do."

She blinked, but seemed to hold her breath.

No time like the present to lay it all on the line.

He caressed her soft lips with his thumb. "You're the woman I love. The woman I want to spend the rest of my life with."

Her lips curved and her eyes shone. "You'd willingly put up with me as a partner?"

"Gladly. In fact, if you're going to be a part-owner of Dawson's Diner, we might as well make it official…"

Could she hear the way his heart pounded in his chest?

She ran her fingers over his jawline. "More official than a signed sheet of paper?"

Before Joel lost his concentration—or courage—he pulled her completely into his arms, her head coming to rest over his heart.

A place she already belonged.

The place he prayed she'd agree to stay.

"I think you should become a Dawson," he whispered.

"A what?" She jolted, then tilted her head back to gaze into his eyes.

A rush of warmth flowed through his limbs, bleeding emotion into his voice.

"I'd better do this right even if I haven't had the chance to buy a ring." He stepped back and dropped to one knee on the linoleum floor not far from a sink full of dirty dishes. "I love you, Lauren Graham. And like I told your dad on Monday, I want nothing more than to spend the rest of my life serving beside you. Will you marry me?"

She almost bounced on her toes.

Would she agree to be partners in the ultimate sense of the word?

Accept Joel and the diner and his family for the rest of her life?

Or was it too soon?

Her smile grew. "That's a no-brainer."

"Is that a yes or a no?" He peered up at her.

"Yes! Of course I'll marry you."

He stood, sweeping Lauren up into his arms as his lips descended to kiss his fiancée for the very first time.

His future wife.

His partner in life.

Beyond the pass-through window, someone cheered.

Someone who sounded suspiciously like his mother. Or his aunt. Or both.

Lauren giggled against his lips. "They almost sound as happy as I am."

"Impossible." Joel chuckled, then after another quick kiss, set Lauren down.

"I love you, Joel, and would gladly stay right here. Or escape out the back door." She pressed a hand over his pounding heart, then tipped her head toward the dining room. "But we should probably get back to the others."

He interlaced their fingers. "You're right."

She winked. "First my dad, then you. Being right is a trend today."

He was still laughing when they stepped through the swinging doors and into a deluge of hugs, back-slaps, handshakes, and congratulations from friends and family alike. Including his female relatives who argued over who got the credit for finding a woman willing to put up with him.

Hugh gave Joel a solemn nod before the man turned to embrace his daughter.

On Monday, her dad had asked about Joel's intentions and eventually given his blessing on a future marriage. A marriage partnership that would eventually replace the agreement they'd been working on just minutes ago.

Except his parents—and the business—couldn't wait for a wedding. They needed the money now.

Hugh obviously thought along the same lines because he led Lauren—followed by the rest—back to the abandoned paperwork. "Before Joel dragged you off to the kitchen, you said there was something you wanted to change."

"Oh, right." She sat and looked over the draft. "Would it be okay if I lowered this dollar amount a bit to keep some for myself?"

"For a wedding?" Hugh raised an eyebrow. "Because as the father of three girls, I've already been saving for that."

Lauren blushed. "Good to know for whenever Joel and I get the chance to talk about the details. But I'd still like to enroll in that online program I told you about." She grinned at Joel. "It appears I could use the knowledge now more than ever."

Joel scooted his chair closer and laced their fingers together. "If that's what you want to do, go for it. Although I wonder if they can teach you anything you don't already know."

Lauren grinned. "It's gotta be better than the last semester's worth of classes I slogged through."

"So it would be money well spent." Her dad made an adjustment to both the investment amount and the percentage of ownership.

Which in turn raised Joel's remaining debt liability to just over a hundred thousand.

But Lauren and his family's legacy were more than worth the sacrifice.

"Now, Dad? About those naming rights you mentioned earlier..."

Joel's gasp was drowned out by others around the table.

Hopefully she wouldn't do something ridiculous.

No. He had to trust her instincts.

Trust that she loved this place as much as he had come to love it. Joel squeezed her hand. "What did you have in mind?"

Lauren's smile became almost wistful as she gazed into his eyes. "As much as I can't wait to become a Dawson, what do you think about the name Hope's Café?"

She looked across the table to where his parents had reclaimed their seats. "It's been on my mind ever since Greta said this was originally the Heartland Café before becoming Dawson's Diner. And I know how often you teased your mom that this was her café."

Lauren's voice hitched. "Whenever I spent time with Julie, Hope used to treat me like I was her granddaughter too. And she introduced me to the source of true hope."

Joel released Lauren's hand, instead wrapping his arm around her shoulders. "I think it would be the perfect way to honor her legacy."

"Hope's Café." Aunt Greta beamed. "I love it. It would always remind us of the true mission here as we serve others and give them a taste of hope."

His dad snorted. "Leave it to my sister to make a joke, but I have to agree. New ownership and a new name."

"But the same great service." Joel nodded.

Lauren laughed. "And coffee. Never forget the coffee."

"Or the pie." Trevor leaned back and rubbed his stomach. "I've heard that everything's better with pie."

A minute later, Hugh pushed the revised partnership agreement over for first Lauren and then Joel to sign.

Joel laid the signed page next to the other two already bearing his signature. "We did it. We really did it."

"Let's pray." Dad bowed his head. "Dear God, we thank You for the answered prayers. For meeting our needs and for showing us a way forward. And now we ask Your blessing on Joel and Lauren as they take on this new challenge. May everyone who steps inside these doors find hope. And find You. Amen."

A moment later, Hugh cleared his throat. "I should reiterate that you'll still need a lawyer to draw up official contracts. Once I receive a notarized copy, I can arrange for the transfer of Lauren's portion of the funds."

"Of course." Joel gathered the rest of the assorted papers together into a neat pile. "I'm sure our lawyer can also advise us on the best way to do the funding so everything is documented correctly."

Once they—he—found a competent lawyer.

Something he'd be doing as soon as they wrapped up this meeting and put the diner back in order for the day.

Lauren leaned forward to peer around her dad who was already putting on his coat to leave. "Speaking of things still to do, if we have a new name, we'll definitely need a new logo. Clarissa, can you possibly squeeze us in for a rush job?"

"Me?" The waitress paused from where she collected drink cups. "I mean, sure. Of course. But why the hurry?"

Lauren shook her head. "We've had a few other things on our minds today, but I just remembered that we need to turn in the team sponsorship packet to the high school very soon."

A brisk knocking against glass shifted Joel's attention to the front door where Matt stood, holding what appeared to be an overstuffed manilla envelope.

Right. The man had said he'd found something interesting and would bring it by.

Joel hurried to unlock the door. 'Thanks for stopping by."

Matt glanced over his shoulder at something across the street, then stepped inside, his gaze drifting across the others in the room. "I hope this isn't a bad time."

"We're just finishing up here." Joel nodded to the envelope. "What's that you're carrying?"

"Didn't you say that buffet was your grandmother's?"

"It was. So maybe my parents and my aunt should also be in this conversation." Joel motioned for Matt to follow him and made quick work of the necessary introductions.

Matt shuffled his work boots. "I won't bore you with all the details, but I had to dismantle a few sections of the buffet and found a false back to a drawer."

"A secret compartment?" Lauren joined them.

Of course her curiosity would be piqued along with everyone else's.

Matt nodded, then lifted the envelope. "Inside I found a stack of what looked like letters. All addressed to someone named Harold."

"To Dad?" Aunt Greta wiggled her fingers. "Let's see them."

Matt passed the envelope and she pulled a few out.

"These are definitely Mom's handwriting, but the dates are all after Dad died." She held one up and read aloud, her voice quavering. "Dear Harold, I can't believe you're gone. How am I supposed to carry on without you?"

"Oh." Lauren sighed. "That almost sounds like a diary."

Aunt Greta hugged the letters close. "I bet she forgot they were in the drawer."

"How many are there?" His mom wrapped an arm around Aunt Greta's waist. "Are they all addressed to him?"

"I don't know. But there's an easy way to find out." Aunt Greta spun on her heel and soon the ladies were sorting the letters by date while his dad watched.

Meanwhile, Trevor and Debbie disappeared into the kitchen, Clarissa on their heels with the last tub of dishes. They'd delayed their usual clean-up routines long enough.

Matt pulled Joel to the side and lowered his voice. "I'm not sure what all you were meeting to discuss, but I sure hope it doesn't have anything to do with Mr. Ridge."

"That developer?" The same one who'd wanted to buy the diner? Who'd practically guaranteed they'd change their mind to sell?

The man would *not* be thrilled to discover their plans for new ownership.

Joel's stomach churned. "What about him?"

Matt frowned. "He's sitting in his car across the street, almost like he's been watching you."

"We can only hope he goes away quietly." Joel blew out a slow breath.

After Matt left, Joel turned back to Lauren.

To his new fiancée.

With God's help, they'd escaped another crisis and his family's legacy would go on.

And best of all, they'd face the next adventure together.

Want to see how Clarissa's logo design leads her to love? Continue reading The Cafe on Hope and Main Series with book 2, *Where Promises Endure*.

What's Next?

The Cafe on Hope and Main Series continues with
Book 2, *Where Promises Endure.*

· ❤ · ❤ · ❤ · ❤ · ❤ ·

Keeping her promise just got a lot more complicated.

As guardian for her younger brothers, waitress Clarissa struggles to hold their family together but knows they need a male role model. However the more the local baseball coach fills in the gaps—and sparks her heart—the more she wishes they'd met a different way.

Zeke wants nothing more than to invest in his team both on and off the field, but his newest player's home life just threw him a curve ball. The more time Zeke spends with Clarissa's unique family, the more he longs to linger... except dating a parent is against school rules.

Maybe her promise to raise the boys could be a team effort, but if their forbidden romance is discovered, he'll have to choose between his dream job and her instant family. Perhaps the wisdom—and community—of Hope's Café can keep them from striking out?

Fans of Becky Wade, Denise Hunter, and Karen Kingsbury will fall in love with the charming world of Hope's Cafe.

Continue this heart-warming, faith-filled series today.

· ❤ · ❤ · ❤ · ❤ · ❤ ·

If you'd like to receive updates about upcoming books or sales, you can sign up for my email list on my website at CandeeFick.com.

(There might be a few surprises headed your way including a free castle novella.)

Dear Reader

♥

Thank you for spending a few hours of your time with the characters who call Hope's Cafe their second home. There are a lot more stories to come, so I hope you can settle in with a cup of coffee and a cinnamon roll to savor the journey.

There is no greater pleasure as an author than knowing that I've encouraged my readers! If you enjoyed this book, please take a few minutes to let the rest of the world know by leaving a review on Amazon or on sites like Goodreads or BookBub. It doesn't have to be long. Just a few words pointing other readers this direction would be much appreciated. And even a simple star rating goes a long way!

Readers always ask what's real in a story and what's made up. While the town of Loveland, Colorado is real—complete with all the Valentine's Day celebrations, a local hockey team, and a college just one town away—this particular diner/cafe and its founding family are fictional. I may have placed it on a corner on "Main" street where real locals used to frequent such a restaurant before it closed, but I took creative license with the surrounding businesses and street names in order to set up future story situations.

In a much-older version of this story, Lauren got clobbered with a baseball at a Little League game and I based a lot of her headaches and lingering confusion on personal experience from when it happened to me! However, when it came time to fit this book into a bigger timeline, I needed a wintery-season for her injury instead. Thankfully, my special-needs Princess loves to follow the local hockey team... and so I was able to shift the scene around a new situation in a unique setting.

As I continue to write stories of faith, hope, and love, my prayer is that you will experience the amazing love of God and find encouragement for the journey called life. That you will latch onto hope as an anchor for your soul and like Lauren, learn how to pray like breathing as you exhale the troubles and inhale His power.

Until we (hopefully) meet again in the pages of a book, happy reading everyone!

Candee

More Fiction

A complete and up-to-date list of all my books can be found on my
website at CandeeFick.com

Cafe on Hope and Main Series

(Contemporary small town romance)
Where Hope Begins (Lauren and Joel)
Where Promises Endure (Clarissa and Zeke)
Where Love Abides (Amanda and Matt)

The Wardrobe Series

(Contemporary romance in theater settings)
Dance Over Me (Dani and Alex)
Focus on Love (Liz and Ryan)
Sing a New Song (Gloria and Nick)
A Picture Perfect Christmas (Liz and Ryan continued)

Home For Christmas (Grace and Tyler)
Complete Series Boxed Set

Within the Castle Gates Series

(Historical romance in various time periods)
Stepping Into the Light (Moira and Evan)
To Win Her Heart (Emma and Grayson)
The Lost Heir (Kathleen and Reuben)
Finding Home (Susannah and Nicholas)
Saving Grace (contemporary - Grace and Drew)
A Castle in the Clouds (Miranda and Josh)
Books 1-4 Boxed Set

Standalone Romance

Catch of a Lifetime (Cassie and Reed)

About Candee

♥

Candee Fick is a mocha latte fueled author who writes heartwarming, hope-filled Christian romance. She knows first-hand that while life is hard, God is good. That's why her stories show relatable characters overcoming real-life problems through their faith in God and the support of their small town communities. When Candee isn't weaving intricate plotlines at her favorite coffee shop, she can be found spending quality time with her family in Colorado or lost in the pages of a captivating story while letting the dust bunnies multiply.

Visit www.CandeeFick.com to learn more and get a free book by signing up for her newsletter.